Grace Livingston Hill
L I B R A R Y

ESTER RIED

LIVING BOOKS®
Tyndale House Publishers, Inc.
Wheaton, Illinois

Copyright © 1995 by Tyndale House Publishers, Inc.
All rights reserved
Cover illustration © 1995 by Corbert Gauthier

Living Books is a registered trademark of Tyndale House
Publishers, Inc.

Library of Congress Catalog Card Number
ISBN 0-8423-3181-6

Printed in the United States of America

01 00 99 98 97 96 95
7   6   5   4   3   2   1

CONTENTS

WELCOME

by Grace Livingston Hill

As long ago as I can remember, there was always a radiant being who was next to my mother and father in my heart and who seemed to me to be a combination of fairy godmother, heroine, and saint. I thought her the most beautiful, wise, and wonderful person in my world, outside of my home. I treasured her smiles, copied her ways, and listened breathlessly to all she had to say, sitting at her feet worshipfully whenever she was near; ready to run any errand for her, no matter how far.

I measured other people by her principles and opinions, and always felt that her word was final. I am afraid I even corrected my beloved parents sometimes when they failed to state some principle or opinion as she had done.

When she came on a visit, the house seemed glorified because of her presence; while she remained, life was one long holiday; when she went away, it seemed as if a blight had fallen.

She was young, gracious, and very good to be with.

This radiant creature was known to me by the name of Auntie Belle, though my mother and my grandmother called her Isabella! Just like that! Even sharply sometimes when they disagreed with her: "Isabella!" I wondered that they dared.

Later I found that others had still other names for her. To the congregation of which her husband was pastor she was known as Mrs. Alden. And there was another world in which she moved and had her being when she went away from us from time to time; or when at certain hours in the day she shut herself within a room that was sacredly known as a "study" and wrote for a long time while we all tried to keep still; and in this other world of hers, she was known as Pansy. It was a world that loved and honored her, a world that gave her homage and wrote her letters by the hundreds each week.

As I grew older and learned to read, I devoured her stories chapter by chapter. Even sometimes page by page as they came hot from the typewriter; occasionally stealing in for an instant when she left the study to snatch the latest page and see what had happened next; or to accost her as her morning's work was done with: "Oh, have you finished another chapter?"

Often the whole family would crowd around when the word went around that the last chapter of something was finished and going to be read aloud. And now we listened, breathless, as she read and made her characters live before us.

The letters that poured in at every mail were overwhelming. Asking for her autograph and her photograph; begging for pieces of her best dress to sew into patchwork; begging for advice on how to become a great author; begging for advice on every possible subject. And she answered them all!

Sometimes I look back upon her long and busy life and marvel at what she has accomplished. She was a marvelous housekeeper, knowing every dainty detail of her home to perfection. And a marvelous pastor's wife! The real old-fashioned kind, who made calls with her husband, knew every member intimately, cared for the sick, gathered the young people into her home, and loved them all as if they had been her brothers and sisters. She was beloved, almost adored, by all the members. And she was a tender, vigilant, wonderful mother, such a mother as few are privileged to have, giving without stint of her time, her strength, her love, and her companionship. She was a speaker and teacher, too.

All these things she did, and *yet wrote books!* Stories out of real life that struck home and showed us to ourselves as God saw us; and sent us to our knees to talk with him.

And so, in her name I greet you all, and commend this story to you.

Grace Livingston Hill

(This is a condensed version of the foreword Mrs. Hill wrote for her aunt's final book, *An Interrupted Night*.)

FOREWORD

Isabella Macdonald Alden, beloved aunt of Grace Livingston Hill, had probably one of the longest writing careers in American literature. Over a period of sixty years, Isabella composed more than one hundred novels, many of which were read worldwide.

Born in 1841, in Rochester, New York, Alden reached the peak of her career around 1900, when her books were selling at the rate of 100, copies a year. Because of her immense popularity, the books were translated into many foreign languages.

Isabella's first book, *Helen Lester,* won first prize in a contest for the best story explaining the principles of Christianity for children ages ten to fourteen. It was then that she dedicated her pen "to the direct and continuous effort to win others for Christ and help others to closer fellowship with him." She noted this in *Memories of Yesterdays,* her final published work, which was edited by her niece, Grace.

Married for more than fifty years to the Reverend Gustavus Rossenberg Alden, Isabella drew the material for most of her stories from her experiences as a pastor's wife. "Whenever things went wrong," she once explained, "I went home and wrote a book to make them come out right." Through stories, or parables, she hoped to teach readers the lessons her husband taught in church and in the homes of parishioners.

Of all her books, the Ester Ried series, which Isabella wrote from the depths of personal experience, had the greatest popular appeal. In a letter dated April 12, 1906, one reader penned, "I remember the impression made upon my mind by the reading of *Ester Ried*. I was but a young girl, and its teachings gave me still higher ideals. I was a professing Christian at the time, and its helpfulness cannot be told in words."

Another reader from Massachusetts wrote, "Since the day of *Ester Ried*, your writings have been a comfort and inspiration to me. . . . It must be such a satisfaction to feel that you have been a power for good in so many, many lives." Yet another reader observed in 1906: "And how much good that book has done, such an inspiration to so many."

Today, many years later, it is our hope that you will discover in *Ester Ried* the same blessings, the same enjoyment, and the same help others have found in the stories of Isabella Macdonald Alden as you draw to closer fellowship with Christ.

1

ESTER'S HOME

SHE did not look very much as if she were asleep, nor acted as though she expected to get a chance to be very soon. There was no end to the things which she had to do, for the kitchen was long and wide, and took many steps to set it in order, and it was drawing toward teatime of a Tuesday evening, and there were fifteen boarders who were, most of them, punctual to a minute.

Sadie, the next oldest sister, was still at the academy, as also were Alfred and Julia, while little Minie, the pet and darling, most certainly was *not*. She was around in the way, putting little fingers into every possible place where little fingers ought not to be. It was well for her that no matter how warm and vexed and out of order Ester might be, she never reached the point in which her voice could take other than a loving tone in speaking to Minie; for Minie, besides being a precious little blessing in herself, was the child of Ester's oldest sister, whose home was far away in a western grave-yard, and the little girl had been with them since her early babyhood three years before.

So Ester hurried to and from the pantry with quick, nervous movements as the sun went toward the west, saying to Maggie, who was ironing with all possible speed:

"Maggie, do *hurry* and get ready to help me, or I shall never have tea ready," saying it in a sharp, fretful tone. Then: "No, no, Birdie, don't touch!" in quite a different tone to Minie, who laid loving hands on a box of raisins.

"I *am* hurrying as fast as I *can!*" Maggie made answer. "But such an ironing as I have every week can't be finished in a minute."

"Well, well! Don't talk; that won't hurry matters any."

Sadie Ried opened the door that led from the dining room to the kitchen and peeped in a thoughtless young head covered with bright brown curls:

"How are you, Ester?"

And she emerged fully into the great, warm kitchen, looking like a bright flower picked from the garden, and put out of place. Her pink gingham dress and white, ruffled apron—yes, and the very schoolbooks which she swung by their strap—waked a smothered sigh in Ester's heart.

"Oh, my patience!" was her greeting. "Are *you* home? Then school is out."

"I guess it *is*," said Sadie. "We've been down to the river since school."

"Sadie, won't you come and cut the beef and cake, and make the tea? I did not know it was so late, and I'm nearly tired to death."

Sadie looked sober. "I would in a minute, Ester, only I've brought Florence Vane home with me, and I should not know what to do with her in the meantime. Besides, Mr. Hammond said he would show me about my algebra if I'd go out on the piazza this minute."

"Well, *go* then, and tell Mr. Hammond to wait for his tea until he gets it!" Ester answered crossly.

"Here, Julia"—to the ten-year-old newcomer—"Go away from that raisin box this minute. Go upstairs out of my way, and Alfred too. Sadie, take Minie with you; I can't have her here another instant. You can afford to do that much, perhaps."

"Oh, Ester, you're cross!" said Sadie in a good-humored tone, coming forward after the little girl.

"Come, Birdie, Auntie Essie's cross, isn't she? Come with Aunt Sadie. We'll go to the piazza and make Mr. Hammond tell us a story."

And Minie—Ester's darling, who never received other than loving words from her—went gleefully off, leaving another heartburn to the weary girl. They *stung* her, those words: "Auntie Essie's cross, isn't she?"

Back and forth, from dining room to pantry, from pantry to dining room, went the quick feet. At last she spoke:

"Maggie, leave the ironing and help me; it is time tea was ready."

"I'm just ironing Mr. Holland's shirt," objected Maggie.

"Well, I don't care if Mr. Holland *never* has another shirt ironed. I want you to go to the spring for water and fill the table pitchers, and do a dozen other things."

The tall clock in the dining room struck five, and the dining bell pealed out its prompt summons through the house. The family gathered promptly and noisily—schoolgirls, half a dozen or more; Mr. Hammond, the principal of the academy; Miss Molten, the preceptress; Mrs. Brookely, the music teacher; Dr. Van

Anden, the new physician; Mr. and Mrs. Holland; and Mr. Arnett, Mr. Holland's clerk. There was a moment's hush while Mr. Hammond asked a blessing on the food; then the merry talk went on. For them all Maggie poured cups of tea, and Ester passed bread and butter, and beef and cheese, and Sadie gave overflowing dishes of blackberries and chattered like a magpie, which last she did everywhere and always.

"This has been one of the scorching days," Mr. Holland said. "It was as much as I could do to keep cool in the store, and we generally are well off for a breeze there."

"It has been more than *I* could do to keep cool anywhere," Mrs. Holland answered. "I gave it up long ago in despair."

Ester's lip curled a little. Mrs. Holland had nothing in the world to do from morning until night but to keep herself cool. She wondered what the lady would have said to the glowing kitchen where *she* had passed most of the day.

"Miss Ester looks as though the heat has been too much for her cheeks," Mrs. Brookley said, laughing. "What *have* you been doing?"

"Something besides keeping cool," Ester answered soberly.

"Which is a difficult thing to do, however," Dr. Van Anden said, speaking soberly too.

"I don't know, sir; if I had nothing to do but that, I think I could manage it."

"I have found trouble sometimes in keeping myself at the right temperature even in January."

Ester's cheeks glowed yet more. She understood Dr. Van Anden, and she knew her face did not look very self-controlled. No one knows what prompted Minie to speak just then.

"Aunt Sadie said Auntie Essie was cross. Were you, Auntie Essie?"

The household laughed, and Sadie came to the rescue.

"Why, Minie! You must not tell what Aunt Sadie says. It is just as sure to be nonsense as it is that you are a chatterbox."

Ester thought that they would *never* all finish their supper and depart, but the latest comer strolled away at last, and she hurried to toast a slice of bread, make a fresh cup of tea, and send Julia after Mrs. Ried.

Sadie hovered around the pale, sad-faced woman while she ate.

"Are you *truly* better, Mother? I've been worried half to pieces about you all day."

"Oh yes, I'm better. Ester, you look dreadfully tired. Have you much more to do?"

"Only to trim the lamps, and make three beds that I had not time for this morning, and get things ready for breakfast, and finish Sadie's dress."

"Can't Maggie do any of these things?"

"Maggie is ironing."

Mrs. Ried sighed. "It is a good thing that I don't have the sick headache very often," she said sadly; "or you would soon wear yourself out. Sadie, are you going to the lyceum tonight?"

"Yes, ma'am. Your worthy daughter has the honor of being editress, you know, tonight. Ester, can't you go down? Never mind that dress; let it go to Guinea."

"You wouldn't think so by tomorrow evening," Ester said shortly. "No, I can't go."

The work was all done at last, and Ester betook herself to her room. How tired she was! Every nerve seemed to quiver with weariness.

It was a pleasant little room, this one which she

entered, with its low windows looking out toward the river and its cozy furniture all neatly arranged by Sadie's tasteful fingers.

Ester seated herself by the open window and looked down on the group who lingered on the piazza below—looked *down* on them with her eyes and with her heart—yet envied while she looked; envied their free and easy life, without a care to harass them, so *she* thought; envied Sadie her daily attendance at the academy, a matter which she *so* early in life had been obliged to have done with; envied Mrs. Holland the very ribbons and laces which fluttered in the evening air. It had grown cooler now, as a strong breeze blew up from the river and freshened the air; and as they sat there below, enjoying it, the sound of their gay voices came up to her.

"What do they know about heat, or care, or trouble?" she said scornfully, thinking over all the weight of *her* eighteen years of life. She hated it, this life of hers, just *hated* it—the sweeping, dusting, making beds, trimming lamps, *working* from morning till night; no time for reading, or study, or pleasure. Sadie had said she was cross, and Sadie had told the truth; she *was* cross most of the time, fretted with her everyday petty cares and fatigues.

"Oh!" she said, over and over, "if something would only *happen;* if I could have one day, just *one* day, different from the others; but no, it's the same old thing—sweep and dust, and clean up, and eat and sleep. I *hate* it all."

Yet, had Ester nothing for which to be thankful that the group on the piazza had not?

If she had but thought, she had a robe, and a crown, and a harp, and a place waiting for her up before the throne of God; and all they had *not*.

Ester did not think of this; so much asleep was she that she did not even know that none of those gay hearts down there below her had been given up to Christ. Not one of them, for the academy teachers and Dr. Van Anden were not among them. Oh, Ester was asleep! She went to church on the Sabbath and to preparatory lecture on a weekday; she read a few verses in her Bible, *frequently,* not every day; she knelt at her bedside every night and said a few words of prayer—and this was all!

She lay at night side by side with a young sister who had no claim to a home in heaven, and never spoke to her of Jesus. She worked daily side by side with a mother who, through many trials and discouragements, was living a Christian life, but never talked with her of their future rest. She met daily, sometimes almost hourly, a large household, and never so much as thought of asking them if they, too, were going, someday, home to God. She helped her young brother and sister with their geography lessons yet never mentioned to them the heavenly country whither they themselves might journey. She took the darling of the family often in her arms and told her stories of "Little Bo Peep," and the "Babes in the Wood," and "Robin Redbreast," and never one of Jesus and his call for the tender lambs!

This was Ester, and this was Ester's home.

2

WHAT SADIE THOUGHT

SADIE Ried was the merriest, most thoughtless young creature of sixteen years that ever brightened and bothered a home. Merry from morning until night, with scarcely ever a pause in her constant flow of fun; thoughtless, nearly always selfish too, as the constantly thoughtless always are. Not sullenly and crossly selfish by any means, only so used to thinking of self, so taught to consider herself utterly useless as regarded home and home cares and duties that she opened her bright brown eyes in wonder whenever she was called upon for help.

It was a very bright and very busy Saturday morning.

"Sadie!" Mrs. Ried called, "can't you come and wash up these baking dishes? Maggie is mopping, and Ester has her hands full with the cake."

"Yes, ma'am," said Sadie, appearing promptly from the dining room with Minie perched triumphantly on her shoulder. "Here I am, at your service. Where are they?"

Ester glanced up. "I'd go and put on my white dress first, if I were you," she said significantly.

And Sadie looked down on her pink gingham, ruffled apron, shining cuffs, and laughed.

"Oh, I'll take off my cuffs and put on this distressingly big apron of yours which hangs behind the door; then I'll do."

"That's my clean apron; I don't wash dishes in it."

"Oh, bless your careful heart! I won't hurt it the least speck in the world. Will I, Birdie?"

And she proceeded to wrap her tiny self in the long, wide apron.

"Not *that* pan, child!" exclaimed her mother. "That's a milk pan."

"Oh," said Sadie, "I thought it was pretty shiny. My! what a great pan. Don't you come near me, Birdie, or you'll tumble in and drown yourself before I could fish you out with the dishcloth. Where is that article? Ester, it needs a patch on it; there's a great hole in the middle, and it twists every way."

"Patch it, then," said Ester dryly.

"Well, now I'm ready; here goes. Do you want *these* washed?" And she seized upon a stack of tins which stood on Ester's table.

"Do let things alone!" said Ester. "Those are my baking tins, ready for use; now you've got them wet, and I shall have to go all over them again."

"How will you go, Ester? On foot? They look pretty greasy; you'll slip."

"I wish you would go upstairs. I'd rather wash dishes all the forenoon than have you in the way."

"Birdie," said Sadie gravely, "you and I mustn't go near Auntie Essie again. She's a bowwow, and I'm afraid she'll bite."

Mrs. Ried laughed. She had no idea how sharply Ester had been tried with petty vexations all that morning, nor how bitter those words sounded to her.

"Come, Sadie," she said; "what a silly child you are. Can't you do *anything* soberly?"

"I should think I might, ma'am, when I have such a sober and solemn employment on hand as dish washing. Does it require a great deal of gravity, Mother? Here, Robin Redbreast, keep your beak out of my dishpan."

Minie, in the meantime, had been seated on the table, directly in front of the dishpan.

Mrs. Ried looked around. "Oh, Sadie! what *possessed* you to put her up there?"

"To keep her out of mischief, Mother. She's Jack Horner's little sister and would have had every plum in your pie down her throat by this time if she could have got to them. See here, Pussy, if you don't keep your feet still, I'll tie them fast to the pan with this long towel; then you'll have to go around all the days of your life with a dishpan clattering after you."

But Minie was bent on a frolic. This time the tiny feet kicked a little too hard; and the pan, being drawn too near the edge in order to be out of her reach, lost its balance—over it went.

"Oh, my patience!" screamed Sadie as the water splashed over her, even down to the white stockings and daintily slippered feet.

Minie lifted up her voice and added to the general uproar. Ester left the eggs she was beating and picked up broken dishes. Mrs. Ried's voice arose above the din:

"Sadie, take Minie and go upstairs. You're too full of play to be in the kitchen."

"Mother, I'm *real* sorry," said Sadie, shaking herself out of the great wet apron, laughing even then at the plight she was in. "Pet, don't cry. We didn't drown after all."

"Well! Miss Sadie," Mr. Hammond said as he met them in the hall. "What have you been up to now?"

"Why, Mr. Hammond, there's been another deluge, this time of dishwater, and Birdie and I are escaping for our lives."

━┼ ┼━

"If there is one class of people in this world more disagreeable than all the rest, it is people who call themselves Christians."

This remark Mr. Harry Arnett made that same Saturday evening as he stood on the piazza, waiting for Mrs. Holland's letters. And he made it to Sadie Ried.

"Why, Harry!" she answered in a shocked tone.

"It's a *fact,* Sadie. You just think a bit, and you'll see it is. They're no better nor pleasanter than other people, and all the while they think they're about right."

"What has put you into that state of mind, Harry?"

"Oh, some things which happened at the store today suggested this matter to me. Never mind that part. Isn't it so?"

"There's my mother," Sadie said thoughtfully. "She is good."

"Not because she's a Christian though; it's because she's your mother. You'd have to look till you were gray to find a better mother than I've got, and she isn't a Christian either."

"Well, I'm sure Mr. Hammond is a good man."

"Not a whit better or pleasanter than Mr. Holland as far as I can see. *I* don't like him half so well. And Holland don't pretend to be any better than the rest of us."

"Well," said Sadie gleefully, *"I* don't know many good people. Miss Molton is a Christian, but I guess she is no better than Mrs. Brookley, and *she* isn't. There's Ester; she's a member of the church."

"And do you see as she gets on any better with her religion than you do without it? For *my* part, I think you are considerably pleasanter to deal with."

Sadie laughed. "We're no more alike than a bee and a butterfly, or any other useless little thing," she said brightly. "But you're very much mistaken if you think I'm the best. Mother would lie down in despair and die, and this house would come to naught at once if it were not for Ester."

Mr. Arnett shrugged his shoulders. "I *always* liked butterflies better than bees," he said. "Bees *sting.*"

"Harry," said Sadie, speaking more gravely, "I'm afraid you're almost an infidel."

"If I'm not, I can tell you one thing—it's not the fault of Christians."

Mrs. Holland tossed her letters down to him from the piazza above, and Mr. Arnett went away.

Florence Vane came over from the cottage across the way—came with slow, feeble steps—and sat down in the door beside her friend. Presently Ester came out to them:

"Sadie, can't you go to the office for me? I forgot to send this letter with the rest."

"Yes," said Sadie. "That is, if you think you can go that little bit, Florence."

"I shall think for her," Dr. Van Anden said, coming down the stairs. "Florence, out here tonight, with the dew falling, and not even anything to protect your head. I am surprised!"

"Oh, Doctor, do let me enjoy this soft air for a few minutes."

"*Positively,* no. Either come in the house, or go

home *directly.* You are very imprudent. Miss Ester, *I'll* mail your letters for you."

"What does Dr. Van Anden want to act like a simpleton about Florence Vane for?" Ester asked this question late in the evening, when the sisters were alone in their room.

Sadie paused in her merry chatter. "Why, Ester, what do you mean? About her being out tonight? Why, you know, she ought to be very careful, and I'm afraid she isn't. The doctor told her father this morning he was afraid she would not live through the season unless she was more careful."

"Fudge!" said Ester. "He thinks he is a wise man; he wants to make her out very sick so that he may have the honor of helping her. I don't see as she looks any worse than she did a year ago."

Sadie turned slowly around toward her sister. "Ester, I don't know what is the matter with you tonight. You know that Florence Vane has the consumption, and you know that she is my *dear* friend."

Ester did not know what was the matter with herself, save that this had been the hardest day, from first to last, that she had ever known, and she was rasped until there was no good feeling left in her heart to touch. Little Minie had given her the last hardening touch of the day by exclaiming as she was being hugged and kissed with eager, passionate kisses:

"Oh, Auntie Essie! You've cried tears on my white apron and put out all the starch."

Ester set her down hastily and went away.

Certainly Ester was cross and miserable. Dr. Van Anden was one of her thorns. He crossed her path quite often, either with close, searching words about self-control, or grave silence. She disliked him.

Sadie, as from her pillow she watched her sister in

the moonlight kneel down hastily and knew that she was repeating a few words of prayer, thought of Mr. Arnett's words spoken that evening, and with her heart throbbing still under the sharp tones concerning Florence, sighed a little and said within herself:

"I should not wonder if Harry were right."

And Ester was so much asleep that she did not know, at least did not realize, that she had dishonored her Master all that day.

3

❖≈❖❖❖≈❖

FLORENCE VANE

OF the same opinion concerning Florence was Ester a few weeks later when, one evening as she was hurrying past him, Dr. Van Anden detained her:

"I want to see you a moment, Miss Ester."

During these weeks Ester had been roused. Sadie was sick; had been sick enough to awaken many anxious fears; sick enough for Ester to discover what a desolate house theirs would have been, supposing her merry music had been hushed forever. She discovered, too, how very much she loved her bright young sister.

She had been very kind and attentive; but the fever was gone now, and Sadie was well enough to rove around the house again. Ester began to think that it couldn't be so very hard to have loving hands ministering to one's simplest want, to be cared for, and watched over, and petted every hour in the day. She was returning to her impatient, irritable life. She forgot how high the fever had been at night and how the young head had ached, and only remembered how thoroughly tired she was, watching and ministering day and night. So when she followed Dr. Van Anden to the sitting room in answer to his "I want to see you, Miss Ester," it was a very sober, not altogether pleasant face which listened to his words.

"Florence Vane is very sick tonight. Someone should be with her besides the housekeeper. I thought of you. Will you watch with her?"

If any reasonable excuse could have been found, Ester would surely have said no, so foolish did this seem to her. Why, only yesterday she had seen Florence sitting beside the open window, looking very well; but then, she was Sadie's friend, and it had been more than two weeks since Sadie had needed watching with at night. So Ester could not plead fatigue.

"I suppose so," she answered slowly to the waiting doctor, hearing which, he wheeled and left her, turning back, though, to say:

"Do not mention this to Sadie in her present state of body. I don't care to have her excited."

"Very careful you are of everybody," muttered Ester as he hastened away. "Tell her *what,* I wonder? That you are making much ado about nothing for the sake of showing your astonishing skill?"

In precisely this state of mind she went, a few hours later, over to the cottage, into the quiet room where Florence lay asleep and, for aught she could see, sleeping as quietly as young, fresh life ever did.

"What do you think of her?" whispered the old lady who acted as housekeeper, nurse, and mother to Florence.

"I think I haven't seen her look better this great while," Ester answered abruptly.

"Well, I can't say as she looks any worse to *me* either; but Dr. Van Anden is in a fidget, and I suppose he knows what he's about."

The doctor came in at eleven o'clock, stood for a moment by the bedside, glanced at the old lady, who was dozing in her rocking chair, then came over to Ester and spoke low:

"I can't trust the nurse. She has been broken of her rest and is weary. I want *you* to keep awake. If she—" nodding toward Florence—"stirs, give her a spoonful from that tumbler on the stand. I shall be back at twelve. If she wakens, you may call her father and send John for me; he's in the kitchen. I shall be around the corner at Vinton's."

Then he went away, softly, as he had come. The lamp burned low over by the window, the nurse slept on in her armchair, and Ester sat with wide-open eyes fixed on Florence. And all this time she thought that the doctor was engaged in getting up a scene, the story of which should go forth next day in honor of his skill and faithfulness. Yet, having come to watch, she would not sleep at her post, even though she believed in her heart that, were she sleeping by Sadie's side and the doctor quiet in his own room, all would go on well until the morning.

But the doctor's evident anxiety had driven sleep from the eyes of the gray-haired old man whose one darling lay quiet on the bed. He came in very soon after the doctor had departed.

"I can't sleep," he said in explanation to Ester. "Some way I feel worried. Does she seem worse to you?"

"Not a bit," Ester said promptly. "I think she looks better than usual."

"Yes," Mr. Vane answered in an encouraged tone; "and she has been quite bright all day; but the doctor is all down about her. He won't say a single cheering word."

Ester's indignation grew upon her. "He might, at least, have let this old man sleep in peace," she said sharply in her heart.

At twelve, precisely, the doctor returned. He went directly to the bedside.

"How has she been?" he asked of Ester in passing.

"Just as she is now." Ester's voice was not only dry, but sarcastic.

Mr. Vane scanned the doctor's face eagerly; but it was grave and sad. Quiet reigned in the room. The two men at Florence's side neither spoke nor stirred. Ester kept her seat across from them and grew every moment more sure that she was right, and more provoked. Suddenly the silence was broken. Dr. Van Anden bent low over the sleeper and spoke in a gentle, anxious tone: "Florence." But she neither stirred nor heeded. He spoke again: "Florence," and the blue eyes unclosed slowly and wearily. The doctor drew back quickly and motioned her father forward.

"Speak to her, Mr. Vane."

"Florence, my darling," the old man said, with inexpressible love and tenderness sounding in his voice. His fair young daughter turned her eyes on him; but the words she spoke were not of him, or of aught around her. So clear and sweet they sounded that Ester, sitting quite across the room from her, heard them distinctly.

"I saw Mother, and I saw my Savior."

Dr. Van Anden sank upon his knees as the drooping lids closed again, and his voice was low and tremulous:

"Father, into thy hands we commit this spirit. Thy will be done."

In a moment more, all was bustle and confusion. The nurse was thoroughly awakened; the doctor cared for the poor childless father with the tenderness of a son; then came back to send John for help and to give directions concerning what was to be done.

Through it all Ester sat motionless, petrified with solemn astonishment. Then the angel of death had *really* been there in that very room, and she had been "so wise in her own conceit" that she did not know it until he had departed with the freed spirit!

Florence really *was* sick, then—dangerously sick. The doctor had not deceived them, had not magnified the trouble as she supposed; but it could not be that she was dead! Dead! Why, only a few minutes ago she was sleeping so quietly! Well, she was very quiet now. Could the heart have ceased its beating?

Sadie's Florence dead! Poor Sadie! What would they say to her? How *could* they tell her?

Sitting there, Ester had some of the most solemn, self-reproachful thoughts that she had ever known. God's angel had been present in that room, and in what a spirit had he found this watcher?

Dr. Van Anden went quietly, promptly, from room to room, until everything in the suddenly stricken household was as it should be; then he came to Ester:

"I will go over home with you now," he said, speaking low and kindly. He seemed to understand just how shocked she felt.

They went, in the night and darkness, across the street, saying nothing. As the doctor applied his key to the door, Ester spoke in low, distressed tones:

"Doctor Van Anden, I did not think—I did not dream—" Then she stopped.

"I know," he said kindly. "It was unexpected. *I* thought she would linger until morning, perhaps through the day. Indeed, I was so sure that I ventured to keep my worst fears from Mr. Vane. I wanted him to rest tonight. I am sorry—it would have been better to have prepared him; but at eleven, or at midnight, or at the cock crowing, or in the morning—you see, we know not which. I thank God that to Florence it did not matter."

Those days which followed were days of great opportunity to Ester, *if* she had but known how to use them. Sadie's sad, softened heart, into which grief had entered, might have been turned by a few kind, skillful words from thoughts of Florence to Florence's Savior. Ester *did* try; she was kinder, more gentle with the young sister than was her wont to be; and once, when Sadie was lingering fondly over memories of her friend, she said, in an awkward, blundering way, something about Florence having been prepared to die and hoping that Sadie would follow her example. Sadie looked surprised, but answered gravely:

"I never expect to be like Florence. She was perfect, or at least I'm sure I could never see anything about her that wasn't perfection. You know, Ester, she never did anything wrong."

And Ester, unused to it and confused with her own attempt, kept silence and let poor Sadie rest upon the thought that it was Florence's goodness which made her ready to die, instead of the blood of Jesus.

So the time passed; the grass grew green over Florence's grave, and Sadie missed her indeed. Yet the serious thoughts grew daily fainter, and Ester's golden opportunity for leading her to Christ was lost.

4

❖⬥❖

THE SUNDAY LESSON

ALFRED and Julia Ried were in the sitting room, studying their Sabbath school lessons. Those two were generally to be found together; being twins, they had commenced *life* together and had thus far gone side by side. It was a quiet October Sabbath afternoon. The twins had a great deal of business on hand during the week, and the Sabbath school lesson used to stand a fair chance of being forgotten; so Mrs. Ried had made a law that half an hour of every Sabbath afternoon should be spent in studying the lesson for the coming Sabbath. Ester sat in the same room, by the window; she had been reading, but her book had fallen idly in her lap, and she seemed lost in thought. Sadie, too, was there, carrying on a whispered conversation with Minie, who was snugged close in her arms, and merry bursts of laughter came every few minutes from the little girl. The idea of Sadie keeping quiet herself, or of keeping anybody else quiet, was simply absurd.

"'But I say unto you that ye resist not evil, but whosoever shall smite thee on thy right cheek, turn to him the other also,'" read Julia slowly and thought-fully. "Alfred, what do you suppose that can mean?"

"Don't know, I'm sure," Alfred said. "The next one is just as queer: 'And if any man will sue thee at the law, and take away thy coat, let him have thy cloak also.' I'd like to see *me* doing that. I'd fight for it, I reckon."

"Oh, Alfred! you wouldn't, if the Bible said you mustn't, would you?"

"I don't suppose this means us at all," said Alfred, using, unconsciously, the well-known argument of all who have tried to slip away from gospel teaching since Adam's time.

"I suppose it's talking to those wicked old fellows who lived before the Flood, or some such time."

"Well, *any*how," said Julia, "I should like to know what it all means. I wish Mother would come home. I wonder how Mrs. Vincent is. Do you suppose she will die, Alfred?"

"Don't know—just hear this, Julia! 'But I say unto you, Love your enemies, bless them that curse you, do good to them that hate you and pray for them which despitefully use you and persecute you.' Wouldn't you like to see anybody who did all that?"

"Sadie," said Julia, rising suddenly and moving over to where the frolic was going on, "won't you tell us about our lesson? We don't understand a bit about it; and I can't learn anything that I don't understand."

"Bless your heart, child! I suspect you know more about the Bible this minute than I do. Mother was too busy taking care of you two, when I was a little chicken, to teach me as she has you."

"Well, but what *can* that mean—'If a man strikes you on one cheek, let him strike the other too'?"

"Yes," said Alfred, chiming in, "and, 'If anybody takes your coat away, give him your cloak too.'"

"I suppose it means just that," said Sadie. "If anybody steals your mittens as that Bush girl did yours last winter, Julia, you are to take your hood right off and give it to her."

"Oh, Sadie, you *don't* ever mean that!"

"And then," continued Sadie gravely, "if that shouldn't satisfy her, you had better take off your shoes and stockings, and give her them."

"Sadie," said Ester, "how *can* you teach those children such nonsense?"

"She isn't teaching *me* anything," interrupted Alfred. "I guess I ain't such a dunce as to swallow all that stuff."

"Well," said Sadie meekly, "I'm sure I'm doing the best I can; and you are all finding fault. I've explained to the best of *my* abilities. Julia, I'll tell you the truth—" and for a moment her laughing face grew sober—"I don't know the least thing about it—don't pretend to. Why don't you ask Ester? She can tell you more about the Bible in a minute, I presume, than I could in a year."

Ester laid her book on the window. "Julia, bring your Bible here," she said gravely. "Now what is the matter? I never heard you make such a commotion over your lesson."

"Mother always explains it," said Alfred, "and she hasn't got back from Mrs. Vincent's; and I don't believe anyone else in this house *can* do it."

"Alfred," said Ester, "don't be impertinent. Julia, what is it that you want to know?"

"About the man being struck on one cheek, how he must let them strike the other too. What does it mean?"

"It means just *that;* when girls are cross and ugly to you, you must be good and kind to them; and when a boy knocks down another, he must forgive him instead of getting angry and knocking back."

"Ho!" said Alfred contemptuously, "I never saw the boy yet who would do it."

"That only proves that boys are naughty, quarrelsome fellows who don't obey what the Bible teaches."

"But, Ester," interrupted Julia anxiously, "was that true what Sadie said about me giving my shoes and stockings and my hood to folks who stole something from me?"

"Of course not. Sadie shouldn't talk such nonsense to you. That is about men going to law. Mother will explain it when she goes over the lesson with you."

Julia was only half satisfied. "What does that verse mean about doing good to them that—"

"Here, I'll read it," said Alfred. "'But I say unto you, Love your enemies, bless them that curse you, do good to them that hate you, and pray for them which despitefully use you and persecute you.'"

"Why, that is plain enough. It means just what it says. When people are ugly to you and act as though they hated you, you must be very good and kind to them, and pray for them, and love them."

"Ester, does God really mean for us to love people who are ugly to us and to be good to them?"

"Of course."

"Well, then, why don't we, if God says so? Ester, why don't you?"

"That's the point!" exclaimed Sadie, in her most roguish tone. "I'm glad you've made the application, Julia."

Now Ester's heart had been softening under the influence of these peaceful Bible words. She believed them; and in her heart was a real, earnest desire to teach her brother and sister Bible truths. Left alone, she would have explained that those who loved Jesus *were* struggling, in a weak, feeble way, to obey these directions; that she herself was trying, trying *hard* sometimes; that *they* ought to. But there was this against Ester—her whole life was so at variance with those plain, searching Bible rules that the youngest child could not but see it; and Sadie's mischievous tones and evident relish of her embarrassment at Julia's question destroyed the self-searching thoughts. She answered, with severe dignity:

"Sadie, if I were you, I wouldn't try to make the children as irreverent as I was myself." Then she went dignifiedly from the room.

Dr. Van Anden paused for a moment before Sadie as she sat alone in the sitting room that same Sabbath evening.

"Sadie," said he, "is there one verse in the Bible which you have never read?"

"Plenty of them, Doctor. I commenced reading the Bible through once; but I stopped at some chapter in Numbers—the thirtieth, I think it is, isn't it? Or somewhere along there where all those hard names are, you know. But why do you ask?"

The doctor opened a large Bible which lay on the stand before them and read aloud: "Ye have perverted the words of the living God."

Sadie looked puzzled. "Now, Doctor, whatever possessed you to think that I had never read that verse?"

"God counts that a solemn thing, Sadie."

"Very likely; what then?"

"I was reading on the piazza when the children came to you for an explanation of their lesson."

Sadie laughed. "Did you hear that conversation, Doctor? I hope you were benefited." Then, more gravely: "Dr. Van Anden, do you really mean me to think that I was perverting Scripture?"

"*I* certainly think so, Sadie. Were you not giving the children wrong ideas concerning the teachings of our Savior?"

Sadie was quite sober now. "I told the truth at last, Doctor. I don't know anything about these matters. People who profess to be Christians do not live according to our Savior's teaching. At least *I* don't see any who do; and it sometimes seems to me that those verses which the children were studying *cannot* mean what they say, or Christian people would surely *try* to follow them."

For an answer, Dr. Van Anden turned the Bible leaves again and pointed with his finger to this verse, which Sadie read:

"'But as he which has called you is holy, so be ye holy in all manner of conversation.'"

After that he went out of the room.

And Sadie, reading the verse over again, could not but understand that she *might* have a perfect pattern, if she would.

5

THE POOR LITTLE FISH

"MOTHER," said Sadie, appearing in the dining room one morning, holding Julia by the hand, "did you ever hear of the fish who fell out of the frying pan into the fire?" Which question her mother answered by asking, without turning her eyes from the great batch of bread which she was molding:

"What mischief are you up to now, Sadie?"

"Why, nothing," said Sadie; "only here is the very fish so renowned in ancient history, and I've brought her for your inspection."

This answer brought Mrs. Ried's eyes around from the dough and fixed them upon Julia; and she said as soon as she caught a glimpse of the forlorn little maiden: "Oh, my *patience!*"

A specimen requiring great patience from anyone coming in contact with her was this same Julia. The pretty blue dress and white apron were covered with great patches of mud; morocco boots and neat white stockings were in the same direful plight; and down her face the salt and muddy tears were running, for her handkerchief was also streaked with mud.

"I should *think* so!" laughed Sadie in answer to her mother's exclamation. "The history of the poor little fish, in brief, is this: She started, immaculate in white apron, white stockings, and the like, for the post office with Ester's letter. She met with temptation in the shape of a little girl with paper dolls; and while admiring them, the letter had the meanness to slip out of her hand into the mud! That, you understand, was the frying pan. Much horrified with this state of things, the two wise young heads were put together, and the brilliant idea conceived of giving the muddy letter a thorough washing in the creek! So to the creek they went; and while they stood ankle deep in the mud, vigorously carrying their idea into effect, the vicious little thing hopped out of Julia's hand and sailed merrily away downstream! So there she was, out of the frying pan into the fire, sure enough! And the letter has sailed for Uncle Ralph's by a different route than that which is usually taken."

Sadie's nonsense was interrupted at this point by Ester, who had listened with darkening face to the rapidly told story:

"She ought to be thoroughly *whipped,* the careless little goose! Mother, if you don't punish her now, I never would again."

Then Julia's tearful sorrow blazed into sudden anger: "I *oughtn't* to be whipped; you're an ugly, mean sister to say so. I tumbled down and hurt my arm *dreadfully,* trying to catch your old *hateful* letter; and you're just as mean as you can be!"

Between tears, and loud tones, and Sadie's laughter, Julia had managed to burst forth these angry sentences before her mother's voice reached her; when it did, she was silenced.

"Julia, I am *astonished!* Is that the way to speak to

your sister? Go up to my room directly; and, when you have put on dry clothes, sit down there and stay until you are ready to tell Ester that you are sorry and ask her to forgive you."

"*Really,* Mother," Sadie said as the little girl went stamping up the stairs, her face buried in her muddy handkerchief, "I'm not sure but you have made a mistake, and Ester is the one to be sent to her room until she can behave better. I don't pretend to be *good* myself; but I must say it seems ridiculous to speak in the way she did to a sorry, frightened child. I never saw a more woeful figure in my life"; and Sadie laughed again at the recollection.

"Yes," said Ester, "you uphold her in all sorts of mischief and insolence; that is the reason she is so troublesome to manage."

Mrs. Ried looked distressed. "Don't, Ester," she said; "don't speak in that loud, sharp tone. Sadie, you should not encourage Julia in speaking improperly to her sister. I think myself that Ester was hard with her. The poor child did not mean any harm; but she must not be rude to anybody."

"Oh yes," Ester said, speaking bitterly, "of course, *I* am the one to blame; I always *am.* No one in this house ever does anything wrong except *me.*"

Mrs. Ried sighed heavily, and Sadie turned away and ran upstairs, humming:

> "*Oh, would I were a buttercup,*
> *A blossom in the meadow.*"

And Julia, in her mother's room, exchanged her wet and muddy garments for clean ones and *cried;* washed her face in the clear, pure water until it was fresh and clean, and cried again, louder and harder; her heart was all bruised and bleeding. She had not meant to be careless. She had been carefully dressed that morning to spend the long, bright Saturday with Vesta Griswold. She had intended to go swiftly and safely to the post office with the small white treasure entrusted to her care; but those paper dolls were *so* pretty, and of course, there was no harm in walking along with Addie and looking at them. How could she know that the hateful letter was going to tumble out of her apron pocket? Right there, too, the only place along the road where there was the least bit of mud to be seen! Then she had honestly supposed that a little clean water from the creek, applied with her smooth white handkerchief, would take the stains right out of the envelope, and the sun would dry it, and it would go safely to Uncle Ralph's after all; but, instead of that, the hateful, *hateful* thing slipped right out of her hand and went floating down the stream; and at this point Julia's sobs burst forth afresh. Presently she took up her broken thread of thought and went on: How very, *very* ugly Ester was; if *she* hadn't been there, her mother would have listened kindly to her story of how very sorry she was and how she meant to do just right. Then she would have forgiven her, and she would have been freshly dressed in her clean blue dress instead of her pink one and would have had her happy day after all. Now she would have to spend this bright day all alone; and, at this point, her tears rolled down in torrents.

"Jule," called a familiar voice under her window, "where are you? Come down and mend my sail for me, won't you?"

Julia went to the window and poured into Alfred's sympathetic ears the story of her grief and her wrongs.

"Just exactly like her," was his comment on Ester's share in the tragedy. "She grows crosser every day. I guess, if I were you, I'd let her wait a spell before I asked her forgiveness."

"I guess I shall," sputtered Julia. "She was meaner than anything, and I'd tell her so this minute if I saw her; that's all the sorry I am."

So the talk went on; and when Alfred was called to get Ester a pail of water and left Julia in solitude, she found her heart very much strengthened in its purpose to tire everybody out in waiting for her apology.

The long, warm, busy day moved on; and the overworked and wearied mother found time to toil up two flights of stairs in search of her young daughter in the hope of soothing and helping her; but Julia was in no mood to be helped. She hated to stay up there alone; she wanted to go down in the garden with Alfred; she wanted to go to the arbor and read her new book; she wanted to take a walk down by the river; she wanted her dinner exceedingly; but to ask Ester's forgiveness was the one thing that she did *not* want to do. No, not if she stayed there alone for a week; not if she *starved,* she said aloud, stamping her foot and growing indignant over the thought. Alfred came as often as his Saturday occupations would admit and held emphatic talks with the little prisoner above, admiring her "pluck" and assuring her that he "wouldn't give in, not he."

"You see, I *can't* do it," said Julia, with a gleam of satisfaction in her eyes, "because it wouldn't be true. I'm *not* sorry; and Mother wouldn't have me tell a lie for anybody."

So the sun went toward the west, and Julia at the window watched the academy girls moving home-ward from their afternoon ramble, listened to the preparations for tea which were being made among the dishes in the dining room, and having no more tears to shed, sighed wearily and wished the miserable day were quite done and she were sound asleep. Only a few moments before she had received a third visit from her mother; and turning to her, fresh from a talk with Alfred, she had answered her mother's question as to whether she were not now ready to ask Ester's forgiveness with quite as sober and determined a "No, ma'am" as she had given that day; and her mother had gravely and sadly answered, "I am very sorry, Julia, I can't come up here again; I am too tired for that. You may come to me if you wish to see me any time before seven o'clock. After that you must go to your room."

And with this Julia had let her depart, only saying as the door closed: "Then I can be asleep before Ester comes up. I'm glad of that. I wouldn't look at her again today for anything." And then Julia was once more summoned to the window.

"Jule," Alfred said, with less decision in his voice than there had been before, "Mother looked awful tired when she came downstairs just now, and there was a tear rolling down her cheek."

"There was?" said Julia, in a shocked and troubled tone.

"And I guess," Alfred continued, "she's had a time of it today. Ester is too cross even to look at; and they've been working pell-mell all day; and Minie tumbled over the icebox and got hurt, and Mother held her most an hour, and I guess she feels real bad about this. She told Sadie she felt sorry for you."

Silence for a little while at the window above and from the boy below; then he broke forth suddenly: "I say, Jule, hadn't you better do it after all—not for Ester—but there's Mother, you know."

"But, Alfred," interrupted the truthful and puzzled Julia, "what can I do about it? You know I'm to tell Ester that I'm sorry; and that will not be true."

This question also troubled Alfred. It did not seem to occur to these two foolish young heads that she *ought* to be sorry for her own angry words, no matter how much in the wrong another had been. So they stood with grave faces and thought about it. Alfred found a way out of the mist at last.

"See here, aren't you sorry that you couldn't go to Vesta's, and had to stay up there alone all day, and that it bothered Mother?"

"Of course," said Julia, "I'm real sorry about Mother. Alfred, did I honestly make her cry?"

"Yes, you did," Alfred answered earnestly. "I saw that tear as plain as day. Now you see, you can tell Ester you're sorry, just as well as not; because if you hadn't said anything to her, Mother could have made it all right; so of course you're sorry."

"Well," said Julia slowly, rather bewildered still, "that sounds as if it was right; and yet, somehow . . . Well, Alfred, you wait for me, and I'll be down right away."

So it happened that a very penitent little face stood at her mother's elbow a few moments after this; and Julia's voice was very earnest: "Mother, I'm so sorry I made you such a great deal of trouble today."

And the patient mother turned and kissed the flushed cheek and answered kindly: "Mother will forgive you. Have you seen Ester, my daughter?"

"No, ma'am," spoken more faintly; "but I'm going to find her right away."

And Ester answered the troubled little voice with a

cold, "Actions speak louder than words. I hope you will show how sorry you are by behaving better in the future. Stand out of my way."

"Is it all done up?" Alfred asked a moment later as she joined him on the piazza to take a last look at the beauty of this day which had opened so brightly for her.

"Yes," with a relieved sigh; "and, Alfred, I never mean to be such a woman as Ester is when I grow up. I wouldn't for the world. I mean to be nice, and good, and kind, like sister Sadie."

6

SOMETHING HAPPENS

NOW the letter which had caused so much trouble
in the Ried family, and especially in Ester's heart, was,
in one sense, not an ordinary letter. It had been
written to Ester's cousin Abbie, her one intimate
friend, Uncle Ralph's only daughter. These two, of the
same age, had been correspondents almost from their
babyhood; and yet they had never seen each other's
faces.

To go to New York, to her uncle's house, to see and
be with Cousin Abbie, had been the one great dream
of Ester's heart—as likely to be realized, she could not
help acknowledging, as a journey to the moon and no
more so. New York was at least five hundred miles
away; and the money necessary to carry her there
seemed like a small fortune to Ester, to say nothing of
the endless additions to her wardrobe which would
have to be made before she would account herself
ready. So she contented herself, or perhaps it would be
more truthful to say she made herself discontented,
with ceaseless dreams over what New York, and her
uncle's family, and above all, Cousin Abbie were like;

and whether she would ever see them; and why it had always happened that something was sure to prevent Abbie's visits to herself; and whether she should like her as well, if she could be with her as she did now; and a hundred other confused and disconnected thoughts about them all.

Ester had no idea what this miserable, restless dreaming of hers was doing for her. She did not see that her very desires after a better life, which were sometimes strong upon her, were colored with impatience and envy.

Cousin Abbie was a Christian and wrote her some earnest letters; but to Ester it seemed a very easy matter indeed for one who was surrounded, as she imagined Abbie to be, by luxury and love, to be a joyous, eager Christian. Into this very letter that poor Julia had sent sailing down the stream, some of her inmost feelings had been poured.

"Don't think me devoid of all aspirations after something higher," so the letter ran. "Dear Abbie, you, in your sunny home, can never imagine how wildly I long sometimes to be free from my surroundings, free from petty cares, and trials, and vexations which, I feel, are eating out my very life. Oh, to be free for one hour, to feel myself at liberty for just one day, to follow my own tastes and inclinations; to be the person I believe God designed me to be; to fill the niche I believe he designed me to fill! Abbie, I *hate* my life. I have not a happy moment. It is all rasped, and warped, and unlovely. I am nothing, and I know it; and I had rather, for my own comfort, be like the most of those who surround me—nothing, and not know it. Sometimes I cannot help asking myself why I was made as I am. Why can't I be a clod, a plodder, and drag my way with stupid good nature through this miserable world, instead of chafing and bruising myself at every step."

Now it would be very natural to suppose that a young lady with a grain of sense left in her brains would, in cooler moments, have been rather glad than otherwise to have such a restless, unhappy, unchristianlike letter hopelessly lost. But Ester felt, as has been seen, thoroughly angry that so much lofty sentiment, which she mistook for religion, was entirely lost. Yet let it not be supposed that one word of this rebellious outbreak was written simply for effect. Ester, when she wrote that she "hated her life," was thoroughly and miserably in earnest. When, in the solitude of her own room, she paced her floor that evening and murmured despairingly: "Oh, if something would *only* happen to rest me for just a little while!" she was more thoroughly in earnest than any human being who feels that Christ has died to save her and that she has an eternal resting place prepared for her and waiting to receive her has any right to feel on such a subject. Yet, though the letter had never reached its destination, the pitying Savior, looking down upon his poor, foolish lamb in tender love, made haste to prepare an answer to her wild, rebellious cry for help, even though she cried blindly, without a thought of the Helper who is sufficient for all human needs.

"Long-looked-for, come at last!" and Sadie's clear voice rang through the dining room, and a moment after, that young lady herself reached the pump room, holding up for Ester's view a dainty envelope, directed in a yet more dainty hand to Miss Ester Ried. "Here's that wonderful letter from Cousin Abbie which you have sent me to the post office after three times a day for as many weeks. It reached here by the way of Cape

Horn, I should say, by its appearance. It has been remailed twice."

Ester set her pail down hastily, seized the letter, and retired to the privacy of the pantry to devour it; and for once was oblivious to the fact that Sadie lunched on bits of cake broken from the smooth, square loaf while she waited to hear the news.

"Anything special?" Mrs. Ried asked, pausing in the doorway, which question Ester answered by turning a flushed and eager face toward them as she passed the letter to Sadie with permission to read it aloud. Surprised into silence by the unusual confidence, Sadie read the dainty epistle without comment:

"MY DEAR ESTER:

"I'm in a grand flurry, and shall therefore not stop for long stories today, but come at the pith of the matter immediately. We want you. That is nothing new, you are aware, as we have been wanting you for many a day. But there is new decision in my plans, and new inducements, this time. We not only want, but *must* have you. Please don't say no to me this once. We are going to have a wedding in our house, and we need your presence, and wisdom, and taste. Father says you can't be your mother's daughter if you haven't exquisite taste. I am very busy helping to get the bride in order, which is a work of time and patience; and I do so much need your aid; besides, the bride is your Uncle Ralph's only daughter, so of course you ought to be interested in her.

"Ester, *do* come. Father says the enclosed fifty dollars is a present from him, which you must honor by letting it pay your fare to New York just as soon as possible. The wedding is fixed for the twenty-second; and we want you here at least three weeks before that. Brother Ralph is to be first groomsman; and he especially needs your assistance as the bride has named you for her first bridesmaid. I'm to dress—I mean the bride is to dress—in white, and Mother has a dress prepared for the bridesmaid to match hers; so that matter need not delay or cause you anxiety.

"This letter is getting too long. I meant it to be very brief and pointed. I designed every other word to be come; but after all I do not believe you will need so much urging to be with us at this time. I flatter myself that you love me enough to come to me if you can. So, leaving Ralph to write directions concerning route and trains, I will run and try on the bride's bonnet, which has just come home.

"P.S. There is to be a groom as well as a bride, though I see I have said nothing concerning him. Never mind, you shall see him when you come. Dear Ester, there isn't a word of sense in this letter, I know; but I haven't time to put any in."

"Really," laughed Sadie as she concluded the reading, "this is almost foolish enough to have been written by me. Isn't it splendid, though? Ester, I'm glad you are *you*. I wish I had corresponded with Cousin Abbie myself. A wedding of any kind is a delicious novelty; but a real New York wedding, and a bridesmaid besides—my! I've a mind to clap my hands for you, seeing you are too dignified to do it yourself."

"Oh," said Ester, from whose face the flush had faded, leaving it actually pale with excitement and expected disappointment, "you don't suppose I am foolish enough to think I can go, do you?"

"Of course you will go, when Uncle Ralph has paid your fare and more too. Fifty dollars will buy a good deal besides a ticket to New York. Mother, don't you ever think of saying that she can't go; there is nothing to hinder her. She is to go, isn't she?"

"Why, I don't know," answered this perplexed mother. "I want her to, I am sure; yet I don't see how she can be spared. She will need a great many things besides a ticket, and fifty dollars do not go as far as you imagine; besides, Ester, you know I depend on you so much."

Ester's lips parted to speak; and had the words come forth which were in her heart, they would have been sharp and bitter ones—about never expecting to go anywhere, never being able to do anything but work; but Sadie's eager voice was quicker than hers:

"Oh, now, Mother, it is no use to talk in that way. I've quite set my heart on Ester's going. I never expect to have an invitation there myself, so I must take my honors secondhand.

"Mother, it is time you learned to depend on me a little. I'm two inches taller than Ester, and I've no doubt I shall develop into a remarkable person when she is where we can't all lean upon her. School closes this very week, you know, and we have vacation until October. Abbie couldn't have chosen a better time. Whom do you suppose she is to marry? What a queer creature, not to tell us. Say she can go, Mother— quick!"

Sadie's last point was a good one in Mrs. Ried's opinion. Perhaps the giddy Sadie, at once her pride and her anxiety, might learn a little self-reliance by feeling a shadow of the weight of care which rested continually on Ester.

"You certainly need the change," she said, her eyes resting pityingly on the young, careworn face of her eldest daughter. "But how could we manage about your wardrobe? Your black silk is nice, to be sure, but you would need one bright evening dress at least, and you know we haven't the money to spare."

Then Sadie, thoughtless, selfish Sadie, who was never supposed to have one care for others and very little for herself—Sadie, who vexed Ester nearly every hour in the day by what, at the time, always seemed some especially selfish, heedless act—suddenly shone out gloriously. She stood still and actually seemed to think for a full minute, while Ester jerked a pan of potatoes toward her and commenced peeling vigorously; then she clapped her hands and gave vent to little gleeful shouts before she exclaimed: "Oh, Mother, Mother! I have it exactly. I wonder we didn't think of it before. There's my blue silk—just the thing! I am tall and she is short, so it will make her a beautiful train dress. Won't that do splendidly!"

The magnitude of this proposal awed even Ester into silence. To be appreciated, it must be understood that Sadie Ried had never in her life possessed a silk dress. Mrs. Ried's best black silk had long ago been cut over for Ester; so had her brown and white plaid. So there had been nothing of the sort to remodel for Sadie; and this elegant sky blue silk had been lying in its satin-paper covering for more than two years. It was the gift of a dear friend of Mrs. Ried's girlhood to the young beauty who bore her name, and had been waiting all this time for Sadie to attain proper growth to admit of its being cut into for her. Meantime she had feasted her eyes upon it and gloried in the prospect of that wonderful day when she should sweep across the platform of Music Hall with this same silk falling in beautiful blue waves around her; for it had long been settled that it was to be worn first on that day when she should graduate.

No wonder, then, that Ester stood in mute astonishment while Mrs. Ried commented:

"Why, Sadie, my dear child, is it possible you are willing to give up your blue silk?"

"Not a bit of it, Mother; I don't intend to give it up the least bit in the world. I'm merely going to lend it. It's too pretty to stay poked up in that drawer by itself any longer. I've set my heart on its coming out this very season. Just as likely as not it will learn to put on airs for me when I graduate. I'm not at all satisfied with my attainments in that line; so Ester shall take it to New York; and if she sits down or stands up, or turns around, or has one minute's peace while she has it on, for fear lest she should spot it, or tear it, or get it stepped on, I'll never forgive her."

And at this harangue Ester laughed a free, glad laugh, such as was seldom heard from her. Some way it began to seem as if she were really to go; Sadie had such a brisk, businesslike way of saying, "Ester shall take it to New York." Oh, if she only, *only* could go, she would be willing to do *anything* after that; but one peep, one little peep into the beautiful magic world that lay outside of that dining room and kitchen she felt as if she must have. Perhaps that laugh did as much for her as anything. It almost startled Mrs. Ried with its sweetness and rarity. What if the change would freshen and brighten her, and bring her back to them with some of the sparkles that continually danced in Sadie's eyes; but what, on the other hand, if she should grow utterly disgusted with the monotony of their very quiet, very busy life and refuse to work in that most necessary treadmill any longer? So the mother argued and hesitated, and the decision, which was to mean so much more than any of those knew, trembled in the balance; for let Mrs. Ried once find voice to say, "Oh, Ester, I don't see but what you will *have* to give it up," and Ester would have turned quickly and with curling lip to that pan of potatoes and have sharply forbidden anyone to mention the subject to her again. Once more Sadie, dear, merry, silly Sadie, came to the rescue.

"Mother, oh, Mother! what an endless time you are in coming to a decision! I could plan an expedition to the North Pole in less time than this. I'm just wild to have her go. I want to hear how a genuine New York bride looks; besides, you know, dear Mother, I want to stay in the kitchen with you. Ester does everything, and I don't have any chance. I perfectly long to bake, and boil, and broil, and brew things. Say yes, there's a darling."

Mrs. Ried looked at the bright, flushed face and thought how little the dear child knew about all these matters and how little patience poor Ester, who was so competent herself, would have with Sadie's ignorance, and said, slowly and hesitatingly, but yet actually said:

"Well, Ester, my daughter, I really think we must try to get along without you for a little while!"

And these three people really seemed to think that they had decided the matter. Though two of them were at least theoretical believers in a "special providence," it never once occurred to them that this little thing, in all its details, had been settled for ages.

7

JOURNEYING

"TWENTY minutes here for refreshments!" "Passengers for New York take south track!" "New York daily papers here!" "Sweet oranges here!" And amid all these yells of discordant tongues, and the screeching of engines, and the ringing of bells, and the intolerable din of a merciless gong, Ester pushed and elbowed her way through the crowd, almost panting with her efforts to keep pace with her traveling companion, a nervous country merchant on his way to New York to buy goods. He hurried her through the crowd and the noise into the dining saloon; stood by her side while, obedient to his orders, she poured down her throat a cup of almost boiling coffee; then, seating her in the ladies' room, charged her on no account to stir from that point while he was gone—he had just time to run around to the post office and mail a forgotten letter; then he vanished, and in the confusion and the crowd Ester was alone. She did not feel in the least flurried or nervous; on the contrary, she liked it, this first experience of hers in a city depot; she would not have had it made known to one of the groups of fashionably attired and very-much-at-ease travelers who thronged past her for the world—but the truth was, Ester had been having her very first ride in the cars! Sadie had made various little trips in company with school friends to adjoining towns, after schoolbooks, or music, or to attend a concert, or for pure fun; but, though Ester had spent her eighteen years of life in a town which had long been an express station, yet want of time, or of money, or of inclination to take the bits of journeys which alone were within her reach had kept her at home.

Now she glanced at herself, at her faultlessly neat and ladylike traveling suit. She could get a full view of it in an opposite mirror, and it was becoming, from the dainty veil which fluttered over her hat to the shining tips of her walking boots. She gave a complacent little sigh as she said to herself: "I don't see but I look as much like a traveler as any of them. I'm sure I don't feel in the least confused. I'm glad I'm not as ridiculously dressed as that pert-looking girl in brown. I should call it in very bad taste to wear such a rich silk as that for traveling. She doesn't look as though she had a single idea beyond dress; probably that is what is occupying her thoughts at this very moment"; and Ester's speaking face betrayed contempt and conscious superiority as she watched the fluttering bit of silk and ribbons opposite. Ester had a very mistaken opinion of herself in this respect; probably she would have been startled and indignant had anyone told her that her supposed contempt for the rich and elegant attire displayed all around her was really the outgrowth of envy; that, when she told herself *she* wouldn't lavish so much time and thought, and above all, *money* on mere outside show, it was mere nonsense—that she already spent all the time at her disposal and all the money she could possibly spare on the very things which she was condemning.

The truth was, Ester had a perfectly royal taste in all these matters. Give her but the wherewithal, and she would speedily have glistened in silk and sparkled with jewels; yet she honestly thought that her bitter denunciation of fashion and folly in this form was outward evidence of a mind elevated far above such trivial subjects, and looked down, accordingly, with cool contempt on those whom she was pleased to denominate "butterflies of fashion."

And, in her flights into a "higher sphere of thought," this absurdly inconsistent Ester never once remembered how, just exactly a week ago that day, she had gone around like a storm king in her own otherwise peaceful home, almost wearing out the long-suffering patience of her weary mother, rendered the house intolerable to Sadie, and actually boxed Julia's ears; and all because she saw with her own commonsense eyes that she really *could* not have her blue silk, or rather Sadie's blue silk, trimmed with netted fringe at twelve shillings a yard, but must do with simple folds and a seventy-five-cent heading!

Such a two weeks as the last had been in the Ried family! The entire household had joined in the commotion produced by Ester's projected visit. It was marvelous how much there was to do. Mrs. Ried toiled early and late, and made many quiet sacrifices, in order that her daughter might not feel too keenly the difference between her own and her cousin's wardrobe. Sadie emptied what she denominated her finery box and donated every article in it, delivering comic little lectures to each bit of lace and ribbon as she smoothed them and patted them, and told them they were going to New York. Julia hemmed pocket handkerchiefs and pricked her poor little fingers unmercifully and uncomplainingly. Alfred ran off errands with remarkable promptness, but confessed to Julia privately that it was because he was in such a hurry to have Ester gone, so he could see how it would seem for everybody to be good natured. Little Minie got in everybody's way as much as such a tiny creature could, and finally brought the tears to Ester's eyes and set everyone else into bursts of laughter by bringing a very smooth little handkerchief about six inches square and offering it as her contribution toward the traveler's outfit. As for Ester, she was hurried and nervous, and almost unendurably cross, through the whole of it, wanting a hundred things which it was impossible for her to have, and scorning not a few little trifles that had been prepared for her by patient, toil-worn fingers.

"Ester, I *do* hope New York, or Cousin Abbie, or somebody, will have a soothing and improving effect upon you," Sadie had said with a sort of good-humored impatience only the night before her departure. "Now that you have reached the summit of your hopes, you seem more uncomfortable about it than you were even to stay at home. Do let us see you look pleasant for just five minutes that we may have something good to remember you by."

"My dear," Mrs. Ried had interposed rebukingly, "Ester is hurried and tired, remember, and has had a great many things to try her today. I don't think it is a good plan, just as a family is about to separate, to say any careless or foolish words that we don't mean. Mother has a great many hard days of toil, which Ester has given, to remember her by." Oh, the patient, tender, forgiving mother! Ester, being asleep to her own faults, never once thought of the sharp, fretful, half-disgusted way in which much of her work had been performed, but only remembered, with a little sigh of satisfaction, the many loaves of cake and the rows of pies which she had baked that very morning in order to save her mother's steps. This was all she thought of now, but there came days when she was wide awake.

Meantime the New York train, after panting and snorting several times to give notice that the twenty minutes were about up, suddenly puffed and rumbled its way out from the depot and left Ester obeying orders, that is, sitting in the corner where she had been placed by Mr. Newton—being still outwardly, but there was in her heart a perfect storm of vexation. *This comes of Mother's absurd fussiness in insisting upon putting me in Mr. Newton's care, instead of letting me travel alone as I wanted to, she fumed to herself. Now we shall not get into New York until after six o'clock! How provoking!*

"How provoking this is!" Mr. Newton exclaimed, reechoing her thoughts as he bustled in, red with haste and heat, and stood penitently before her. "I hadn't the least idea it would take so long to go to the post office. I am very sorry!

"Well," he continued, recovering his good humor, notwithstanding Ester's provoking silence, "what can't be cured must be endured, Miss Ester; and it isn't as bad as it might be, either. We've only to wait an hour and a quarter. I've some errands to do, and I'll show you the city with pleasure; or would you prefer sitting here and looking around you?"

"I should decidedly prefer not running the chance of missing the next train," Ester answered very shortly. "So I think it will be wiser to stay where I am."

In truth Mr. Newton endured the results of his own

carelessness with too much complacency to suit Ester's state of mind; but he took no notice of her broadly given hint further than to assure her that she need give herself no uneasiness on that score; he should certainly be on time. Then he went off, looking immensely relieved; for Mr. Newton frankly confessed to himself that he did not know how to take care of a lady. "If she were a parcel of goods now that one could get stored or checked and knew that she would come on all right, why—but a lady. I'm not used to it. How easily I could have caught that train if I hadn't been obliged to run back after her; but, bless me, I wouldn't have her know that for the world." This he said meditatively as he walked down South Street.

The New York train had carried away the greater portion of the throng at the depot so that Ester and the dozen or twenty people who occupied the great sitting room with her had comparative quiet. The wearer of the condemned brown silk and blue ribbons was still there and awoke Ester's vexation still further by seeming utterly unable to keep herself quiet; she fluttered from seat to seat, and from window to window, like an uneasy bird in a cage. Presently she addressed Ester in a bright little tone: "Doesn't it bore you dreadfully to wait in a depot?"

"Yes," said Ester briefly and truthfully, notwithstanding the fact that she was having her first experience in that boredom.

"Are you going to New York?"

"I hope so," she answered with energy. "I expected to have been almost there by this time; but the gentleman who is supposed to be taking care of me had to rush off and stay just long enough to miss the train."

"How annoying!" answered the blue ribbons with

a soft laugh. "I missed it, too, in such a silly way. I just ran around the corner to get some chocolate drops, and a little matter detained me a few moments; and when I came back, the train had gone. I was so sorry, for I'm in such a hurry to get home. Do you live in New York?"

Ester shook her head and thought within herself: *That is just as much sense as I should suppose you to have—risk the chance of missing a train for the sake of a paper of candy.*

Of course Ester could not be expected to know that the chocolate drops were for the wee sister at home, whose heart would be nearly broken if sister Fanny came home, after an absence of twenty-four hours, without bringing her anything; and the "little matter" which detained her a few moments was joining the search after a twenty-five-cent bill which the ruthless wind had snatched from the hand of a barefooted, bareheaded, and almost forlorn little girl, who cried as violently as though her last hope in life had been blown away with it; nor how, failing in finding the treasure, the gold-clasped purse had been opened, and a crisp, new bill had been taken out to fill its place; neither am I at all certain as to whether it would have made any difference at all in Ester's verdict if she had known all the circumstances.

The side door opened quietly just at this point, and a middle-aged man came in, carrying in one hand a toolbox, and in the other a two-story tin pail. Both girls watched him curiously as he set these down on the floor, and taking tacks from his pocket and a hammer from his box, he proceeded to tack a piece of paper to the wall. Ester, from where she sat, could see that the paper was small and that something was printed on it in close, fine type. It didn't look in the least like a handbill or indeed like a notice of any sort. Her desire to know what it could be grew strong; two tiny tacks held it firmly in its place. Then the man turned and eyed the inmates of the room, who were by this time giving undivided attention to him and his bit of paper. Presently he spoke, in a quiet, respectful tone:

"I've tacked up a nice little tract. I thought maybe while you was waiting you might like something to read. If one of you would read it aloud, all the rest could hear it." So saying, the man stooped and took up his toolbox and his tin pail and went away, leaving the influences connected with those two or three strokes of his hammer to work for him through all time and meet him at the judgment. But if a bombshell had suddenly come down and laid itself in ruins at their feet, it could not have made a much more startled company than the tract-tacker left behind him. A tract!—actually tacked up on the wall and waiting for some human voice to give it utterance! A tract in a railroad depot! How queer! How singular! How almost improper! Why? Oh, Ester didn't know; it was so unusual. Yes, but then that didn't make it improper. No; but—then, she—it— Well, it was fanatical. Oh yes, that was it. She knew it was improper in some way. It was strange that that very convenient word should have escaped her for a little. This talk Ester held hurriedly with her conscience. It was asleep, you know; but just then it nestled as in a dream and gave her a little prick; but that industrious, important word, *fanatical,* lulled it back to its rest. Meantime there hung the tract, and fluttered a little in the summer air as the door opened and closed. Was no one to give it voice?

"I'd like dreadful well to hear it," an old lady said,

nodding her gray head toward the little leaf on the wall; "but I've packed up my specs and might just as well have no eyes at all as far as readin' goes, when I haven't got my specs on. There's some young eyes 'round here though, one would think," she added, looking inquiringly around. "You won't need glasses, I should say now, for a spell of years!"

This remark, or hint, or inquiry was directed squarely at Ester and received no other answer than a shrug of the shoulder and an impatient tapping of her heels on the bare floor. Under her breath Ester muttered, "Disagreeable old woman!"

The brown silk rustled, and the blue ribbons fluttered restlessly for a minute; then their owner's clear voice suddenly broke the silence: "I'll read it for you, ma'am, if you really would like to hear it."

The wrinkled, homely, happy old face broke into a beaming smile as she turned toward the pink-cheeked, blue-eyed maiden. "That I would," she answered heartily, "dreadful well. I ain't heard nothing good, 'pears to me, since I started; and I've come two hundred miles. It seems as if it might kind of lift me up, and rest me like, to hear something real good again."

With the flush on her face a little heightened, the young girl promptly crossed to where the tract hung; and a strange stillness settled over the listeners as her clear voice sounded distinctly down the long room. This was what she read:

"Dear Friend: Are you a Christian? What have you done today for Christ? Are the friends with whom you have been talking traveling toward the New Jerusalem? Did you compare notes with them as to how you were all prospering on the way? Is that stranger by your side a fellow pilgrim? Did you ask him if he *would* be? Have you been careful to recommend the religion of Jesus Christ by your words, by your acts, by your looks, this day? If danger comes to you, have you this day asked Christ to be your helper? If death comes to you this night, are you prepared to give up your account? What would your record of this last day be? A blank? What! Have you done *nothing* for the Master? Then what have you done against him? Nothing? Nay, verily! Is not the Bible doctrine, He that is not for me is against me?

"Remember that every neglected opportunity, every idle word, every wrong thought of yours has been written down this day. You cannot take back the thoughts or words; you cannot recall the opportunity. This day, with all its mistakes and blots and mars, you can never live over again. It must go up to the judgment just as it is. Have you begged the blood of Jesus to be spread over it all? Have you resolved that no other day shall witness a repetition of the same mistakes? Have you resolved in your own strength or in his?"

During the reading of the tract, a young man had entered, paused a moment in surprise at the unwonted scene, then moved with very quiet tread across the room and took the vacant seat near Ester. As the reader came back to her former seat with the pink on her cheek deepened into warm crimson, the newcomer greeted her with:

"Good evening, Miss Fannie. Have you been finding work to do for the Master?"

"Only a very little thing," she answered with a voice in which there was a slight tremble.

"I don't know about that, my dear." This was the old woman's voice. "I'm sure I thank you a great deal. They're kind of startling questions like; enough to most scare a body, unless you was trying pretty hard, now ain't they?"

"Very solemn questions, indeed," answered the gentleman to whom this question seemed to be addressed. "I wonder, if we were each obliged to write truthful answers to each one of them, how many we should be ashamed to have each other see?"

"How many would be ashamed to have *him* see?" The old woman spoke with an emphatic shake of her gray head and a reverent touch of the pronoun.

"That is the vital point," he said. "Yet how much more ashamed we often seem to be of man's judgment than of God's."

Then he turned suddenly to Ester and spoke in a quiet, respectful tone:

"Is the stranger by my side a fellow pilgrim?"

Ester was startled and confused. The whole scene had been a very strange one to her. She tried to think the blue-ribboned girl was dreadfully out of her sphere; but the questions following each other in such quick succession were so very solemn, and personal, and searching—and now this one. She hesitated, and stammered, and flushed like a schoolgirl as at last she faltered: "I—I think—I believe—I am."

"Then I trust you are wide awake and a faithful worker in the vineyard," he said earnestly. "These are times when the Master needs true and faithful workmen."

"He's a minister," said Ester positively, to herself, when she had recovered from her confusion sufficiently to observe him closely as he carefully folded the old woman's shawl for her, took her box and basket in his care, and courteously offered his hand to assist her into the cars, for the New York train thundered in at last, and Mr. Newton presented himself; and they rushed and jostled each other out of the depot and into the train. And the little tract hung quietly in its corner; and the carpenter who had left it there, hammered, and sawed, and planed—yes, and prayed that God would use it; and knew not then, nor afterward, that it had already awakened thoughts that would tell for eternity.

8

THE JOURNEY'S END

"YES, he's a minister," Ester repeated even more decidedly as, being seated in the swift-moving train directly behind the old lady and the young gentleman who had become the subject of her thoughts, she found leisure to observe him more closely. Mr. Newton was absorbed in the *Tribune;* so she gave her undivided attention to the two and could hear snatches of the conversation which passed between them as well as note the courteous care with which he brought her a cup of water and attended to all her simple wants. During the stopping of the train at a station, their talk became distinct.

"And I haven't seen my boy, don't you think, in ten years," the old lady was saying. "Won't he be glad, though, to see his mother once more? And he's got children—two of them; one is named after me, Sabrina. It's an awful homely name, I think, don't you? But then, you see, it was Grandma's."

"And that makes all the difference in the world," her companion answered. "So the old home is broken up, and you are going to make a new one."

"Yes, and I'll show you *everything* I've got to remember my old garden by."

With eager, trembling fingers, she untied the string which held down the cover of her basket and, rummaging within, brought to light a withered bouquet of the very commonest and, perhaps, the very homeliest flowers that grew, if there *are* any homely flowers.

"There," she said, holding it tenderly and speaking with quivering lip and trembling voice. "I picked 'em the very last thing I did, out in my own little garden patch by the back door. Oh, times and times I've sat and weeded and dug around them, with him sitting on the stoop and reading out loud to me. I thought all about just how it was while I was picking these. I didn't stay no longer, and I didn't go back to the house after that. I couldn't; I just pulled my sunbonnet over my eyes and went across lots to where I was going to get my breakfast."

Ester felt very sorry for the poor homeless, friendless old woman—felt as though she would have been willing to do a good deal just then to make her comfortable; yet it must be confessed that that awkward bunch of faded flowers, arranged without the slightest regard to colors, looked rather ridiculous; and she felt surprised, and not a little puzzled, to see actual tears standing in the eyes of her companion as he handled the bouquet with gentle care.

"Well," he said after a moment of quiet, "you are not leaving your best friend after all. Does it comfort your heart very much to remember that, in all your partings and trials, you are never called upon to bid Jesus good-bye?"

"What a way he has of bringing that subject into every conversation," commented Ester, who was now sure that he was a minister. Someway Ester had fallen into a way of thinking that everyone who spoke freely concerning these matters must be either a fanatic or a minister.

"Oh, that's about all the comfort I've got left." This answer came forth from a full heart and eyes brimming with tears. "And I don't s'pose I need any other if I've got Jesus left. I oughtn't to need anything else; but sometimes I get impatient—it seems to me I've been here long enough, and it's time I got home."

"How is it with the boy who is expecting you; has he this same friend?"

The gray head was slowly and sorrowfully shaken. "Oh, I'm afraid he don't know nothing about *him.*"

"Ah! then you have work to do; you can't be spared to rest yet. I presume the Master is waiting for you to lead that son to himself."

"I mean to, I mean to, sir," she said earnestly; "but sometimes I think maybe my coffin could do it better than I; but God knows—and I'm trying to be patient."

Then the train whirred on again, and Ester missed the rest; but one sentence thrilled her—"Maybe my coffin could do it better than I." How earnestly she spoke, as if she were willing to die at once, if by that she could save her son. How earnest they both were, anyway—the wrinkled, homely, ignorant old woman and the cultivated, courtly gentleman. Ester was ill at ease—conscience was arousing her to unwonted thought. These two were different from her. She was a Christian—at least she supposed so, hoped so; but she was not like them. There was a very decided difference. Were they right, and was she all wrong? Wasn't she a Christian after all? And at this thought she actually shivered. She was not willing to give up her title, weak though it might be.

Oh, well! she decided after a little, *she is an old woman, almost through with life. Of course she looks at everything through a different aspect from what a young girl like me naturally would; and as for him, ministers always are different from other people, of course.*

Foolish Ester! Did she suppose that ministers have a private Bible of their own, with rules of life set down therein for them, quite different from those written for her! And as for the old woman, almost through with life, how near might Ester be to the edge of her own life at that very moment! When the train stopped again the two were still talking.

"I just hope my boy will look like you," the old lady said suddenly, fixing admiring eyes on the tall form that stood beside her, patiently waiting for the cup from which she was drinking the tea which he had procured for her.

Ester followed the glance of her eye and laughed softly at the extreme improbability of her hope being realized, while he answered gravely:

"I hope he will be a noble boy and love his mother as she deserves; then it will matter very little who he looks like."

While the cup was being returned there was a bit of toilet making going on; the gray hair was smoothed back under the plain cap, and the faded, twisted shawl rearranged and carefully pinned. Meantime her thoughts seemed troubled, and she looked up anxiously into the face of her comforter as he again took his seat beside her.

"I'm just thinking I'm such a homely old thing, and New York is such a grand place, I've heard them say. I *do* hope he won't be ashamed of his mother."

"No danger," was the hearty answer; "he'll think

you are the most beautiful woman he has seen in ten years."

There is no way to describe the happy look which shone in the faded blue eyes at this answer; and she laughed a soft, pleased laugh as she said:

"Maybe he'll be like the man I read about the other day. Some mean old scamp told him how homely his mother was; and he said, says he, 'Yes, she's a homely woman, sure enough; but oh, she's such a *beautiful* mother!' Whatever will I do when I get in New York?" she added quickly, seized with a sudden anxiety. "Just as like as not, now, he never got a bit of my letter and won't be there to get me!"

"Do you know where your son lives?"

"Oh yes, I've got it on a piece of paper, the street and the number; but bless your heart, I shouldn't know whether to go up, or down, or across."

Just the shadow of a smile flitted over her friend's face as the thought of the poor old lady, trying to make her way through the city, came to him. Then he hastened to reassure her.

"Then we are all right, whether he meets you or not; we can take a carriage and drive there. I will see you safe at home before I leave you."

This crowning act of kindness brought the tears.

"I don't know why you are so good to me," she said simply, "unless you are the friend I prayed for to help me through this journey. If you are, it's all right; God will see that you are paid for it."

And before Ester had done wondering over the singular quaintness of this last remark, there was a sudden triumphant shriek from the engine and a tremendous din, made up of a confusion of more sounds than she had ever heard in her life before; then all was hurry and bustle around her, and she suddenly awakened to the fact that as soon as they had crossed the ferry she would actually be in New York. Even then she bethought herself to take a curious parting look at the oddly matched couple who were carefully making their way through the crowd, and wonder if she would ever see them again.

The next hour was made up of bewilderment to Ester. She had a confused remembrance afterward of floating across a silver river in a palace; of reaching a place where everybody screamed instead of talked and where all the bells were ringing for fire, or something else. She looked eagerly about for her uncle and saw at least fifty men who resembled him as she saw him last, about ten years ago. She fumbled nervously for his address in her pocketbook and gave Mr. Newton a recipe for making mince pies instead; finally she found herself tumbled in among cushions and driving right into carriages and carts and people, who all got themselves mysteriously out of the way; down streets that she thought must surely be the ones that the bells were ringing for, as they were all ablaze. It had been arranged that Ester's escort should see her safely set down at her uncle's door, as she had been unable to state the precise time of her arrival; and besides, as she was an entire stranger to her uncle's family, they could not determine any convenient plan for meeting each other at the depot. So Ester was whirled through the streets at a dizzying rate and, with eyes and ears filled with bewildering sights and sounds, was finally deposited before a great building aglow with gas and gleaming with marble. Mr. Newton rang the bell, and Ester, making confused adieus to him, was meantime ushered into a hall looking not unlike Judge Warren's best parlor. A sense of awe, not unmixed with loneliness and almost terror, stole over her as the man who opened the door stood waiting, after a civil, "Whom do you wish to see, and what name shall I send up?"

Whom *did* she wish to see, and what *was* her name, anyway? Could this be her uncle's house? Did she want to see any of them? She felt half afraid of them all. Suddenly the dignity and grandeur seemed to melt into gentleness before her as the tiniest of little women appeared and a bright young voice broke into hearty welcome:

"Is this really my cousin Ester? And so you have come! How perfectly splendid. Where is Mr. Newton? Gone? Why, John, you ought to have smuggled him in to dinner. We are *so* much obliged to him for taking care of *you*. John, send those trunks up to my room. You'll room with me, Ester, won't you? Mother thought I ought to put you in solitary state in a spare chamber, but I couldn't. You see, I have been so many years waiting for you that now I want you every bit of the time."

All this while she was giving her loving little pats and kisses on their way upstairs, whither she at once carried the traveler. Such a perfect gem of a room as that was into which she was ushered. Ester's love of beauty seemed likely to be fully gratified; she cast one eager glance around her, took in all the charming little details in a second of time, and then gave her undivided attention to this wonderful person before her, who certainly was, in veritable flesh and blood, the much-dreamed-over, much-longed-for Cousin Abbie. A hundred times had Ester painted her portrait—tall and dark and grand, with a perfectly regal form and queenly air, hair black as midnight, coiled in heavy masses around her head, eyes blacker if possible than her hair. As to dress, it was very difficult to determine; sometimes it was velvet and diamonds, or if the season would not possibly admit of that, then a rich, dark silk; never, by any chance, a material lighter than silk. This had been her picture. Now she could not suppress a laugh as she noted the contrast between it and the original. She was even two inches shorter than Ester herself, with a manner much more like a fairy's than a queen's; instead of heavy coils of black hair, there were little rings of brown curls clustering around a fair, pale forehead and continually peeping over into the bluest of eyes; then her dress was the softest and quietest of muslins, with a pale blue tint. Ester's soft laugh chimed merrily; she turned quickly.

"Now have you found something to laugh at in me already?" she said gleefully.

"Why," said Ester, forgetting to be startled over the idea that she should laugh at Cousin Abbie, "I'm only laughing to think how totally different you are from your picture."

"From my picture!"

"Yes, the one which I had drawn of you in my own mind. I thought you were tall, and had black hair, and dressed in silks, like a grand lady."

Abbie laughed again.

"Don't condemn me to silks in such weather as this, at least," she said gaily. "Mother thinks I am barbarous to summon friends to the city in August; but the circumstances are such that it could not well be avoided. So put on your coolest dress and be as comfortable as possible."

This question of how she should appear on this first evening had been one of Ester's puzzles. It would hardly do to don her blue silk at once, and she had almost decided to choose the black one; but Abbie's laugh and shrug of the shoulder had settled the ques-

tion of silks. So now she stood in confused indecision
before her open trunk.

Abbie came to the rescue.

"Shall I help you?" she said, coming forward. "I'll
not ring for Maggie tonight, but will be waiting maid
myself. Suppose I hang up some of these dresses? And
which shall I leave for you? This looks the coolest,"
and she held up to Ester's view the pink-and-white
muslin which did duty as an afternoon dress at home.

"Well," said Ester with a relieved smile, "I'll take
that."

And she thought within her heart: *They are not so
grand after all.*

Presently they went down to dinner, and in view of
the splendor of the dining room and the sparkle of gas
and the glitter of silver, she changed her mind again
and thought them very grand indeed.

Her uncle's greeting was very cordial; and though
Ester found it impossible to realize that her Aunt
Helen was actually three years older than her own
mother or indeed that she was a middle-aged lady at
all, so very bright and gay and altogether unsuitable
did her attire appear; yet, on the whole, she enjoyed
the first two hours of her visit very much and surprised and delighted herself at the ease with which she
slipped into the many new ways which she saw
around her. Only once did she find herself very much
confused; to her great astonishment and dismay she
was served with a glass of wine. Now Ester, among the
staunch temperance friends with whom she had hitherto passed her life, had met with no such trial of her
temperance principles, which she supposed were
sound and strong; yet here she was at her uncle's table,
sitting near her aunt, who was contentedly sipping
from her glass. Would it be proper, under the circum-

stances, to refuse? Yet would it be proper to do violence to her sense of right?

Ester had no pledge to break, except the pledge with her own conscience; and it is most sadly true that that sort of pledge does not seem to be so very binding in the estimation of some people. So Ester sat and toyed with hers, and came to the very unwarrantable conclusion that what her uncle offered for her entertainment must be proper for her to take! Do Ester's good sense the justice of understanding that she didn't believe any such thing; that she knew it was her own conscience by which she was to be judged, not her uncle's; that such smooth-sounding arguments honestly meant that whatever her uncle offered for her entertainment she had not the moral courage to refuse. So she raised the dainty wineglass to her lips and never once bethought herself to look at Abbie and notice how the color mounted and deepened on her face, nor how her glass remained untouched beside her plate. On the whole Ester was glad when all the bewildering ceremony of the dinner was concluded, and she, on the strength of her being wearied with her journey, was permitted to retire with Abbie to their room.

9

COUSIN ABBIE

"NOW I have you all to myself," that young lady said with a happy smile as she turned the key on the retreating Maggie and wheeled an ottoman to Ester's side.

"Where shall we commence? I have so very much to say and hear; I want to know all about Aunt Laura, and Sadie, and the twins. Oh, Ester, you have a little brother; aren't you so glad he is a *little* boy?"

"Why, I don't know," Ester said hesitatingly; then more decidedly, "No, I am always thinking how glad I should be if he were a young man, old enough to go out with me and be company for me."

"I know that is pleasant; but there are very serious drawbacks. Now, there's our Ralph; it is very pleasant to have him for company; and yet—well, Ester, he isn't a Christian, and it seems all the time to me that he is walking on quicksand. I am in one continual tremble for him, and I wish so often that he was just a little boy, no older than your brother, Alfred; then I could learn his tastes and indeed mold them in a measure by having him with me a great deal; and it does seem to me that I could make religion appear such a pleasant thing to him that he couldn't help seeking Jesus for himself. Don't you enjoy teaching Alfred?"

Poor puzzled Ester! With what a matter-of-course air her cousin asked this question. Could she possibly tell her that she sometimes never gave Alfred a thought from one week's end to another and that she never in her life thought of teaching him a single thing?

"I am not his teacher," she said at length. "I have no time for any such thing; he goes to school, you know, and Mother helps him."

"Well," said Abbie with a thoughtful air, "I don't quite mean teaching, either; at least not lessons and things of that sort, though I think I should enjoy having him depend on me in all his needs; but I was thinking more especially of winning him to Jesus; it seems so much easier to do it while one is young. Perhaps he is a Christian now; is he?"

Ester merely shook her head in answer. She could not look in those earnest blue eyes and say that she had never, by word or act, asked him to come to Jesus.

"Well, that is what I mean; you have so much more chance than I, it seems to me. Oh, my heart is so heavy for Ralph! I am all alone. Ester, do you know that neither my mother nor my father are Christians, and our home influence is—well, is not what a young man needs. He is very—gay they call it. There are his friends here in the city, and his friends in college— none of them the style of people that *I* like him to be with—and only poor little me to stem the tide of worldliness all around him. There is one thing in particular that troubles me—he is, or rather he is not—" And here poor Abbie stopped, and a little silence followed. After a moment she spoke again:

"Oh, Ester, you will learn what I mean without my telling you; it is something in which I greatly need your help. I depend upon you; I have looked forward to your coming, on his account as well as on my own. I know it will be better for him."

Ester longed to ask what the "something" was and what was expected of her; but the pained look on Abbie's face deterred her, and she contented herself by saying:

"Where is he now?"

"In college; coming next week. I long, on his account, to have a home of my own. I believe I can show him a style of life which will appear better to him than the one he is leading now."

This led to a long talk on the coming wedding.

"Mother is very much disturbed that it should occur in August," Abbie said; "and of course, it is not pleasant as it would be later; but the trouble is, Mr. Foster is obliged to go abroad in September."

"Who is Mr. Foster? Can't you be married if he isn't here?"

"Not very well," Abbie said with a bright little laugh. "You see, he is the one who has asked me to marry him."

"Why, is he?" and Ester laughed at her former question; then, as a sudden thought occurred to her, she asked: "Is he a minister?"

"Oh, dear no, he is only a merchant."

"Is he a . . . a Christian?" was her next query, and so utterly unused was she to conversation on this subject that she actually stammered over the simple sentence.

Such a bright, earnest face as was turned toward her at this question!

"Ester," said Abbie quickly, "I couldn't marry a man who was not a Christian."

"Why," Ester asked, startled a little at the energy of her tone, "do you think it is wrong?"

"Perhaps not for everyone. I think one's own carefully enlightened conscience should prayerfully decide the question; but it would be wrong for me. I am too weak; it would hinder my own growth in grace. I feel that I need all the human helps I can get. Yes, Mr. Foster is an earnest Christian."

"Do you suppose," said Ester, growing metaphysical, "that if Mr. Foster were not a Christian you would marry him?"

A little shiver quivered through Abbie's frame as she answered:

"I hope I should have strength to do what I thought right; and I believe I should."

"Yes, you think so now," persisted Ester, "because there is no danger of any such trial; but I tell you I don't believe, if you were brought to the test, that you would do any such thing."

Abbie's tone in reply was very humble.

"Perhaps not—I might miserably fail; and yet, Ester, *he* has said, 'My grace is sufficient for thee.'"

Then, after a little silence, the bright look returned to her face as she added:

"I am very glad that I am not to be tried in that furnace; and do you know, Ester, I never believed in making myself a martyr to what might have been, or even what *may* be in the future; sufficient unto the day is my motto. If it should ever be my duty to burn at the stake, I believe I should go to my Savior and plead for the sufficient grace; but as long as I have no such known trial before me, I don't know why I should be asking for what I do not need or grow unhappy over improbabilities, though I *do* pray every day to be prepared for whatever the future has for me."

Then the talk drifted back again to the various details connected with the wedding, until suddenly Abbie came to her feet with a spring.

"Why, Ester!" she exclaimed penitently, "what a thoughtless wretch I am! Here I have been chattering you fairly into midnight, without a thought of your tired body and brain. This session must adjourn immediately. Shall you and I have prayers together to-night? Will it seem homelike to you? Can you play I am Sadie for just a little while?"

"I should like it," Ester answered faintly.

"Shall I read, as you are so weary?" And, without waiting for a reply, she unclasped the lids of her little Bible. "Are you reading the Bible by course? Where do you like best to read, for devotional reading I mean?"

"I don't know that I have any choice." Ester's voice was fainter still.

"Haven't you? I have my special verses that I turn to in my various needs. Where are you and Sadie reading?"

"Nowhere," said Ester desperately.

Abbie's face expressed only innocent surprise. "Don't you read together? You are roommates, aren't you? Now I always thought it would be so delightful to have a nice little time, like family worship, in one's own room."

"Sadie doesn't care anything about these things; she isn't a Christian," Ester said at length.

"Oh, dear! isn't she?" What a very sad and troubled tone it was in which Abbie spoke. "Then you know something of my anxiety; and yet it is different. She is younger than you, and you can have her so much under your influence. At least it seems different to me.

How prone we are to consider our own anxieties peculiarly trying."

Ester never remembered giving a half hour's anxious thought to this which was supposed to be an anxiety with her in all her life; but she did not say so, and Abbie continued: "Who is your particular Christian friend, then?"

What an exceedingly trying and troublesome talk this was to Ester! What *was* she to say?

Clearly nothing but the truth.

"Abbie, I haven't a friend in the world."

"You poor, dear child; then we are situated very much alike after all—though I have dear friends outside of my own family; but what a heavy responsibility you must feel in your large household, and you the only Christian. Do you shrink from responsibility of that kind, Ester? Does it seem, sometimes, as if it would almost rush you?"

"Oh, there are some Christians in the family," Ester answered, preferring to avoid the last part of the sentence; "but then—"

"They are halfway Christians, perhaps. I understand how that is; it really seems sadder to me than even thoughtless neglect."

Be it recorded that Ester's conscience pricked her. This supposition on Abbie's part was not true. Dr. Van Anden, for instance, always had seemed to her most horribly and fanatically in earnest. But in what rank should she place this young, and beautiful, and wealthy city lady? Surely, she could not be a fanatic?

Ester was troubled.

"Well," said Abbie, "suppose I read you some of my sweet verses. Do you know I always feel a temptation to read in John? There is so much in that book about Jesus, and John seemed to love him so."

Ester almost laughed. What an exceedingly queer idea—a *temptation* to read in any part of the Bible. What a strange girl her cousin was.

Now the reading began.

"This is my verse when I am discouraged—'Wait on the Lord; be of good courage and he shall strengthen thine heart; wait, I say, on the Lord.' Isn't that reassuring? And then these two. Oh, Ester, these are wonderful! 'I have blotted out, as a thick cloud, thy transgressions, and, as a cloud, thy sins; return unto me; for I have redeemed thee. Sing, O ye heavens; for the Lord hath done it; shout, ye lower parts of the earth; break forth in singing, ye mountains, O forest, and every tree therein; for the Lord hath redeemed Jacob, and glorified himself in Israel.' And in that glorious old prophet's book is my jubilant verse—'And the ransomed of the Lord shall return and come to Zion with songs and everlasting joy upon their heads; they shall obtain joy and gladness, and sorrow and sighing shall flee away.'

"Now, Ester, you are very tired, aren't you? And I keep dipping into my treasure like a thoughtless, selfish girl as I am. You and I will have some precious readings out of this book, shall we not? Now I'll read you my sweet good-night psalm. Don't you think the Psalms are wonderful, Ester?"

And without waiting for reply, the low-toned, musical voice read on through that marvel of simplicity and grandeur, the 121st Psalm: "'I will lift up mine eyes unto the hills, from whence cometh my help. My help cometh from the Lord which made heaven and earth. He will not suffer thy foot to be moved: he that keepeth thee will not slumber. Behold, he that keepeth Israel shall neither slumber nor sleep. The Lord is thy keeper, the Lord is thy shade upon thy right hand. The sun shall not smite thee by day, nor the moon by night. The Lord shall preserve thee from all evil: he shall preserve thy soul. The Lord shall preserve thy going out and thy coming in, from this time forth, and even for evermore.'

"Ester, will you pray?" questioned her cousin as the reading ceased and she softly closed her tiny book.

Ester gave her head a nervous, hurried shake.

"Then shall I? Or, dear Ester, would you prefer to be alone?"

"No," said Ester; "I should like to hear you." And so they knelt, and Abbie's simple, earnest, tender prayer Ester carried with her for many a day.

After both heads were resting on their pillows, and quiet reigned in the room, Ester's eyes were wide open. Her Cousin Abbie had astonished her; she was totally unlike the Cousin Abbie of her dreams in every particular; in nothing more so than the strangely childlike matter-of-course way in which she talked about this matter of religion. Ester had never in her life heard anyone talk like that, except perhaps that minister who had spoken to her in the depot. His religion seemed not unlike Abbie's. Thinking of him, she suddenly addressed Abbie again.

"There was a minister in the depot today, and he spoke to me"; then the entire story of the man with his tract, and the girl with blue ribbons, and the old lady, and the young minister, and bits of the conversation were gone over for Abbie's benefit.

And Abbie listened, and commented, and enjoyed every word of it, until the little clock on the mantel spoke in silver tones and said, one, two. Then Abbie grew penitent again.

"Positively, Ester, I won't speak again: you will be

sleepy all day tomorrow, and you needn't think I shall give you a chance even to wink. Good night."

"Good night," repeated Ester; but she still kept her eyes wide open. Her journey, and her arrival, and Abbie, and the newness and strangeness of everything around her had banished all thought of sleep. So she went over in detail everything which had occurred that day; but persistently her thoughts returned to the question which had so startled her, coming from the lips of a stranger, and to the singleness of heart which seemed to possess her Cousin Abbie.

Was *she a fellow pilgrim after all?* she queried. If so, what caused the difference between Abbie and herself? It was but a few hours since she first beheld her cousin; and yet she distinctly *felt* the difference between them in that matter. *We are as unlike,* thought Ester, turning restlessly on her pillow, *well, as unlike as two people can be.*

What *would* Abbie say could she know that it was actually months since Ester had read as much connectedly in her Bible as she had heard read that evening? Yes, Ester had gone backward, even as far as that! Farther! What would Abbie say to the fact that there were many, many prayerless days in her life? Not very many, perhaps, in which she had not used a form of prayer; but their names were legion in which she had risen from her knees unhelped and unrefreshed; in which she knew that she had not *prayed* a single one of the sentences which she had been repeating. And just at this point she was stunned with a sudden thought—a thought which too often escapes us all. She would not for the world, it seemed to her, have made known to Abbie just how matters stood with her; and yet, and yet—Christ knew it all. She lay very still and breathed heavily. It came to her with all the thrill of an entirely new idea.

Then that unwearied and ever-watchful Satan came to her aid.

"Oh, well," said he, "your Cousin Abbie's surroundings are very different from yours. Give you all the time which she has at her disposal, and I dare say you would be quite as familiar with your Bible as she is with hers. What does she know about the petty vexations and temptations and bewildering, everpressing duties which every hour of every day beset your path? The circumstances are very different. Her life is in the sunshine, yours in the shadow. Besides, you do not know her; it is easy enough to talk; *very* easy to read a chapter in the Bible; but after all, there are other things quite as important, and it is more than likely that your cousin is not quite perfect yet."

Ester did not know that this was the soothing lullaby of the old serpent. Well for her if she had, and had answered it with that solemn, all-powerful "Get thee behind me, Satan." But she gave her own poor brain the benefit of every thought; and having thus lulled, and patted, and coaxed her half-roused and startled conscience into quiet rest again, she turned on her pillow and went to sleep.

10

ESTER'S MINISTER

ESTER was dreaming that the old lady on the cars had become a fairy and that her voice sounded like a silver bell, when she suddenly opened her eyes and found that it was either the voice of the marble clock on the mantel or of her Cousin Abbie, who was bending over her.

"Do you feel able to get up to breakfast, Ester dear, or had you rather lie and rest?"

"Breakfast!" echoed Ester, in a sleepy bewilderment, raising herself on one elbow and gazing at her cousin.

"Yes, breakfast!"—this with a merry laugh. "Did you suppose that people in New York lived without such inconveniences?"

Oh! to be sure; she was in New York, and Ester repeated the laugh—it had sounded so queer to hear anyone talk to her about getting up to breakfast; it had not seemed possible that that meal could be prepared without her assistance.

"Yes, certainly, I'll get up at once. Have I kept you waiting, Abbie?"

"Oh no, not at all; generally we breakfast at nine, but Mother gave orders last night to delay until half past nine this morning."

Ester turned to the little clock in great amazement; it was actually ten minutes to nine! What an idea! She never remembered sleeping so late in her life before. Why, at home the work in the dining room and kitchen must all be done by this time, and Sadie was probably making beds. Poor Sadie! What a time she would have! *She will learn a little about life while I am away,* thought Ester complacently as she stood before the mirror and pinned the dainty frill on her new pink cambric wrapper, which Sadie's deft fingers had fashioned for her.

Ester had declined the assistance of Maggie—feeling that though she knew perfectly well how to make her own toilet, she did *not* know how to receive assistance in the matter.

"Now I will leave you for a little," Abbie said, taking up her tiny Bible. "Ester, where is your Bible? I suppose you have it with you?"

Ester looked annoyed.

"I don't believe I have," she said hurriedly. "I packed in such haste, you see, and I don't remember putting it in at all."

"Oh, I am sorry—you will miss it so much! Do you have a thousand little private marks in your Bible that nobody else understands? I have a great habit of reading in that way. Well, I'll bring you one from the library that you may mark just as much as you please."

Ester sat herself down, with a very complacent air, beside the open window, with the Bible which had just been brought her in her lap. Clearly she had been left alone that she might have opportunity for private devotion, and she liked the idea very much; to be sure, she had not been in the habit of reading in the Bible in the morning, but that, she told herself, was simply because she never had time hardly to breathe in the mornings at home; there she had beefsteak to cook and breakfast rolls to attend to, she said disdainfully as if beefsteak and breakfast rolls were the most contemptible articles in the world, entirely beneath the notice of a rational being; but now she was in a very different atmosphere; and at nine o'clock of a summer morning was attired in a very becoming pink wrapper, finished with the whitest of frills, and sat at her window, a young lady of elegant leisure, waiting for the breakfast bell. Of course she could read a chapter in the Bible now and should enjoy it quite as much as Abbie did. She had never learned that happy little habit of having a much-used, much-worn, much-loved Bible for her own personal and private use; full of pencil marks and sacred meanings, grown dear from association, and teeming with memories of precious communings. She had one, of course—a nice, proper-looking Bible—and if it chanced to be convenient when she was ready to read, she used it; if not, she took Sadie's, or picked up Julia's from under the table or the old one on a shelf in the corner with one cover and part of Revelation missing—it mattered not one whit to her which—for there were no pencil marks, and no leaves turned down, and no special verses to find. She thought the idea of marking certain verses an excellent one and, deciding to commence doing so at once, cast about her for a pencil. There was one on the round table by the other window; but there were also many other things. Abbie's watch lay ticking softly in its marble and velvet bed and had to be examined and sighed over; and Abbie's diamond pin in the jewel case also demanded attention—then there were some blue and gold volumes to be peeped at, and Longfellow received more than a peep; then, most witching of all, *Say and Seal* in two volumes—the very books Sadie had borrowed once, and returned before Ester had a chance to discover how Faith managed about the ring. Longfellow and the Bible slid on the table together, and *Say and Seal* was eagerly seized upon, just to be glanced over, and the glances continued until there pealed a bell through the house; and with a start and a confused sense of having neglected her opportunities, this Christian young lady followed her cousin downstairs to meet all the temptations and bewilderments of a new day, unstrengthened by communion with either her Bible or her Savior.

That breakfast, in all its details, was a most bewitching affair. Ester felt that she could never enjoy that meal again at a table that was not small and round and covered with damask, nor drink coffee that had not first flowed gracefully down from a silver urn. As for Aunt Helen, she could have dispensed with her; she even caught herself drawing unfavorable comparisons between her and the patient, hardworking mother far away.

"Where is Uncle Ralph?" she asked suddenly, becoming conscious that there were only three, when last evening there were four.

"Gone downtown some hours ago," Abbie answered. "He is a businessman, you know, and cannot keep such late hours."

"But does he go without breakfast?"

"No—takes it at seven, instead of nine, like our lazy selves."

"He used to breakfast at a restaurant downtown, like other businessmen," further explained Aunt Helen, observing the bewildered look of this novice in city life. "But it is one of Abbie's recent whims that she can make him more comfortable at home, so they rehearse the interesting scene of breakfast by gaslight every morning."

Abbie's clear laugh rang out merrily at this.

"My dear mother, don't, I beg of you, insult the sun in that manner! Ester, fancy gaslight at seven o'clock on an August morning!"

"Do you get downstairs at seven o'clock?" was Ester's only reply.

"Yes, at six or, at most, half past. You see, if I am to make Father as comfortable at home as he would be at a restaurant, I must flutter around a little."

"Burns her cheeks and her fingers over the stove," continued Aunt Helen in a disgusted tone, "in order that her father may have burnt toast prepared by her hands."

"You've blundered in one item, Mother," was Abbie's good-humored reply. "My toast is *never* burnt, and only this morning Father pronounced it perfect."

"Oh, she is developing!" answered Mrs. Ried with a curious mixture of annoyance and amusement in look and tone. "If Mr. Foster fails in business soon, as I presume he will, judging from his present rate of proceeding, we shall find her advertising for the position of first-class cook in a small family."

If Abbie felt wounded or vexed over this thrust at Mr. Foster, it showed itself only by a slight deepening of the pink on her cheek as she answered in the brightest of tones: "If I do, Mother, and you engage me, I'll promise you that the eggs shall not be boiled as hard as these are."

All this impressed two thoughts on Ester's mind—one, that Abbie, for some great reason unknown to and unimagined by herself, actually of her own free will arose early every morning and busied herself over preparations for her father's breakfast; the other, that Abbie's mother said some disagreeable things to her in a disagreeable way—a way that would exceedingly provoke *her* and that she *wouldn't endure,* she said to herself with energy.

These two thoughts so impressed themselves that when she and Abbie were alone again, they led her to ask two questions:

"Why do you get breakfast at home for your father, Abbie? Is it necessary?"

"No, only I like it, and he likes it. You see, he has very little time to spend at home, and I like that little to be homelike; besides, Ester, it is my one hour of opportunity with my father. I almost *never* see him alone at any other time, and I am constantly praying that the Spirit will make use of some little word or act of mine to lead him to the cross."

There was no reply to be made to this, so Ester turned to the other question:

"What does your mother mean by her reference to Mr. Foster?"

"She thinks some of his schemes of benevolence are on too large a scale to be prudent. But he is a very prudent man and doesn't seem to think so at all."

"Doesn't it annoy you to have her speak in that manner about him?"

The ever-ready color flushed into Abbie's cheeks again, and after a moment's hesitation, she answered gently: "I think it would, Ester, if she were not my *own mother,* you know."

Another rebuke. Ester felt vexed anyway. This new strange cousin of hers was going to prove painfully good.

But her first day in New York, despite the strangeness of everything, was full of delight to her. They did not go out, as Ester was supposed to be wearied from her journey, though, in reality, she never felt better; and she reveled all day in a sense of freedom—of doing exactly what she pleased, and indeed of doing nothing; this last was an experience so new and strange to her that it seemed delightful. Ester's round of home duties had been so constant and pressing, the rebound was extreme; it seemed to her that she could never bake any more pies and cakes in that great oven, and she actually shuddered over the thought that, if she were at home, she would probably be engaged in ironing, while Maggie did the heavier work.

She went to fanning most vigorously as this occurred to her and sank back among the luxurious cushions of Abbie's easy chair as if exhausted; then she pitied herself most industriously and envied Abbie more than ever, and gave no thought at all to Mother and Sadie, who were working so much harder than usual, in order that she might sit here at ease. At last she decided to dismiss every one of these uncomfortable thoughts, to forget that she had ever spent an hour of her life in a miserable, hot kitchen, but to give herself entirely and unreservedly to the charmed life, which stretched out before her for three beautiful weeks. "Three weeks is quite a little time, after all," she told herself hopefully. "Three weeks ago I hadn't the least idea of being here; and who knows what may happen in the next three weeks?" Ah! sure enough, Ester, who knows?

"When am I to see Mr. Foster?" she inquired of Abbie as they came up together from the dining room after lunch.

"Why, you will see him tonight if you are not too

tired to go out with me. I was going to ask about that."

"I'm ready for anything; don't feel as if I ever experienced the meaning of that word," said Ester briskly, rejoicing at the prospect of going anywhere.

"Well, then, I shall carry you off to our Thursday evening prayer meeting—it's just *our* meeting, you see—we teachers in the mission—there are fifty of us, and we do have the most delightful times. It is like a family—rather a large family, perhaps, you think—but it doesn't seem so when we come on Sabbath, from the great congregation, and gather in our dear little chapel—we seem like a company of brothers and sisters, shutting ourselves in at home, to talk and pray together for a little, before we go out into the world again. Is Thursday your regular prayer meeting evening, Ester?"

Now it would have been very difficult for Ester to tell when *her* regular prayer meeting evening was, as it was so long ago that she grew out of the habit of regularly attending that now she scarcely ever gave it a thought. But she had sufficient conscience left to be ashamed of this state of things and to understand that Abbie referred to the church prayer meeting, so she answered simply—"No, Wednesday."

"That is our church prayer meeting night. I missed it last evening because I wanted to welcome you. And Tuesday is our Bible class night."

"Do you give three evenings a week to religious meetings, Abbie?"

"Yes," said Abbie with soft glee; "isn't it splendid? I appreciate my privileges, I assure you; so many people *could not* do it."

And so many people would not, Ester thought.

So they were not in to dinner with the family, but

took theirs an hour earlier; and with David, whom Abbie called her bodyguard, for escort, made their way to Abbie's dear little chapel, which proved to be a good-sized church, very prettily finished and furnished.

That meeting, from first to last, was a succession of surprises to Ester, commencing with the leader and being announced to Abbie in undertone:

"Your minister is the very man who spoke to me yesterday in the depot."

Abbie nodded and smiled her surprise at this information; and Ester looked about her. Presently another whisper:

"Why, Abbie, there is the blue-ribboned girl I told you about, sitting in the third seat from the front."

"That," said Abbie, looking and whispering back, "is Fanny Ames; one of our teachers."

Presently Ester set to work to select Mr. Foster from the rows of young men who were rapidly filling the front seats in the left aisle.

"I believe that one in glasses and brown kids is he," she said to herself, regarding him curiously; and as if to reward her penetration, he rose suddenly and came over, book in hand, to the seat directly in front of where they were sitting.

"Good evening, Abbie," was his greeting. "We want to sing this hymn and have not the tune. Can you lead it without the notes?"

"Why, yes," answered Abbie slowly and with a little hesitation. "That is, if you will help me."

"We'll all help," he said, smiling and returning to his seat.

"Yes, I'm sure that is he," commented Ester. Then the meeting commenced; it was a novel one. One person at least had never attended any just like it.

Instead of the chapter of proper length, which Ester thought all ministers selected for public reading, this reader read just three verses, and he did not even rise from his seat to do it, nor use the pulpit Bible, but read from a bit of a book which he took from his pocket. Then the man in spectacles started a hymn, which Ester judged was the one which had no notes attached from the prompt manner in which Abbie took up the very first word.

"Now," said the leader briskly, "before we pray let us have requests." And almost before he had concluded the sentence a young man responded.

"Remember, especially, a boy in my class, who seems disposed to turn every serious word into ridicule."

What a queer subject for prayer, Ester thought.

"Remember my little brother, who is thinking earnestly of those things," another gentleman said, speaking quickly, as if he realized that he must hasten or lose his chance.

"Pray for every one of my class. I want them all." And at this Ester actually started, for the petition came from the lips of blue-ribboned Fanny in the corner. A lady actually taking part in a prayer meeting when gentlemen were present! How very improper. She glanced around her nervously, but no one else seemed in the least surprised or disturbed; and indeed another young lady immediately followed her with a similar request.

"Now," said the leader, "let us pray." And that prayer was so strange in its sounding to Ester. It did not commence by reminding God that he was the Maker and Ruler of the universe, or that he was omnipotent and omnipresent and eternal, or any of the solemn forms of prayer to which her ears were used, but simply: "Oh, dear Savior, receive these petitions which we bring. Turn to thyself the heart of the lad who ridicules the efforts of his teacher; lead the little brother into the strait and narrow way; gather that entire class into thy heart of love"—and thus for each separate request a separate petition; and as the meeting progressed it grew more strange every moment to Ester. Each one seemed to have a word that he was eager to utter; and the prayers, while very brief, were so pointed as to be almost startling. They sang, too, a great deal, only a verse at a time, and whenever they seemed to feel like it. Her amazement reached its height when she felt a little rustle beside her and turned in time to see the eager light in Abbie's eyes as she said:

"One of my class has decided for Christ."

"Good news," responded the leader. "Don't let us forget this item of thanksgiving when we pray."

As for Ester, she was almost inclined not to believe her ears. Had her cousin Abbie actually spoken in meeting? She was about to sink into a reverie over this, but hadn't time, for at this point the leader arose.

"I am sorry," said he, "to cut the thread that binds us, but the hour is gone. Another week will soon pass, though, and, God willing, we shall take up the story— sing." And a soft, sweet chant stole through the room: "Let my prayer be set forth before thee as incense; and the lifting of my hands as evening sacrifice." Then the little company moved with a quiet cheerfulness toward the door.

"Have you enjoyed the evening?" Abbie asked in an eager tone as they passed down the aisle.

"Why, yes, I believe so; only it was rather queer."

"Queer, was it? How?"

"Oh, I'll tell you when we get home. Your minister

is exactly behind us, Abbie, and I guess he wants to speak with you."

There was a bright flush on Abbie's face, and a little sparkle in her eye as she turned and gave her hand to the minister and then said in a demure and soft tone: "Cousin Ester, let me make you acquainted with my friend, Mr. Foster."

11

THE NEW BOARDER

"I DON'T know what to decide, really," Mrs. Ried said thoughtfully, standing with an irresolute air beside the pantry door. "Sadie, hadn't I better make these pies?"

"Is that the momentous question which you can't decide, Mother?"

Mrs. Ried laughed. "Not quite; it is about the new boarder. We have room enough for another certainly, and seven dollars a week is quite an item just now. If Ester were at home, I shouldn't hesitate."

"Mother, if I weren't the meekest and most enduring of mortals, I should be hopelessly vexed by this time at the constancy with which your thoughts turn to Ester; it is positively insulting, as if I were not doing remarkably. Do you put anything else in apple pies? I never mean to have one, by the way, in my house. I think they're horrid; crust—apples—nutmeg—little lumps of butter all over it. Is there anything else, Mother, before I put the top on?"

"Sometimes I sweeten mine a little," Mrs. Ried answered demurely.

"Oh, sure enough; it was that new boarder that took all thoughts of sweetness out of me. How much sugar, Mother? Do let him come. We are such a stupid family now, it is time we had a new element in it; besides, you know I broke the largest platter yesterday, and his seven dollars will help buy another. I wish he was anything but a doctor, though; one ingredient of that kind is enough in a family, especially of the stamp which we have at present."

"Sadie," said Mrs. Ried gravely and reprovingly; "I never knew a young man for whom I have greater respect than I have for Dr. Van Anden."

"Yes, ma'am," answered Sadie with equal gravity; "I have an immense respect for him I assure you, and so I have for the president, and I feel about as intimate with the one as the other. I hope Dr. Douglass will be delightfully wild and wicked. How will Dr. Van Anden enjoy the idea of a rival?"

"I spoke of it to him yesterday. I told him we wouldn't give the matter another thought if it would be in any way unpleasant to him. I thought we owed him that consideration in return for all his kindness to us; but he assured me that it could make not the slightest difference to him."

"Do let him come, then. I believe I need another bed to make; I'm growing thin for want of exercise, and by the way, that suggests an item in his favor; being a doctor, he will be out all night occasionally, perhaps, and the bed won't need making so often. Mother, I do believe I didn't put a speck of soda in that cake I made this morning. What will that do to it? Or more properly speaking, what will it *not* do, inasmuch as it is not there to *do*? As for Ester, I shall consider it a personal insult if you refer to her again when I am so magnificently filling her place."

And this much-enduring Mother laughed and groaned at nearly the same time. Poor Ester never forgot the soda, nor indeed anything else in her life; but then Sadie was so overflowing with sparkle and good humor.

Finally the question was decided, and the new boarder came and was duly installed in the family; and thence commenced a new era in Sadie's life. Merry clerks and schoolboys she counted among her acquaintances by the score. Grave, dignified, slightly taciturn men of the Dr. Van Anden stamp she numbered also among her friends; but never one quite like Dr. Douglass. This easy, graceful, courteous gentleman, who seemed always to have just the right thing to say or do at just the right moment; who was neither wild nor sober; who seemed the furthest possible removed from wicked, yet who was never by any chance disagreeably good. His acquaintance with Sadie progressed rapidly. A new element had come to mix in with her life. The golden days wherein the two sisters had been much together, wherein the Christian sister might have planted much seed for the Master in Sadie's bright young heart, had all gone by. Perchance that sleeping Christian, nestled so cozily among the cushions in Cousin Abbie's morning room, might have been startled and aroused, could she have realized that days like those would never come back to her; that being misspent they had passed away; that a new worker had come to drop seed into the unoccupied heart; that never again would Sadie be as fresh, and as guileless, and as easily won as in those days which she had let slip in idle, aye, worse than idle, slumber.

Sadie sealed and directed a letter to Ester and ran with it downstairs. Dr. Douglass stood in the doorway, hat in hand.

"Shall I have the pleasure of being your carrier?" he said courteously.

"Do you suppose you are to be trusted?" Sadie questioned as she quietly deposited the letter in his hat.

"That depends in a great measure on whether you repose trust in me. The world is safer in general than we are inclined to think it. Who lives in that little bird's nest of a cottage just across the way?"

"A dear old gentleman, Mr. Vane," Sadie answered, her voice taking a tender tone as it always did when any chance word reminded her of Florence. "That is he standing in the gateway. Doesn't he look like a grand old patriarch?"

As they looked, Dr. Van Anden drove suddenly from around the corner and reined in his horses in front of the opposite gateway. They could hear his words distinctly.

"Mr. Vane, let me advise you to avoid this evening breeze; it is blowing up strongly from the river."

"Is Dr. Van Anden the old gentleman's nurse, or guardian, or what?" questioned Sadie's companion.

"Physician," was her brief reply. Then, after a moment, she laughed mischievously. "You don't like Dr. Van Anden, Dr. Douglass?"

"I! Oh yes, I like him; the trouble is, he doesn't like me, for which he is not to blame, to be sure. Probably he cannot help it. I have in some way succeeded in gaining his ill will. Why do you think I am not one of his admirers?"

"Oh," answered this rude and lawless girl, "I thought it would be very natural for you to be slightly jealous of him, professionally, you know."

If her object was to embarrass or annoy Dr. Douglass, apparently she did not gain her point. He laughed good humoredly as he replied:

"Professionally, he is certainly worthy of envy; I regard him as a very skillful physician, Miss Ried."

Ere Sadie could reply, the horses were stopped before the door, and Dr. Van Anden addressed her:

"Sadie, do you want to take a ride?"

Now, although Sadie had no special interest in, or friendship for, Dr. Van Anden, she did exceedingly like his horses and cultivated their acquaintance whenever she had an opportunity. So within five minutes after this invitation was received she was skimming over the road in a high state of glee. Sadie marked that night afterward as the last one in which she rode after those black ponies for many a day. The doctor seemed more at leisure than usual and in a much more talkative mood; so it was quite a merry ride until he broke a moment's silence by an abrupt question:

"Sadie, haven't your mother and you always considered me a sincere friend to your family?"

Sadie's reply was prompt and to the point.

"Certainly, Dr. Van Anden; I assure you I have as much respect for, and confidence in, you as I should have had for my grandfather, if I had ever known him."

"That being the case," continued the doctor gravely, "you will give me credit for sincerity and earnestness in what I am about to say. I want to give you a word of warning concerning Dr. Douglass. He is not a man whom *I* can respect; not a man with whom I should like to see my sister on terms of friendship. I have known him well and long, Sadie; therefore I speak."

Sadie Ried was never fretful, never petulant, and very rarely angry; but when she was, it was a genuine case of unrestrained rage, and woe to the individual who fell a victim to her blazing eyes and sarcastic tongue. Tonight Dr. Van Anden was that victim. What right had he to arraign her before him and say with whom she should, or should not, associate, as if he were indeed to think that she was too friendly with Dr. Douglass!

With the usual honesty belonging to very angry people, it had not once occurred to her that Dr. Van Anden had said and done none of these things. When she felt that her voice was sufficiently steady, she spoke:

"I am happy to be able to reassure you, Dr. Van Anden, you are *very* kind—extremely so; but as yet I really feel myself in no danger from Dr. Douglass's fascinations, however remarkable they may be. My mother and I enjoy excellent health at present, so you need have no anxiety as regards our choice of physicians, although it is but natural that you should feel nervous, perhaps; but you will pardon me for saying that I consider your interference with my affairs unwarrantable and uncalled for."

If Dr. Van Anden desired to reply to this insulting harangue, there was no opportunity, for at this moment they whirled around the corner and were at home.

Sadie flung aside her hat with an angry vehemence and, seating herself at the piano, literally stormed the keys, while the doctor reentered his carriage and quietly proceeded to his evening round of calls.

What a whirlwind of rage there was in Sadie's heart! What earthly right had this man whom she *detested* to give *her* advice? Was she a child, to be commanded by anyone? What right had anyone to speak in that way of Dr. Douglass? He was a gentleman, *certainly*, much more of a one than Dr. Van Anden had shown himself to be—and she liked him; yes, and she would like him, in spite of a whole legion of envious doctors.

A light step crossed the hall and entered the parlor. Sadie merely raised her eyes long enough to be certain that Dr. Douglass stood beside her, and continued her playing. He leaned over the piano and listened.

"Had you a pleasant ride?" he asked as the tone of the music lulled a little.

"Charming." Sadie's voice was full of emphasis and sarcasm.

"I judged, by the style of music which you were playing that there must have been a hurricane."

"Nothing of the sort; only a little paternal advice."

"Indeed! Have you been taken into his kindly care? I congratulate you."

Sadie was still very angry, or she would never have been guilty of the shocking impropriety of her next remark. But it is a lamentable fact that people will say and do very strange things when they are angry—things of which they have occasion to repent in cooler moments.

Fixing her bright eyes full and searchingly on Dr. Douglass, she said abruptly:

"He was warning me against the impropriety of associating with your dangerous self."

A look as of sadness and deep pain crossed Dr. Douglass's face, and he thought aloud, rather than said: "Is that man determined I shall have no friends?"

Sadie was touched; she struck soft, sweet chords with a slow and gentle movement as she asked:

"What is your offense in his eyes, Dr. Douglass?"

Then, indeed, Dr. Douglass seemed embarrassed;

maintaining, though, a sort of hesitating dignity as he attempted a reply.

"Why—I—he—I would rather not tell you, Miss Ried; it sounds badly." Then, with a little, slightly mournful laugh: "And that half-admission sounds badly, too; worse than the simple truth, perhaps. Well, then, I had the misfortune to cross his path professionally, once; a little matter, a slight mistake, not worth repeating—neither would I repeat it if it were, in honor to him. He is a man of skill and since then has risen high; one would not suppose that he would give that little incident of the past a thought now; but he seems never to have forgiven me."

The music stopped entirely, and Sadie's great truthful eyes were fixed in horror on his face. "Is it possible," she said at length, "that *that* is all, and he can bear such determined ill will toward you? And they call him an earnest Christian!"

At which remark Dr. Douglass laughed a low, quick laugh, as if he found it quite impossible to restrain his mirth, and then became instantly grave and said:

"I beg your pardon."

"For what, Dr. Douglass; and why did you laugh?"

"For laughing; and I laughed because I could not restrain a feeling of amusement at your innocently connecting his unpleasant state of mind with his professions of Christianity."

"Should they not be connected?"

"Well, that depends upon how much importance you attach to them."

"Dr. Douglass, what do you mean?"

"Treason, I suspect, viewed from your standpoint; and therefore it would be much more proper for me not to talk about it."

"But I want you to talk about it. Do you mean to say that you have no faith in anyone's religion?"

"How much have you?"

"Dr. Douglass, that is a very Yankee way of answering a question."

"I know; but it is the easiest way of reaching my point; so I repeat: How much faith have you in these Christian professions? Or, in other words, how many professing Christians do you know who are particularly improved in your estimation by their professions?"

The old questioning of Sadie's own heart brought before her again! Oh, Christian sister, with whom so many years of her life had been spent, with whom she had been so closely connected, if she could but have turned to you, and remembering your earnest life, your honest endeavors toward the right, your earnest struggles with sin and self, the evident marks of the Lord Jesus all about you; and, remembering this, have quelled the tempter in human form, who stood waiting for a verdict with a determined—"I have known *one*"—what might not have been gained for your side that night?

12

THREE PEOPLE

AS it was, she hesitated and thought—not of Ester, *her* life had not been such as to be counted for a moment—of her mother.

Well, Mrs. Ried's religion had been of a negative rather than of a positive sort, at least outwardly. She never spoke much of these matters, and Sadie positively did not know whether she ever prayed or not. How was she to decide whether the gentle, patient life was the outgrowth of religion in her heart, or whether it was a natural sweetness of disposition and tenderness of feeling?

Then there was Dr. Van Anden; an hour ago she would surely have said him, but now it was impossible; so as the silence, and the peculiar smile on Dr. Douglass's face, grew uncomfortable, she answered hurriedly: "I don't know many Christian people, Doctor." And then, more truthfully: "But I don't consider those with whom I am acquainted in any degree remarkable; yet at the same time I don't choose to set down the entire Christian world as a company of miserable hypocrites."

"Not at all," the doctor answered quickly. "I assure you I have many friends among that class of people whom I respect and esteem; but since you have pressed me to continue this conversation I must frankly confess to you that my esteem is not based on the fact that they are called Christians. I—but, Miss Ried, this is entirely unlike and beneath me, to interfere with and shake your innocent, trusting faith. I would not do it for the world."

Sadie interrupted him with an impatient shake of her head.

"Don't talk nonsense, Dr. Douglass, if you can help it. I don't feel innocent at all, just now at least, and I have no particular faith to shake; if I had, I hope you would not consider it such a flimsy material as to be shaken by anything which you have said as yet. I certainly have heard no arguments. Occasionally I think of these matters, and I have been surprised, and not a little puzzled, to note the strange inconsistency existing between the profession and practice of these people. If you have any explanation I should like to hear it, that is all."

Clearly this man must use at least the semblance of sense if he were going to continue the conversation. His answer was grave and guarded.

"I have offered no arguments, nor do I mean to. I was apologizing for having touched upon this matter at all. I am unfortunate in my belief, or rather disbelief; but it is no part of my intention to press it upon others. I incline to the opinion that there are some very good, nice, pleasant people in the world, whom the accidents of birth and education have taught to believe that they are aided in this goodness and pleasantness by a more-than-human power, and this belief rather helps than otherwise to mature their naturally sweet, pure lives. My explanation of their seeming inconsistencies is that they have never realized the full moral force of the rules which they profess to follow. I divide the world into two distinct classes—the so-called Christian world, I mean. Those whom I have just named constitute one class, and the other is composed of unmitigated hypocrites. Now, my friend, I have talked longer on this subject than I like or than I ought. I beg you will forget all I have said and give me some music to close the scene."

Sadie laughed and ran her fingers lightly over the keys; but she asked:

"In which class do you place your brother in the profession, Doctor?"

Dr. Douglass drew his shoulder into a very slight though expressive shrug as he answered:

"It is exceedingly proper, and also rather rare, for a physician to be eminent not only for skill but piety, and my brother practitioner is a wise and wary man, who—" and here he paused abruptly—"Miss Ried," he added after a moment, in an entirely changed tone: "Which of us is at fault tonight, you or myself, that I seem bent on making uncharitable remarks? I really did not imagine myself so totally depraved. And to be serious, I am very sorry that this style of conversation was ever commenced. I did not intend it. I do not believe in interfering with the beliefs or controverting the opinions of others."

Apparently Sadie had recovered her good humor, for her laugh was as light and careless as usual when she made answer:

"Don't distress yourself unnecessarily, Dr. Douglass; you haven't done me the least harm. I assure you I don't believe a word you say, and I do you the honor of believing that you don't credit more than two-thirds of it yourself. Now, I'm going to play you the stormiest piece of music you ever heard in your life." And the keys rattled and rang under her touch, and drew half a dozen loungers from the halls to the parlor, and effectually ended the conversation.

Three people belonging to that household held each a conversation with their own thoughts that night, which to finite eyes would have aided the right wonderfully had it been said before the assembled three, instead of in the quiet and privacy of their own rooms.

Sadie had calmed down and, as a natural consequence, was somewhat ashamed of herself; and as she rolled up and pinned and otherwise snugged her curls into order for the night, scolded herself after this fashion:

"Sadie Ried, you made a simpleton of yourself in that speech which you made to Dr. Van Anden tonight; because you think a man interferes with what doesn't concern him is no reason why you should grow flushed and angry, and forget that you're a lady. You said some very rude and insulting words, and you know your poor dear mother would tell you so if she knew anything about it, which she won't; that's one comfort; and besides, you have probably offended those delightful black ponies, and it will be forever before they will take you for another ride, and that's worse than all the rest. But who would think of Dr. Van Anden being such a man? I wish Dr. Douglass had gone to Europe before he told me—it was rather pleasant to believe in the extreme goodness of somebody. I wonder how much of that nonsense which Dr. Douglass talks he believes, anyway? Perhaps he is half right; only I'm not going to think any such thing, because it would be wicked, and I'm good. And because—" in a graver tone, and with a little reverent touch of an old worn book which lay on her bureau—"this is my father's Bible, and he lived and died by its precepts."

Up another flight of stairs, in his own room, Dr. Douglass lighted his cigar, fixed himself comfortably in his armchair, with his feet on the dressing table, and, between the puffs, talked after this fashion:

"Sorry we ran into this miserable train of talk tonight; but that young witch leads a man on so. I'm glad she has a decided mind of her own; one feels less conscience-stricken. I'm what they call a skeptic myself, but after all, I don't quite like to see a lady become one. *I* shan't lead her astray. I wouldn't have said anything tonight if it hadn't been for that miserable hypocrite of a Van Anden; the fellow must learn not to pitch into me if he wants to be let alone; but I doubt if he accomplished much this time. What a witch she is!" And Dr. Douglass removed his cigar long enough to give vent to a hearty laugh in remembrance of some of Sadie's remarks.

Just across the hall, Dr. Van Anden sat before his table, one hand partly shading his eyes from the gaslight while he read. And the words which he read were these: "'O let not the oppressed return ashamed: let the poor and needy praise thy name. Arise, O God, plead thine own cause; remember how the foolish man reproacheth thee daily. Forget not the voice of thine enemies; the tumult of those that rise up against thee increaseth continually.'"

Something troubled the doctor tonight; his usually grave face was tinged with sadness. Presently he arose and paced with slow measured tread up and down the room.

"I ought to have done it," he said at last. "I ought

to have told her mother that he was in many ways an unsafe companion for Sadie, especially in this matter; he is a very cautious, guarded, fascinating skeptic—all the more fascinating because he will be careful not to shock her taste with any boldly spoken errors. I should have warned them—how came I to shrink so miserably from my duty? What mattered it that they would be likely to ascribe a wrong motive to my caution? It was none the less my duty on that account." And the sad look deepened on his face as he marched slowly back and forth; but he was nearer a solution of his difficulties than was either of those others, for at last he came over to his chair again and sank before it on his knees.

Now, let us understand these three people; each of them, in their separate ways, was making mistakes. Sadie had said that she was not going to believe any of the nonsense which Dr. Douglass talked; she honestly supposed that she was not influenced in the least. And yet she was mistaken; the poison had entered her soul. As the days passed on, she found herself more frequently caviling over the shortcomings of professing Christians; more quick to detect their mistakes and failures; more willing to admit the half uttered thought that this entire matter might be a smooth-sounding fable. Sadie was the child of many prayers, and her father's much-used Bible lay on her dressing table, speaking for him, now that his tongue was silent in the grave; so she did not *quite* yield to the enemy—but she was walking in the way of temptation—and the Christian tongues around her, which the grave had *not* silenced, yet remained as mute as though their lips were already sealed; and so the path in which Sadie walked grew daily broader and more dangerous.

Then there was Dr. Douglass—not by any means

the worst man that the world can produce. He was, or fancied himself to be, a skeptic. Like many a young man, wise in his own conceit, he had no very distinct idea of what he was skeptical about, nor to what heights of illogical nonsense his own supposed view, carried out, would lead him; like many another, too, he had studied rhetoric, and logic, and mathematics, and medicine, thoroughly and well; he would have hesitated long, and studied hard, and pondered deeply before he had ventured to dispute an established point in surgery. And yet, with the inconsistent folly of the age, he had absurdly set his seal to the falsity of the Bible after giving it, at most, but a careless reading here and there, and without having ever once honestly made use of the means by which God has promised to enlighten the seekers after knowledge. And yet, his eyes being blinded, he did not realize how absurd and unreasonable, how utterly foolish, was his conduct. He thought himself sincere; he had no desire to lead Sadie astray from her early education, and like most skeptical natures, he quite prided himself upon the care with which he guarded his peculiar views, although I could never see why that was being any other than miserably selfish or inconsistent; for it is saying, in effect, one of two things, either: "My belief is sacred to myself alone, and nobody else shall have the benefit of it if I can help it"; or else: "I am very much ashamed of my position as a skeptic, and I shall keep it to myself as much as possible." Be that as it may, Dr. Douglass so thought, and was sincere in his intentions to do Sadie no harm; yet, as the days came and went, he was continually doing her injury. They were much in each other's society, and the subject which he meant should be avoided was constantly intruding. Both were so constantly on the alert to see and hear the unwise, and inconsistent, and unchristian acts and words, and also, alas! there were so many to be seen and heard that these two made rapid strides in the broad road.

Finally, there was Dr. Van Anden, carrying about with him a sad and heavy heart. He could but feel that he had shrunken from his duty, hidden behind that most miserable of all excuses: "What will people think?" If Dr. Van Anden had had any title but that particular one prefixed to his name, he would not have hesitated to have advised Mrs. Ried concerning him; but how could he endure the suspicion that he was jealous of Dr. Douglass? Then, in trying to right the wrong by warning Sadie, he was made to realize as many a poor Christian has realized before him, that he was making the sacrifice too late, and in vain. There was yet another thing—Dr. Douglass's statements to Sadie had been colored with truth. Among his other honest mistakes was the belief that Dr. Van Anden was a hypocrite. They had clashed in former years. Dr. Douglass had been most in the wrong, though what man, unhelped by Christ, was ever known to believe this of himself? But there had been wrong also on the other side, hasty words spoken— words which rankled, and were rankling still, after the lapse of years. Dr. Van Anden had never said: "I should not have spoken thus; I am sorry." He had taught himself to believe that it would be an unnecessary humiliation for him to say this to a man who had so deeply wronged him!

But, to do our doctor justice, time had healed the wound with him; it was not personal enmity which prompted his warning, neither had he any idea of the injury which those sharp words of his were doing in the unsanctified heart. And when he dropped upon his knees that night, he prayed earnestly for the conversion of Sadie and Dr. Douglass.

So these three lived their lives under that same roof and guessed not what the end might be.

13

THE STRANGE CHRISTIAN

"ABBIE," said Ester, wriggling herself around from before an open trunk and letting a mass of collars and cuffs slide to the floor in her earnestness, "do you know I think you're the very strangest girl I ever knew in my life?"

"I'm sure I did not," Abbie answered gaily. "If it's a nice strange, do tell me about it. I like to be nice—ever so much."

"Well, but I am in earnest, Abbie; you certainly are. These very collars made me think of it. Oh, dear me! They are all on the floor." And she reached after the shining, sliding things.

Abbie came and sat down beside her, presently, with a mass of puffy lace in her hands, which she was putting into shape.

"Suppose we have a little talk, all about myself," she said gently and seriously. "And please tell me, Ester, plainly and simply, what you mean by the term *strange*. Do you know I have heard it so often that sometimes I fear I really am painfully unlike other people. You are just the one to enlighten me."

Ester laughed a little as she answered: "You are taking the matter very seriously. I did not mean anything dreadful."

"Ah! but you are not to be excused in that way, my dear Ester. I look to you for information. Mother has made the remark a great many times, but it is generally connected in some way with religious topics, and Mother, you know, is not a Christian; therefore I have thought that perhaps some things seemed strange to her which would not to—*you,* for instance. But since you have been here you have spoken your surprise concerning me several times, and looked it oftener; and today I find that even my stiff and glossy, and every way proper, collars and cuffs excite it. So do please tell me, ought I to be in a lunatic asylum somewhere instead of preparing to go to Europe?"

Now although Ester laughed again at the mixture of comic and pathetic in Abbie's tone, yet something in the words had evidently embarrassed her. There was a little struggle in her mind, and then she came boldly forth with her honest thoughts.

"Well, the strangeness is connected with religious topics in my mind also; even though I am a professing Christian, I do not understand you. I am an economist in dress, you know, Abbie. I don't care for these things in the least; but if I had the money, as you have, there are a great many things which I should certainly have. You see, there is no earthly sense in your economy, and yet you hesitate over expenses almost as much as I do."

There was a little gleam of mischief in Abbie's eyes as she answered: "Will you tell me, Ester, why you would take the trouble to get these things if you do not care for them in the least?"

"Why, because—because—they would be proper and befitting my station in life."

"Do I dress in a manner unbecoming to my station in life?"

"No," said Ester promptly, admiring even then the crimson finishings of her cousin's morning robe. "But then—well, Abbie, do you think it is wicked to like nice things?"

"No," Abbie answered very gently; "but I think it is wrong to school ourselves into believing that we do not care for anything of the kind when, in reality, it is a higher, better motive which deters us from having many things. Forgive me, Ester, but I think you are unjust sometimes to your better self in this very way."

Ester gave a little start and realized for the first time in her life that, truth-loving girl though she was, she had been practicing a pretty little deception of this kind and actually palming it off on herself. In a moment, however, she returned to the charge.

"But, Abbie, did Aunt Helen really want you to have that pearl velvet we saw at Stewart's?"

"She really did."

"And you refused it?"

"And I refused it."

"Well, is that to be set down as a matter of religion too?" This question was asked with very much of Ester's old sharpness of tone.

Abbie answered her with a look of amazement. "I think we don't understand each other," she said at length, with the gentlest of tones. "That dress, Ester, with all its belongings could not have cost less than seven hundred dollars. Could I, a follower of the meek and lowly Jesus, living in a world where so many of his poor are suffering, have been guilty of wearing such a dress as that? My dear, I don't think you sustain the charge against me thus far. I see now how these pretty little collars (and, by the way, Ester, you are crushing one of them against that green box) suggested the thought; but you surely do not consider it strange, when I have such an array of collars already, that I did not pay thirty dollars for that bit of a cobweb which we saw yesterday?"

"But Aunt Helen wanted you to."

A sad and troubled look stole over Abbie's face as she answered: "My mother, remember, dear Ester, does not realize that she is not her own, but has been bought with a price. You and I know and feel that we must give an account of our stewardship. Ester, do you see how people who ask God to help them in every little thing which they have to decide—in the least expenditure of money—cannot after that deliberately fritter it away?"

"Do you ask God's help in these matters?"

"Why, certainly—" with the wondering look in her eyes which Ester had learned to know and dislike— "'Whatsoever therefore ye do'—you know."

"But, Abbie, going out shopping to buy—handkerchiefs, for instance; that seems to me a very small thing to pray about."

"Even the purchase of handkerchiefs may involve a question of conscience, my dear Ester, as you would realize if you had seen the wicked purchases that I have in that line; and in some way I never can feel that anything that has to do with me is of less importance than a tiny sparrow, and yet, you know, he looks after them."

"Abbie, do you mean to say that in every little thing that you buy you weigh the subject and discuss the right and wrong of it?"

"I certainly do try to find out just exactly what is

right and then do it; and it seems to me there is no act in this world so small as to be neither right nor wrong."

"Then," said Ester, with an impatient twitch of her dress from under Abbie's rocker, "I don't see the use in being rich."

"Nobody is rich, Ester, only God; but I'm so glad sometimes that he has trusted me with so much of his wealth that I feel like praying a prayer about the one thing—a thanksgiving. What else am I strange about, Ester?"

"Everything," with growing impatience. "I think it was as queer in you as possible not to go to the concert last evening with Uncle Ralph."

"But, Ester, it was prayer meeting evening."

"Well, suppose it was. There is prayer meeting every week, and there isn't this particular singer very often, and Uncle Ralph was disappointed. I thought you believed in honoring your parents."

"You forget, dear Ester, that Father said he was particularly anxious that I should do as I thought right, and that he should not have purchased the tickets if he had remembered the meeting. Father likes consistency."

"Well, that is just the point. I want to know if you call it inconsistent to leave your prayer meeting for just one evening, no matter for what reason?"

Abbie laughed in answer. "Do you know, Ester, you wouldn't make a good lawyer; you don't stick to the point. It isn't a great many reasons that might be suggested that we are talking about; it is simply a concert." Then more gravely—"I try to be very careful about this matter. So many detentions are constantly occurring in the city that unless the line were very closely drawn I should not get to prayer meeting at all. There are occasions, of course, when I must be detained; but under ordinary circumstances it must be more than a concert that detains me."

"I don't believe in making religion such a very solemn matter as that all amounts to; it has a tendency to drive people away from it."

The look on Abbie's face, in answer to this testily spoken sentence, was a mixture of bewilderment and pain.

"I don't understand," she said at length. "How is that a solemn matter? If we really expect to meet our Savior at a prayer meeting, isn't it a delightful thought? I am very happy when I can go to the place of prayer."

Ester's voice savored decidedly of the one which she was wont to use in her very worst moods in that long dining room at home.

"Of course, I should have remembered that Mr. Foster would be at the prayer meeting and not at the concert; that was reason enough for your enjoyment."

The rich blood surged in waves over Abbie's face during this rude address; but she said not a single word in answer. After a little silence, she spoke in a voice that trembled with feeling.

"Ester, there is one thought in connection with this subject that troubles me very much. Do you really think as you have intimated, that I am selfish, that I consult my own tastes and desires too much, and so do injury to the cause? For instance, do you think I prejudiced my father?"

What a sweet, humble, even tearful, face it was! And what a question to ask of Ester! What had developed this disagreeable state of mind save the confused upbraidings of her hitherto quiet conscience over the contrast between Cousin Abbie's life and hers.

Here, in the very face of her theories to the contrary, in very defiance to her belief in the folly, and fashion, and worldliness that prevailed in the city, in the very heart of this great city, set down in the midst of wealth and temptation, had she found this young lady, daughter of one of the merchant princes, the almost bride of one of the brightest stars in the New York galaxy on the eve of a brilliant departure for foreign shores, with a whirl of preparation and excitement about her enough to dizzy the brain of a dozen ordinary mortals; yet moving sweetly, brightly, quietly through it all, and manifestly finding her highest source of enjoyment in the presence of, and daily communion with, her Savior.

All Ester's speculations concerning her had come to naught. She had planned the wardrobe of the bride, over and over again, for days before she saw her; and while she had prepared proper little lectures for her on the folly and sinfulness of fashionable attire, had yet delighted in the prospect of the beauty and elegance around her. How had her prospects been blighted! Beauty there certainly was in everything, but it was the beauty of simplicity, not at all such a display of silks and velvets and jewels as Ester had planned. It certainly could not be wealth which made Abbie's life such a happy one, for she regulated her expenses with a care and forethought such as Ester had never even dreamed of. It could not be a life of ease, a freedom from annoyance, which kept her bright and sparkling, for it had only taken a week's sojourn in her Aunt Helen's home to discover to Ester the fact that all wealthy people were not necessarily amiable and delightful. Abbie was evidently rasped and thwarted in a hundred little ways, having a hundred little trials which *she* had never been called upon to endure. In short, Ester had discovered that the mere fact of living in a great city was not in itself calculated to make the Christian race more easy or more pleasant. She had begun to suspect that it might not even be quite so easy as it was in a quiet country home; and so one by one all her explanations of Abbie's peculiar character had become bubbles and had vanished as bubbles do. What, then, sustained and guided her cousin? Clearly Ester was shut up to this one conclusion—it was an ever-abiding, all-pervading Christian faith and trust. But then had not *she* this same faith? And yet could any contrast be greater than was Abbie's life contrasted with hers?

There was no use in denying it, no use in lulling and coaxing her conscience any longer; it had been for one whole week in a new atmosphere; it had roused itself; it was not thoroughly awake as yet, but restless and nervous and on the alert—and *would not* be hushed back into its lethargic state.

This it was which made Ester the uncomfortable companion which she was this morning. She was not willing to be shaken and roused; she had been saying very unkind, rude things to Abbie, and now, instead of flouncing off in an uncontrollable fit of indignation, which course Ester could but think would be the most comfortable thing which could happen next, so far as she was concerned, Abbie sat still, with that look of meek inquiry on her face, humbly awaiting her verdict. How Ester wished she had never asked that last question! How ridiculous it would make her appear, after all that had been said, to admit that her cousin's life had been one continual reproach of her own; that concerning this very matter of the concert, she had heard Uncle Ralph remark that if all the world matched what they did with what they said as well as Abbie did, he was not sure but he might be a

Christian himself. Then suppose she should add that this very pointed remark had been made to her when they were on their way to the concert in question.

Altogether, Ester was disgusted and wished she could get back to where the conversation commenced, feeling certain now that she would leave a great many things unsaid.

I do not know how the conversation would have ended, whether Ester could have brought herself to the plain truth, and been led on and on to explain the unrest and dissatisfaction of her own heart, and thus have saved herself much of the sharp future in store for her; but one of those unfortunate interruptions which seem to finite eyes to be constantly occurring now came to them. There was an unusual bang to the front door, the sound of strange footsteps in the hall, the echo of a strange voice floating up to her, and Abbie, with a sudden flinging of thimble and scissors and an exclamation of "Ralph has come," vanished.

14

THE LITTLE CARD

LEFT to herself, Ester found her train of thought so thoroughly disagreeable that she hastened to rid herself of it and seized upon the newcomer to afford her a substitute.

This cousin, whom she had expected to influence for good, had at last arrived. Ester's interest in him had been very strong ever since that evening of her arrival, when she had been appealed to to use her influence on him—just in what way she hadn't an idea. Abbie had never spoken of it since and seemed to have lost much of her eager desire that the cousins should meet. Ester mused about all this now; she wished she knew just in what way she was expected to be of benefit. Abbie was evidently troubled about him. Perhaps he was rough and awkward; schoolboys often were, even those born in a city. Very much of Ralph's life had been spent away from home, she knew; and she had often heard that boys away from home influences grew rude and coarse oftentimes. Yes, that was undoubtedly it. Shy, too, he was of course; he was of about the age to be that. She could imagine just how he looked—he felt out of place in the grand mansion which he called home, but where he had passed so small a portion of his time. Probably he didn't know what to do with his hands, nor his feet; and just as likely as not he sat on the edge of his chair and ate with his knife—school was a horrid place for picking up all sorts of ill manners. Of course all these things must annoy Abbie very much, especially at this time when he must necessarily come so often in contact with that perfection of gentlemanliness, Mr. Foster. *I wish,* thought Ester at this point, growing a little anxious, *I wish there was more than a week before the wedding; however, I'll do my best. Abbie shall see I'm good for something. Although I do differ with her somewhat in her peculiar views, I believe I know how to conduct myself with ease in almost any position, even if I have been brought up in the country.* And by the time the lunch bell rang, a girl more thoroughly satisfied with herself and her benevolent intentions than was this same Ester could hardly have been found. She stood before the glass, smoothing the shining bands of hair, preparatory to tying a blue satin ribbon over them, when Abbie fluttered in.

"Forgive me, a great many times, for rushing off in the flutter I did, and leaving you behind, and staying away so long. You see, I haven't seen Ralph in quite a little time, and I forgot everything else. Your hair doesn't need another bit of brushing, Ester, it's as smooth as velvet; they are all waiting for us in the dining room, and I want to show you to Ralph." And before the blue satin ribbon was tied quite to her satisfaction, Ester was hurried to the dining room to take up her new role of guide and general assistant to the awkward youth.

I suppose he hasn't an idea what to say to me, was her

last compassionate thought as Abbie's hand rested on the knob. *I hope he won't be hopelessly quiet, but I'll manage in some way.*

At first he was nowhere to be seen; but as Abbie said eagerly: "Ralph, here is Cousin Ester!" the door swung back into its place and revealed a tall, well-proportioned young man with a full-bearded face and the brightest of dancing eyes. He came forward immediately, extending both hands and speaking in a rapid voice.

"Long-hoped-for, come at last! I don't refer to myself, you understand, but to this much-waited-for, eagerly-looked-forward-to prospect of greeting my Cousin Ester. Ought I to welcome you, or you me—which is it? I'm somewhat bewildered as to proprieties. This fearfully near approach to a wedding has confused my brain. Sis—" turning suddenly to Abbie—"have you prepared Ester for her fate? Does she fully understand that she and I are to officiate? That is, if we don't evaporate before the eventful day. Sis, how could you have the conscience to perpetrate a wedding in August? Whatever takes Foster abroad just now, anyway?" And without waiting for answer to his ceaseless questions he ran gaily on.

Clearly, whatever might be his shortcomings, inability to talk was *not* one of them. And Ester, confused, bewildered, utterly thrown out of her prepared part in the entertainment, was more silent and awkward than she had ever known herself to be; provoked, too, with Abbie, with Ralph, with herself. *How could I have been such a simpleton?* she asked herself as, seated opposite her cousin at the table, she had opportunity to watch the handsome face, with its changeful play of expression, and note the air of pleased attention with which even her Uncle Ralph listened to his ceaseless flow of words. *I knew he was older than Abbie and that this was his third year in college. What could I have expected from Uncle Ralph's son? A pretty dunce he must think me, blushing and stammering like an awkward country girl. What on earth could Abbie mean about needing my help for him and being troubled about him? It is some of her ridiculous fanatical nonsense, I suppose. I wish she could ever talk or act like anybody else.*

"I don't know that such is the case, however," Ralph was saying when Ester returned from this rehearsal of her own thoughts. "I can simply guess at it, which is as near an approach to an exertion as a fellow ought to be obliged to make in this weather. John, you may fill my glass, if you please. Father, this is even better wine than your cellar usually affords, and that is saying a great deal. Sis, has Foster made a temperance man of you entirely? I see you are devoted to ice water."

"Oh, certainly," Mrs. Ried answered for her, in the half-contemptuous tone she was wont to assume on such occasions. "I warn you, Ralph, to get all the enjoyment you can out of the present, for Abbie intends to keep you with her entirely after she has a home of her own—out of the reach of temptation."

Ester glanced hurriedly and anxiously toward her cousin. How did this pet scheme of hers become known to Mrs. Ried, and how could Abbie possibly retain her habitual self-control under this sarcastic ridicule, which was so apparent in her mother's voice?

The pink on her cheek did deepen perceptibly, but she answered with the most perfect good humor: "Ralph, don't be frightened, please. I shall let you out once in a long while if you are very good."

Ralph bent loving eyes on the young, sweet face

and made prompt reply: "I don't know that I shall care for even that reprieve, since you're to be jailer."

What could there be in this young man to cause anxiety or to wish changed? Yet even while Ester queried, he passed his glass for a third filling, and taking note just then of Abbie's quick, pained look, then downcast eyes and deeply flushing face, the knowledge came suddenly that in that wineglass the mischief lay. Abbie thought him in danger, and this was the meaning of her unfinished sentence on that first evening and her embarrassed silence since; for Ester, with her filled glass always beside her plate, untouched indeed sometimes, but oftener sipped from in response to her uncle's invitation, was not the one from whom help could be expected in this matter. And Ester wondered if the handsome face opposite her could really be in absolute danger, or whether this was another of Abbie's whims—at least it wasn't pleasant to be drinking wine before him, and she left her glass untouched that day and felt thoroughly troubled about that and everything.

The next morning there was a shopping excursion, and Ralph was smuggled in as an attendant. Abbie turned over the endless sets of handkerchiefs in bewildering indecision.

"Take this box; do, Abbie," Ester urged. "This monogram in the corner is lovely, and that is the dearest little sprig in the world."

"Which is precisely what troubles me," laughed Abbie. "It is entirely too dear. Think of paying such an enormous sum for just handkerchiefs!"

Ralph, who was lounging near her, trying hard not to look bored, elevated his eyebrows as his ear caught the sentence and addressed her in undertone: "Is Foster hard up? If he is, you are not on his hands yet,

Sis; and I'm inclined to think Father is good for all the finery you may happen to fancy."

"That only shows your ignorance of the subject or your high opinion of me. I assure you, were I so disposed I could bring Father's affairs into a fearful tangle this very day, just by indulging a fancy for finery."

"Are his affairs precarious, Abbie, or is finery prodigious?"

Abbie laid her hand on a square of cobwebby lace. "That is seventy-five dollars, Ralph."

"What of that? Do you want it?" And Ralph's hand was in his pocket.

Abbie turned with almost a shiver from the counter. "I hope not, Ralph," she said with sudden energy. "I hope I may never be so unworthy of my trust as to make such a wicked use of money." Then more lightly, "You are worse than Queen Ester here, and her advice is bewildering enough."

"But, Abbie, how can you be so absurd," said that young lady, returning to the charge. "Those are not very expensive, I am sure, at least not for you; and you certainly want some very nice ones. I'm sure if I had one-third of your spending money I shouldn't need to hesitate."

Abbie's voice was very low and sweet, and reached only her cousin's ear. "Ester, the silver and the gold are *his,* and I have asked him this very morning to help me in every little item to be careful of his trust. Now do you think—" But Ester had turned away in a vexed uncomfortable state of mind and walked quite to the other end of the store, leaving Abbie to complete her purchases as she might see fit. She leaned against the door, tapping her fingers in a very soft, but very nervous manner against the glass. How queer it was that in the smallest matters she and Abbie could not agree. How was it possible that the same set of rules could govern them both? And the old ever-recurring question came up to be thought over afresh. Clearly they were unlike—utterly unlike. Now was Abbie right and she wrong? Or was Abbie—no, not wrong, the word would certainly not apply; there absolutely *could* be no wrong connected with Abbie's way. Well, then, queer!—unlike other people, unnecessarily precise—studying the right and wrong of matters, which she had been wont to suppose had no moral bearing of any sort, rather which she had never given any attention to. While she waited and queried, her eye caught a neat little card receiver hanging near her, apparently filled with cards, and bearing in gilt lettering, just above them, the winning words: "FREE TO ALL. TAKE ONE." This was certainly a kindly invitation; and Ester's curiosity being aroused as to what all this might be for, she availed herself of the invitation, and drew with dainty fingers a small, neat card from the case, and read:

I SOLEMNLY AGREE,
>   *As God Shall Help Me*:
>   1. To observe regular seasons of secret prayer, at least in the morning and evening of each day.
>   2. To read daily at least a small portion of the Bible.
>   3. To attend at one or more prayer meetings every week, if I have strength to get there.
>   4. To stand up for Jesus always and everywhere.
>   5. To try to save at least one soul each year.
>   6. To engage in no amusement where my Savior could not be a guest.

Had the small bit of cardboard been a coal of fire it could not have been more suddenly dropped upon the marble before her than was this as Ester's startled eyes took in its meaning. Who could have written those sentences? And to be placed there in a conspicuous corner of a fashionable store? Was she never to be at peace again? Had the world gone wild? Was this an emanation from Cousin Abbie's brain, or were there many more Cousin Abbies in what she had supposed was a wicked city, or—oh painful question, which came back hourly nowadays and seemed fairly to chill her blood—was this religion, and had she none of it? Was her profession a mockery, her life a miserably acted lie?

"Is that thing hot?" It was Ralph's amused voice which asked this question close beside her.

"What? Where?" And Ester turned in dire confusion.

"Why, that bit of paper—or is it a ghostly communication from the world of spirits? You look startled enough for me to suppose anything, and it spun away from your grasp very suddenly. Oh," he added as he glanced it through, "rather ghostly, I must confess, or would be if one were inclined that way; but I imagined your nerves were stronger. Did the pronoun startle you?"

"How?"

"Why I thought perhaps you considered yourself committed to all this solemnity before your time, or willy-nilly, as the children say. What a comical idea to hang oneself up in a store in this fashion. I must have one of these. Are you going to keep yours?" And as he spoke he reached forward and possessed himself of one of the cards. "Rather odd things to be found in our possession, wouldn't they be? Abbie, now, would be just one of this sort."

That cold shiver trembled again through Ester's frame as she listened. Clearly he did not reckon her one of "that sort." He had known her but one day, and yet he seemed positive that she stood on an equal footing with himself. Oh, why was it? How did he know? Was her manner then utterly unlike that of a Christian, so much so that this young man saw [it] already, or was it that glass of wine from which she had sipped last evening? And at this moment she would have given much to be back where she thought herself two weeks ago on the wine question; but she stood silent and let him talk on, not once attempting to define her position—partly because there had crept into her mind this fearful doubt, unaccompanied by the prayer:

> "If I've never loved before,
> Help me to begin today"—

and partly, oh poor Ester, because she was utterly unused to confessing her Savior; and though not exactly ashamed of him, at least she would have indignantly denied the charge, yet it was much less confusing to keep silence and let others think as they would—this had been her rule; she followed it now, and Ralph continued:

"Queer world this? Isn't it? How do you imagine our army would have prospered if one-fourth of the soldiers had been detailed for the purpose of coaxing the rest to follow their leader and obey orders? That's what it seems to me the so-called Christian world is up to. Does the comical side of it ever strike you, Ester? Positively I can hardly keep from laughing now and then to hear the way in which Dr. Downing pitches into his church members, and they sit and take it as meekly as lambs brought to the slaughter. It does them about as much good, apparently, as it does me—no, not so much, for it amuses me and serves to make me good-natured, on good terms with myself for half an hour or so. I'm so thoroughly rejoiced, you see, to think that I don't belong to that set of miserable sinners."

"Dr. Downing does preach very sharp, harsh sermons," Ester said at last, feeling the necessity of saying something. "I have often wondered at it. I think them calculated to do more harm than good."

"Oh, *I* don't wonder at it in the least. I'd make it sharper yet if I were he; the necessity exists evidently. The wonder lies in *that* to my mind. If a fellow really means to do a thing, what does he wait to be punched up about it everlastingly for? Hang me if I don't like to see people act as though they meant it, even if the question is a religious one. Ester, how many times ought I to beg your pardon for using an unknown tongue—in other words, slang phrases? I fancied myself talking to my chum, delivering a lecture on theology, which is somewhat out of my sphere, as you have doubtless observed. Yet such people as you and I can't help having eyes and ears, and using them now and then, can we?"

Still silence on Ester's part, so far as defining her position was concerned. She was not ashamed of her Savior now, but of herself. If this gay cousin's eyes were critical, she knew she could not bear the test. Yet she rallied sufficiently to condemn within her own mind the poor little cards.

"They will do more harm than good," she told herself positively. To such young men as Ralph, for instance, what could he possibly want with one of them, save to make it the subject of ridicule when he got with some of his wild companions? But it transpired that his designs were not so very wicked after all, for as they left the store he took the little card from his pocket and handed it to Abbie with a quiet: "Sis, here is something that you will like."

And Abbie read it and said: "How solemn that is. Did you get it for me, Ralph? Thank you." And Ralph bowed and smiled on her, a kind, almost tender smile, very unlike the roguish twinkle that had shone in his eyes while he talked with Ester.

All through the busy day that silent, solemn card haunted Ester. It pertinaciously refused to be lost. She dropped it twice in their transit from store to store, but Ralph promptly returned it to her. At home she laid it on her dressing table, but pile scarves and handkerchiefs and gloves over it as high as she might, it was sure to flutter to the floor at her feet as she sought hurriedly in the mass of confusion for some missing article. Once she seized and flung it from the window in dire vexation and was rewarded by having Maggie present it to her about two minutes thereafter as a "something that landed square on my head, ma'am, as I was coming around the corner." At last she actually grew nervous over it, felt almost afraid to touch it, so thoroughly had it fastened itself on her conscience. These great black letters in that first sentence seemed burned into her brain: "I solemnly agree, as God shall help me."

At last she deposited the unwelcome little monitor at the very bottom of her collar box, under some unused collars, telling herself that it was for safekeeping that she might not lose it again, not letting her conscience say for a moment that it was because she wanted to bury the haunting words out of her sight.

that opportunity for tumbling over the floor and showering its contents right and left.

"What next, I wonder?" Ester muttered as she stooped to scoop up the disordered mass of collars, ruffles, cuffs, laces, and the like, and with them came, faceup and bright black letters scorching into her very soul, the little card with its: "I solemnly agree, as God shall help me." Ester paused in her work and stood upright with a strange beating at her heart. What *did* this mean? Was it merely chance that this sentence had so persistently met her eye all this day, put the card where she would? And what was the matter with her anyway? Why should those words have such strange power over her? Why had she tried to rid herself of the sight of them? She read each sentence aloud slowly and carefully. "Now," she said decisively, half irritated that she was allowing herself to be hindered, "it is time to put an end to this nonsense. I am sick and tired of feeling as I have of late—these are all very reasonable and proper pledges, at least the most of them are. I believe I'll adopt this card. Yes, I will—that is what has been the trouble with me. I've neglected my duty—rather, I have so much care and work at home that I haven't time to attend to it properly—but here it is different. It is quite time I commenced right in these things. Tonight, when I come to my room, I will begin. No, I cannot do that either, for Abbie will be with me. Well, the first opportunity then that I have—or no—I'll stop now, this minute, and read a chapter in the Bible and pray; there is nothing like the present moment for keeping a good resolution. I like decision in everything—and, I dare say, Abbie will be very willing to have a quiet talk with Mr. Foster before I come down."

And sincerely desirous to be at peace with her newly troubled conscience—and sincerely sure that she was in the right way for securing that peace—Ester closed and locked her door and sat herself down by the open window in a thoroughly self-satisfied state of mind to read the Bible and to pray.

Poor human heart, so utterly unconscious of its own deep sickness—so willing to plaster over the unhealed wound! Where should she read? She was at all times a random reader of the Bible; but now with this new era it was important that there should be a more definite aim in her reading. She turned the leaves rapidly, eager to find a book which looked inviting for the occasion, and finally seized upon the Gospel of John as entirely proper and appropriate, and industriously commenced: "In the beginning was the Word, and the Word was with God, and the Word was God. The same was in the beginning with God." *Now that wretched hairpin is falling out again, as sure as I live; I don't see what is the matter with my hair today. I never had so much trouble with it.* "All things were made by him; and without him was not anything made that was made. In him was life; and the life was the light of men." *There are Mr. and Miss Hastings. I wonder if they are going to call here? I wish they would. I should like to get a nearer view of that trimming around her sack; it is lovely whatever it is.* "And the light shineth in darkness; and the darkness comprehended it not."

Now it was doubtful if it had once occurred to Ester who this glorious "Word" was, or that He had aught to do with her. Certainly the wonderful and gracious truths embodied in these precious verses, truths which had to do with every hour of her life, had not this evening so much as made an entrance into her busy grain; and yet she actually thought herself in the way of getting rid of the troublesome thoughts that had haunted her the days just past. The verses were being read aloud; the thoughts about the troublesome hair and the trimmings on Miss Hastings' sack were suffered to remain thoughts, not to be put into words—had they been, perhaps even Ester would have noticed the glaring incongruity. As it was, she continued her two occupations, reading the verses, thinking the thoughts, until at last she came to a sudden pause, and silence reigned in the room for several minutes; then there flushed over Ester's face a sudden glow as she realized that she sat, Bible in hand, one corner of the solemnly worded card marking the verse at which she had paused, and that verse was: "He came unto his own, and his own received him not." And she realized that her thoughts during the silence had been: *Suppose Miss Hastings should call and should inquire for her, and she should go with Aunt Helen to return the call, should she wear Mother's black lace shawl with her blue silk dress or simply the little ruffled cape which matched the dress!* She read that last verse over again with an uncomfortable consciousness that she was not getting on very well; but try as she would, Ester's thoughts seemed resolved not to stay with that first chapter of John—they roved all over New York, visited all the places that she had seen and a great many that she wanted to see, and that seemed beyond her grasp, going on meantime with the verses and keeping up a disagreeable undercurrent of disgust. Over those same restless thoughts there came a tap at the door and Maggie's voice outside.

"Miss Ried, Miss Abbie sent me to say that there was company waiting to see you, and if you please, would you come down as soon as you could?"

Ester sprang up. "Very well," she responded to Maggie. "I'll be down immediately."

Then she waited to shut the card into her Bible to

keep the place, took a parting peep in the mirror to see that the brown hair and blue ribbon were in order, wondered if it were really the Hastings who called on her, unlocked her door, and made a rapid passage down the stairs—most unpleasantly conscious, however, at that very moment that her intentions of setting herself right had not been carried out, and also that so far as she had gone, it had been a failure. Truly, after the lapse of so many years, the light was still shining in darkness.

In the parlor, after the other company had departed, Ester found herself the sole companion of Mr. Foster at the further end of the long room. Abbie, half sitting, half kneeling on an ottoman near her father, seemed to be engaged in a very earnest conversation with him, in which her mother occasionally joined and at which Ralph appeared occasionally to laugh; but what was the subject of debate they at their distance were unable to determine, and at last Mr. Foster turned to his nearest neighbor.

"And so, Miss Ester, you manufactured me into a minister at our first meeting?"

In view of their nearness to cousinship, the ceremony of surname had been promptly discarded by Mr. Foster, but Ester was unable to recover from a sort of awe with which he had at first inspired her, and this opening sentence appeared to be a confusing one, for she flushed deeply and only bowed her answer.

"I don't know but it is a most unworthy curiosity on my part," continued Mr. Foster, "but I have an overwhelming desire to know why—or, rather, to know in what respect—I am ministerial. Won't you enlighten me, Miss Ester?"

"Why," said Ester, growing still more confused, "I thought—I said—I—no, I mean, I heard your talk with that queer old woman, some of it; and some things that you said made me think you must be a minister."

"What things, Miss Ester?"

"Everything," said Ester desperately. "You talked, you know, about—about religion nearly all the time."

A look of absolute pain rested for a moment on Mr. Foster's face as he said: "Is it possible that your experience with Christian men has been so unfortunate that you believe none but ministers ever converse on that subject?"

"I never hear any," Ester answered positively.

"But your example as a Christian lady, I trust, is such that it puts to shame your experience among gentlemen?"

"Oh, but," said Ester, still in great confusion, "I didn't mean to confine my statement to gentlemen. I never hear anything of the sort from ladies."

"Not from that dear old friend of ours on the cars?"

"Oh yes; she was different from other people too. I thought she had a very queer way of speaking; but then she was old and ignorant. I don't suppose she knew how to talk about anything else, and she is my one exception."

Mr. Foster glanced in the direction of the golden brown head that was still in eager debate at the other end of the room before he asked his next question. "How is it with your cousin?"

"Oh, she!" said Ester, brought suddenly and painfully back to all her troublesome thoughts—and then, after a moment's hesitation, making a quick resolution to probe this matter to its foundation, if it had one. "Mr. Foster, don't you think she is *very* peculiar?"

At which question Mr. Foster laughed, then

answered good-humoredly: "Do you think me a competent witness in that matter?"

"Yes," Ester answered gravely, too thoroughly in earnest to be amused now: "she is entirely different from any person that I ever saw in my life. She doesn't seem to think about anything else—at least she thinks more about this matter than any other."

"And that is being peculiar?"

"Why, I think so—unnatural, I mean—unlike other people."

"Well, let us see. Do you call it being peculiarly good or peculiarly bad?"

"Why," said Ester in great perplexity, "it isn't *bad* of course. But she—no, she is very good, the best person I ever knew; but it is being like nobody else, and nobody *can* be like her. Don't you think so?"

"I certainly do," he answered with the utmost gravity, and then he laughed again; but presently noting her perplexed look, he grew sober and spoke with quiet gravity. "I think I understand you, Miss Ester. If you mean, Do I not think Abbie has attained to a rare growth in spirituality for one of her age, I most certainly do; but if you mean, Do I not think it almost impossible for people in general to reach as high a foothold on the rock as she has gained, I certainly do not. I believe it is within the power, and not only that, but it is the blessed privilege, and not only that, but it is the sacred duty of every follower of the Cross to cling as close and climb as high as she has."

"*I* don't think so," Ester said, with a decided shake of the head. "It is much easier for some people to be good Christians than it is for others."

"Granted—that is, there is a difference of temperament certainly. But do you rank Abbie among those for whom it was naturally easy?"

"I think so."

This time Mr. Foster's head was very gravely shaken. "If you had known her when I did you would not think so. It was very hard for her to yield. Her natural temperament, her former life, her circle of friends, her home influences were all against her, and yet Christ triumphed."

"Yes, but having once decided the matter, it is smooth sailing with her now."

"Do you think so? Has Abbie no trials to meet, no battles with Satan to fight, so far as you can discover?"

"Only trifles," said Ester, thinking of Aunt Helen and Ralph, but deciding that Abbie had luxuries enough to offset both these anxieties.

"I believe you will find that it needs precisely the same help to meet trifles that it does to conquer mountains of difficulty. The difference is in degree, not in kind. But I happen to know that some of Abbie's trifles have been very heavy and hard to bear. However, the matter rests just here, Miss Ester. I believe we are all too willing to be conquered, too willing to be martyrs, not willing to reach after and obtain the settled and ever-growing joys of the Christian."

Ester was thoroughly ill at ease; all this condemned her—and at last, resolved to escape from this network of her awakening conscience, she pushed boldly on. "People have different views on this subject as well as on all others. Now Abbie and I do not agree in our opinions. There are things which she thinks right that seem to me quite out of place and improper."

"Yes," he said inquiringly and with the most quiet and courteous air; "would you object to mentioning some of those things?"

"Well, as an instance, it seemed to me very queer indeed to hear her and other young ladies speaking in your teachers' prayer meeting. *I* never heard of such a thing, at least not among cultivated people."

"And you thought it improper?"

"Almost—yes, quite—perhaps. At least *I* should never do it."

"Were you at Mrs. Burton's on the evening in which our society met?"

This, to Ester's surprise, was her companion's next very-wide-of-the-mark question. She opened her eyes inquiringly; then concluding that he was absentminded, or else had no reply to make and was weary of the subject, answered simply and briefly in the affirmative.

"I was detained that night. Were there many out?"

"Quite a full society, Abbie said. The rooms were almost crowded."

"Pleasant?"

"Oh, very. I hardly wished to go, as they were strangers to me; but I was very happily disappointed and enjoyed the evening exceedingly."

"Were there reports?"

"Very full ones, and Mrs. Burton was particularly interesting. She had forgotten her notes, but gave her reports from memory very beautifully."

"Ah, I am sorry for that. It must have destroyed the pleasure of the evening for you."

"I don't understand, Mr. Foster."

"Why, you remarked that you considered it improper for ladies to take part in such matters; and of course, what is an impropriety you cannot have enjoyed."

"Oh, that is a very different matter. It was not a prayer meeting."

"I beg pardon. I did not understand. It is only at

prayer meetings that it is improper for ladies to speak. May I ask why?"

Ester was growing vexed. "Mr. Foster," she said sharply, "you know that it is quite another thing. There are gentlemen enough present, or ought to be, to do the talking in a prayer meeting."

"There is generally a large proportion of gentlemen at the society. I presume there were those present capable of giving Mrs. Burton's report."

"Well *I* consider a society a very different thing from a gathering in a church."

"Ah, then it's the church that is at fault. If that is the case, I should propose holding prayer meetings in private parlors. Would that obviate your difficulty?"

"No," said Ester sharply, "not if there were gentlemen present. It is their business to conduct a religious meeting."

"Then, after all, it is religion that is at the foundation of this trouble. Pray, Miss Ester, was Mrs. Burton's report irreligious?"

"Mr. Foster," said Ester, with flushing cheeks and in a whirl of vexation, *"don't* you understand me?"

"I think I do, Miss Ester. The question is, do you understand yourself? Let me state the case. You are decidedly not a woman's rights lady. I am decidedly not a woman's rights gentleman—that is, in the general acceptation of that term. You would think, for instance, that Abbie was out of her sphere in the pulpit or pleading a case at the bar. So should I. In fact, there are many public places in which you and I, for what we consider good and sufficient reasons, would not like to see her. But, on the other hand, we both enjoy Mrs. Burton's reports, either verbal or written, as she may choose. We, in company with many other ladies and gentlemen, listen respectfully; we both greatly enjoy hearing Miss Ames sing; we both consider it perfectly proper that she should so entertain us at our social gatherings. At our literary society we have both enjoyed to the utmost Miss Hanley's exquisite recitation from *Kathrina*. I am sure not a thought of impropriety occurred to either of us. We both enjoyed the familiar talk on the subject for the evening after the society proper had adjourned. So the question resolves itself into this: It seems that it is pleasant and proper for fifty or more of us to hear Mrs. Burton's report in Mrs. Burton's parlor—to hear ladies sing—to hear ladies recite in their own parlors, or in those of their friends— to converse familiarly on any sensible topic; but the moment the very same company are gathered in our chapel, and Mrs. Burton says, 'Pray for my class,' and Miss Ames says, 'I love Jesus,' and Miss Hanley says, 'The Lord is the strength of my heart, and my portion forever,' it becomes improper. Will you pardon my obtuseness and explain to me the wherefore?"

But Ester was not in a mood to explain, if indeed she had aught to say, and she only answered with great decision and emphasis: "*I* have never been accustomed to it."

"No! I think you told me that you were unaccustomed to hearing poetical recitations from young ladies. Does that condemn them?"

To which question Ester made no sort of answer, but sat looking confused, ashamed, and annoyed all in one. Her companion roused himself from his half-reclining attitude on the sofa and gave her the benefit of a very searching look; then he came to an erect posture and spoke with entire change of tone.

"Miss Ester, forgive me if I have seemed severe in my questionings and sarcastic in my replies. I am afraid I have. The subject is one which awakens sarcasm in me. It is so persistently twisted and befogged and misunderstood, some of the very best people seem inclined to make our prayer meetings into formidable church meetings, for the purpose of hearing a succession of not *very* short sermons, rather than a social gathering of Christians, to sympathize with and pray for and help each other, as I believe the Master intended them to be. But may I say a word to you personally? Are you quite happy as a Christian? Do you find your love growing stronger and your hopes brighter from day to day?"

Ester struggled with herself, tore bits of down from the edge of her fan, tried to regain her composure and her voice, but the tender, gentle, yet searching tone seemed to have probed her very soul—and the eyes that at last were raised to meet his were melting into tears, and the voice which answered him quivered perceptibly. "No, Mr. Foster, I am not happy."

"Why? May I ask you? Is the Savior untrue to his promises, or is his professed servant untrue to him?"

Ester's heart was giving heavy throbs of pain, and her conscience was whispering loudly, "Untrue, untrue"; but she had made no answer when Ralph came with brisk step toward where they sat.

"Two against one isn't fair play," he said, with a mixture of mischief and vexation in his tone. "Foster, don't shirk; you have taught Abbie, now go and help her fight it out like a man. Come, take yourself over there and get her out of this scrape. I'll take care of Ester; she looks as though she had been to camp meeting."

And Mr. Foster, with a wondering look for Ralph and a troubled one for Ester, moved slowly toward that end of the long parlor where the voices were growing louder, and one of them excited.

16

A VICTORY

"THIS is really the most absurd of all your late absurdities," Mrs. Ried was saying, in rather a loud tone, and with a look of dignified disgust bestowed upon Abbie as Mr. Foster joined the group.

"Will you receive me into this circle and enlighten me as regards this particular absurdity," he said, seating himself near Mrs. Ried.

"Oh, it was nothing remarkable," that lady replied in her most sarcastic tone. "At least it is quite time we were growing accustomed to this new order of things. Abbie is trying to enlighten her father on the new and interesting question of temperance, especially as it is connected with wedding parties, in which she is particularly interested just at present."

Abbie bestowed an appealing glance on Mr. Foster and remained entirely silent.

"I believe I can claim equal interest then in the matter," he answered brightly, "and will petition you, Mrs. Ried, to explain the point at issue."

"Indeed, Mr. Foster, I'm not a temperance lecturer and do not consider myself competent to perform the awful task. I defer to Abbie, who seems to be thoroughly posted and very desirous of displaying her argumentative powers."

Still silence on Abbie's part, and only a little tremble of the lip told a close observer how deeply she felt the sharp tones and unmotherly words. Mrs. Ried spoke at last, in calm, measured accents.

"My daughter and I, Mr. Foster, differ somewhat in regard to the duties and privileges of a host. I claim the right to set before my guests whatever *I* consider proper. She objects to the use of wine, as, perhaps, you are aware. Indeed, I believe she has imbibed her very peculiar views from you; but I say to her that as I have always been in the habit of entertaining my guests with that beverage, I presume I shall continue to do so."

Mr. Foster did not seem in the mood to argue the question, but responded with genial good humor. "Ah, but, Mrs. Ried, you ought to gratify your daughter in her parting request. That is only natural and courteous, is it not?"

Mrs. Ried felt called upon to reply. "We have gratified so many of her requests already that the whole thing bids fair to be the most ridiculous proceeding that New York has ever witnessed. Fancy a dozen rough boys banging and shouting through my house, eating cake enough to make them sick for a month, to say nothing of the quantity which they will stamp into my carpets, and all because they chance to belong to Abbie's mission class!"

Ralph and Ester had joined the group in the meantime, and the former here interposed.

"That last argument isn't valid, Mother. Haven't I promised to hoe out the rooms myself, immediately after the conclusion of the solemn services?"

And Mr. Foster bestowed a sudden troubled look on Abbie, which she answered by saying in a low voice, "I should recall my invitations to them under such circumstances."

"You will do no such thing," her father replied sharply. "The invitations are issued in your parents' names, and we shall have no such senseless proceedings connected with them. When you are in your own house you will doubtless be at liberty to do as you please; but in the meantime it would be well to remember that you belong to your father's family at present."

Ralph was watching the flushing cheek and quivering lip of his young sister, and at this point flung down the book with which he had been idly playing, with an impatient exclamation: "It strikes me, Father, that you are making a tremendous din about a little matter. I don't object to a glass of wine myself, almost under any circumstances, and I think this excruciating sensitiveness on the subject is absurd and ridiculous, and all that sort of thing; but at the same time I should be willing to undertake the job of smashing every wine bottle there is in the cellar at this moment, if I thought that Sis's last hours in the body, or at least in the paternal mansion, would be made any more peaceful thereby."

During this harangue the elder Mr. Ried had time to grow ashamed of his sharpness and answered in his natural tone. "I am precisely of your opinion, my son. We are making much ado about nothing. We certainly have often entertained company before, and Abbie has sipped her wine with the rest of us without sustaining very material injury thereby, so far as I can see. And here is Ester, as staunch a church member as any of you, I believe, but that doesn't seem to forbid her behaving in a rational manner and partaking of whatever her friends provide for her entertainment. Why cannot the rest of you be equally sensible?"

During the swift second of time which intervened between that sentence and her reply, Ester had three hard things to endure—a sting from her restless conscience, a look of mingled pain and anxiety from Mr. Foster, and one of open-eyed and mischievous surprise from Ralph. The she spoke rapidly and earnestly. "Indeed, Uncle Ralph, I beg you will not judge any other person by my conduct in this matter. I am very sorry and very much ashamed that I have been so weak and wicked. I think just as Abbie does, only I am not like her, and have been tempted to do wrong, for fear you would think me foolish."

No one but Ester knew how much these sentences cost her; but the swift, bright look telegraphed her from Abbie's eyes seemed to repay her.

Ralph laughed outright. "Four against one," he said gaily. "I've gone over to the enemy's side myself, you see, on account of the pressure. Father, I advise you to yield while you can do it gracefully, and also to save me the trouble of smashing the aforesaid bottles."

"But," persisted Mr. Ried, "I haven't heard an argument this evening. What is there so shocking in a quiet glass of wine enjoyed with a select gathering of one's friends?"

John now presented himself at the door with a respectful, "If you please, sir, there is a person in the hall who persists in seeing Mr. Foster."

"Show him in, then," was Mr. Ried's prompt reply.

John hesitated and then added: "He is a very common-looking person, sir, and—"

"I said show him in, I believe," interrupted the gentleman of the house, in a tone which plainly indicated that he was expending on John the irritation which he did not like to bestow further on either his children or his guests.

John vanished, and Mr. Ried added: "You can take your *friend* into the library, Mr. Foster, if it proves to be a private matter."

There was a marked emphasis on the word *friend* in this sentence; but Mr. Foster only bowed his reply, and presently John returned, ushering in a short, stout man dressed in a rough working suit, twirling his hat in his hand, and looking extremely embarrassed and out of place in the elegant parlor. Mr. Foster turned toward him immediately and gave him a greeting both prompt and cordial. "Ah, Mr. Jones, good evening. I have been in search of you today, but some way managed to miss you."

At this point Abbie advanced and placed a small white hand in Mr. Jones's great hard brown one as she repeated the friendly greeting and inquired at once: "How is Sallie tonight, Mr. Jones?"

"Well, ma'am, it is about her that I've come, and I beg your pardon, sir (turning to Mr. Foster), for making so bold as to come up here after you; but she is just that bad tonight that I could not find it in me to deny her anything, and she is in a real taking to see you. She has sighed and cried about it most of this day, and tonight we felt, her mother and me, that we couldn't stand it any longer, and I said I'd not come home till I found you and told you how much she wanted to see you. It's asking a good deal, sir, but she is going fast, she is; and—" Here Mr. Jones's voice choked, and he rubbed his hard hand across his eyes.

"I will be down immediately," was Mr. Foster's prompt reply. "Certainly you should have come for me. I should have been very sorry indeed to disappoint Sallie. Tell her I will be there in half an hour, Mr. Jones."

And with a few added words of kindness from Abbie, Mr. Jones departed, looking relieved and thankful.

"That man," said Mr. Foster, turning to Ester as the door closed after him, "is the son of our old lady, don't you think! You remember I engaged to see her conveyed to his home in safety, and my anxiety for her future welfare was such that my pleasure was very great in discovering that the son was a faithful member of our mission Sabbath school and a thoroughly good man."

"And who is Sallie?" Ester inquired, very much interested.

Mr. Foster's face grew graver. "Sallie is his one treasure, a dear little girl, one of our mission scholars, and a beautiful example of how faithful Christ can be to his little lambs."

"What is supposed to be the matter with Sallie?" This question came from Ralph, who had been half amused, half interested, with the entire scene.

The gravity on Mr. Foster's face deepened into sternness as he answered: "Sallie is only one of the many victims of our beautiful system of public poisoning. The son of her mother's employer, in a fit of drunken rage, threw her from the very top of a long flight of stairs, and now she lies warped and misshapen, mourning her life away. By the way," he continued, turning suddenly toward Mr. Ried, "I believe you were asking for arguments to sustain my peculiar views. Here is one of them: This man of whom I speak, whose crazed brain has this young sad life and death to answer for, I chance to know to a certainty commenced his downward career in a certain pleasant parlor in this city, among a select gathering of friends, taking a quiet glass of wine!" And Mr. Foster made his adieus very brief and departed.

Ralph's laugh was just a little nervous as he said, when the family was alone: "Foster is very fortunate in having an incident come to our very door with which to point his theories."

Abbie had deserted her ottoman and taken one close by her father's side. Now she laid her bright head lovingly against his breast and looked with eager, coaxing eyes into his stern gray ones. "Father," she said softly, "you'll let your little curly have her own way just this time, won't you? I will promise not to coax you again until I want something very bad indeed."

Mr. Ried had decided his plan of action some moments before. He was prepared to remind his daughter in tones of haughty dignity that he was "not in the habit of playing the part of a despot in his own family, and that as she and her future husband were so very positive in their very singular opinions, and so entirely regardless of his wishes or feelings, he should, of course, not force his hospitalities on her guests."

He made one mistake. For just a moment he allowed his eyes to meet the sweet blue ones, looking lovingly and trustingly into his, and whatever it was, whether the remembrance that his one daughter was so soon to go out from her home, or the thought of all the tender and patient love and care which she had bestowed on him in those early morning hours, the stern gray eyes grew tender, the haughty lines about the mouth relaxed, and with a sudden caressing movement of his hand among the brown curls, he said in a half-moved, half-playful tone:

"Did you ever ask anything of anybody in your life

that you didn't get?" Then more gravely: "You shall have your way once more, Abbie. It would be a pity to despoil you of your scepter at this late day."

"Fiddlesticks!" ejaculated Mrs. Ried.

Before she had added anything to that original sentiment, Abbie was behind her chair, both arms wound around her neck, and then came soft, quick, loving kisses on her cheeks, on her lips, on her chin, and even on her nose.

"Nonsense!" added her mother. Then she laughed. "Your father would consent to have the ceremony performed in the attic if you should take a fancy that the parlors are too nicely furnished to suit your puritanic views, and I don't know but I should be just as foolish."

"That man has gained complete control over her," Mrs. Ried said, looking after Abbie with a little sigh and addressing her remarks to Ester as they stood together for a moment in the further parlor. "He is a first-class fanatic, grows wilder and more incomprehensible in his whims every day, and bends Abbie to his slightest wish. My only consolation is that he is a man of wealth and culture, and indeed in every other respect, entirely unexceptionable."

A new light dawned upon Ester. This was the secret of Abbie's "strangeness." Mr. Foster was one of those rare and wonderful men about whom one occasionally reads but almost never meets, and of course Abbie, being so constantly under his influence, was constantly led by him. Very few could expect to attain to such a height; certainly she, with her social disadvantages and helpful surroundings, must not hope for it.

She was rapidly returning to her former state of self-satisfaction. There were certain things to be done. For instance, that first chapter of John should receive more close attention at her next reading; and there were various other duties which should be taken up and carefully observed. But, on the whole, Ester felt that she had been rather unnecessarily exercised and that she must not expect to be perfect. And so once more, there was raised a flag of truce between her conscience and her life.

17

STEPPING BETWEEN

THEY lingered together for a few minutes in the sitting room, Abbie, Ester, Ralph, and Mr. Foster. They had been having a half-sad, half-merry talk. It was the evening before the wedding. Ere this time tomorrow Abbie would have left them, and in just a little while the ocean would roll between them. Ester drew a heavy sigh as she thought of it all. This magic three weeks, which had glowed in beauty for her, such, as she told herself, her life would never see again, were just on the eve of departure; only two days now before she would carry that same restless, unhappy heart back among the clattering dishes in that pantry and dining room at home. Ralph broke the little moment of silence which had fallen between them.

"Foster, listen to the sweet tones of that distant clock. It is the last time that you, being a free man, will hear it strike five."

"Unless I prove to be an early riser on the morrow, which necessity will compel me to become if I tarry longer here at present. Abbie, I must be busy this entire evening. That funeral obliged me to defer some important business matters that I meant should have been dispatched early in the day."

"It isn't possible that you have been to a funeral today! How you do mix things." Ralph uttered this sentence in real or pretended horror.

"Why not?" Mr. Foster answered gently and added: "It is true though; life and death are very strangely mixed. It was our little Sabbath school girl, Sallie, whom we laid to rest today. It didn't jar as some funerals would have done; one had simply to remember that she had reached home. Miss Ester, if you will get that package for me I will execute your commission with pleasure."

Ester went away to do his bidding, and Ralph, promising to meet him at the store in an hour, sauntered away, and for a few moments Abbie and Mr. Foster talked together alone.

"Good-bye all of you," he said, smiling as he glanced back at the two girls a few moments later. "Take care of her, Ester, until I relieve you. It will not be long now."

"Take care," Ester answered gaily; "you have forgotten the slip that there may be between the cup and the lip."

But he answered with an almost solemn gravity: "I never forget that more worthy expression of the same idea, We know not what a day may bring forth; but I always remember with exceeding joy that God knows and will lead us."

"He is graver than ten ministers," Ester said as they turned from the window. "Come, Abbie, let us go upstairs."

It was two hours later when Abbie entered the sitting room where Ester awaited her and curled herself into a small heap of white muslin at Ester's feet.

"There!" said she with a musical little laugh, "Mother has sent me away. The measure of her disgust is complete now. Dr. Downing is in the sitting room, and I have been guilty of going in to see him. Imagine such a fearful breach of etiquette taking place in the house of Ried! Do you know, I don't quite know what to do with myself. There is really nothing more to busy myself about, unless I eat the wedding cake."

"You don't act in the least like a young lady who is to be married tomorrow," was Ester's answer as she regarded her cousin with a half-amused, half-puzzled air.

"Don't I?" said Abbie, trying to look alarmed. "What *have* I done now? I'm forever treading on bits of propriety and crushing them. It will be a real relief to me when I am safely married and can relapse into a common mortal again. Why, Ester, what have I been guilty of just now?"

"You are not a bit sentimental, are you, Abbie?" And at this gravely put question Abbie's laugh rang out again.

"Now don't, please, add that item to the list," she said merrily. "Ester, is it very important that one should be sentimental on such an occasion? I wish you were married, I really do, so that I might be told just how to conduct myself. How can you and Mother be so unreasonable as to expect perfection when it is all new, and I really never practiced in my life?" Then a change, as sudden as it was sweet, flushed over Abbie's face. The merry look died out, and in its place a gentle, tender softness rested in the bright blue eyes, and her voice was low and quiet. "You think my mood a strange one, I fancy, dear Ester; almost unbecoming in its gaiety. Perhaps it is, and yet I feel it bright and glad and happy. The change is a solemn one, but it seems to me that I have considered it long and well. I remember that my new home is to be very near my old one; that my brother will have a patient, faithful, lifelong friend in Mr. Foster, and this makes me feel more hopeful for him—and, indeed, it seems to me that I feel like repeating, 'The lines have fallen unto me in pleasant places.' I do not, therefore, affect a gravity that I do not feel. I am gloriously happy tonight, and the strongest feeling in my heart is thankfulness. My heavenly Father has brimmed my earthly cup, so that it seems to me there is not room in my heart for another throb of joy; and so you see—Ester, what on earth can be going on downstairs? Have you noticed the banging of doors and the general confusion that reigns through the house? Positively if I wasn't afraid of shocking Mother into a fainting fit I would start on a voyage of discovery."

"Suppose I go," Ester answered, laughing. "Inasmuch as I am not going to be married, there can be no harm in seeing what new developments there are belowstairs. I mean to go. I'll send you word if it is anything very amazing."

And with a laughing adieu Ester closed the door on the young bride-elect and ran swiftly downstairs. There did seem to be a good deal of confusion in the orderly household, and the very air of the hall seemed to be pervaded with a singular subdued excitement; voices of suppressed loudness issued from the front parlor, and as Ester knocked, she heard a half scream from Mrs. Ried, mingled with cries of, "Don't let her in." Growing thoroughly alarmed, Ester now abruptly pushed open the door and entered.

"Oh, for mercy's sake, don't let her come," almost screamed Mrs. Ried, starting wildly forward.

"Mother, *hush!*" said Ralph's voice in solemn sternness. "It is only Ester. Where is Abbie?"

"In her room. What is the matter? Why do you all act so strangely? I came to see what caused so much noise."

And then her eyes and voice were arrested by a group around the sofa: Mr. Ried and Dr. Downing, and stooping over some object which was hidden from her was the man who had been pointed out to her as the great Dr. Archer. As she looked in terrified amazement, he raised his head and spoke.

"It is as I feared, Mr. Ried. The pulse has ceased."

"It is not possible!" And the hollow, awestruck tone in which Mr. Ried spoke cannot be described.

And then Ester saw stretched on that sofa a perfectly motionless form, a perfectly pale and quiet face, rapidly settling into the strange solemn calm of death, and that face and form were Mr. Foster's! And she stood as if riveted to the spot; stood in speechless, moveless horror and amazement—and then the swift-coming thoughts shaped themselves into two woe-charged words: "Oh, Abbie!"

What a household was this into which death had so swiftly and silently entered! The very rooms in which the quiet form lay sleeping, all decked in festive beauty in honor of the bridal morning; but oh! there was to come no bride.

Ester shrank back in awful terror from the petition that she would go to Abbie.

"I cannot—I *cannot!*" she repeated again and again. "It will kill her; and oh! it would kill me to tell her."

Mrs. Ried was even more hopeless a dependence than Ester; and Mr. Ried cried out in the very agony of despair: "What *shall* we do? Is there *nobody* to help us?"

Then Ralph came forward, grave almost to sternness, but very calm. "Dr. Downing," he said, addressing the gentleman who had withdrawn a little from the family group. "It seems to me that you are our only hope in this time of trial. My sister and you are sustained, I verily believe, by the same power. The rest of us seem to *have* no sustaining power. Would you go to my sister, sir?"

Dr. Downing turned his eyes slowly away from the calm, moveless face which seemed to have fascinated him and said simply: "I will do what I can for Abbie. It is blessed to think what a Helper she has. One who never faileth. God pity those who have no such friend."

So they showed him up to the brightly lighted library and sent a message to the unsuspecting Abbie.

"Dr. Downing," she said, turning briskly from the window in answer to Maggie's summons. "Whatever does he want of me do you suppose, Maggie? I'm half afraid of him tonight. However, I'll endeavor to brave the ordeal. Tell Miss Ester to come up to me as soon as she can, and be ready to defend me if I am to receive a lecture."

This, as she flitted by toward the door; and a pitying cloud just then hid the face of the August moon and veiled from the glance of the poor young creature the white, frightened face of Maggie.

With that unutterable agony of fear did the family below wait and long for and dread the return of Dr. Downing or some message from that dreadful room. The moments that seemed hours to them dragged on, and no sound came to them.

"She has not fainted then," muttered Ralph at last, "or he would have rung. Ester, you know what Maggie said. Could you not go to her?"

Ester cowered and shrunk. "Oh, Ralph, don't ask me. I *cannot!*"

Then they waited again in silence; and at last shivered with fear as Dr. Downing softly opened the door. There were traces of deep emotion on his face, but just now it was wonderful for its calmness.

"She knows all," he said, addressing Mr. Ried. "And the widow's God is hers. Mrs. Ried, she makes special request that she need see no living soul tonight; and, indeed, I think it will be best. And now, my friends, may I pray with you in this hour of trial?"

So while quick, skillful fingers prepared the sleeper in that front parlor for his long, long rest, a group such as had never bowed the knee together before knelt in the room just across the hall, and amid tears and moans they were commended to the care of him who waits to help us all.

By and by a solemn quiet settled down upon that strangely stricken household. In the front parlor the folding doors were closed, and the angel of death kept guard over his quiet victim. From the chamber overhead came forth no sound, and none knew save God how fared the struggle between despair and submission in that young heart. In the sitting room Ester waited breathlessly while Ralph gave the particulars, which she had not until now been able to hear.

"We were crossing just above the store; had nearly got across. He was just saying that his preparations were entirely perfected for a long absence. 'It is a long journey,' he added, 'and if I never come back I have the satisfaction of thinking that I have left everything ready even for that. It is well to be ready for death, Ralph,' he said, with one of his glorious smiles; 'it makes life pleasanter.' I don't know how I can tell you the rest." And Ralph's lips grew white and tremulous.

"Indeed, I hardly know how it was. There was an old bent woman crossing just behind us, and there was a carriage, and a wretch of a drunken driver pushing his way through. I don't know how Foster came to look around, but he did, and said, 'There is my dear old lady behind us, Ralph; she ought not to be out with a mere child for a companion.' And then he uttered an exclamation of terror and sprang forward—and I know nothing clearly that followed. I saw him drag that old woman fairly from under the horses' feet. I heard the driver curse and saw him strike his frightened horses, and they reared and plunged, and I saw him fall; but it all seemed to happen in one second of time—and how I got him home, and got Dr. Archer, and kept it from Abbie, I don't seem to know. Oh, God, help my poor little fair darling." And Ralph choked and stopped, and wiped from his eyes great burning tears.

"Oh, Ralph!" said Ester as soon as she could speak. "Then all this misery comes because that driver was intoxicated."

"Yes," said Ralph, with compressed lips and flashing eyes.

> "And that, knowing the time, that now it is high time to awake out of sleep: for now is our salvation nearer than when we believed."
>
> *Rom. 13:11*

18

LIGHT OUT OF DARKNESS

SLOWLY, slowly, the night wore away, and the eastern sky grew rosy with the blush of a new morning—the bridal morning!

How strangely unreal, how even impossible did it seem to Ester, as she raised the curtains and looked drearily out upon the dawn that this was actually the day upon which her thoughts had centered during the last three weeks. What a sudden shutting down had there been to all their plans and preparations! How strange the house looked—here a room bedecked in festive beauty for the wedding; there one with shrouded mirrors and floating folds of crape! Life and death, a wedding and a funeral—they had never either of them touched so close to her before; and now the one had suddenly glided backward and left her heart heavy with the coming of the other. Mechanically, she turned to look upon the silvery garment gleaming among the white furnishings of the bed, for she was that very morning to have assisted in arraying the bride in those robes of beauty. Her own careful fingers had laid out all the bewildering paraphernalia of the dressing room—sash and gloves, and handkerchief and laces. Just in that very spot had she stood only yesterday and, talking the while with Abbie, had altered a knot of ribbons and given the ends a more graceful droop, and just at that moment Abbie had been summoned belowstairs to see Mr. Foster—and now he was waiting down there, not for Abbie, but for the coffin and the grave, and Abbie was—

And here Ester gave a low, shuddering moan and covered her eyes with her hands. Why had she come into that room at all? And why was all this fearful time allowed to come to Abbie? Poor, poor Abbie! she had been so bright and so good, and Mr. Foster had been so entirely her guide—how could she ever endure it? Ester doubted much whether Abbie could ever bear to see *her* again, she had been so closely connected with all these bright days over which so fearful a pall had fallen. It would be very natural if she should refuse even to *see* her—and, indeed, Ester almost hoped she would. It seemed to her that this was a woe too deep to be spoken of or endured, only she said with a kind of desperation, "Things *must* be endured"; and there was a wild thought in her heart that if she could but have the ordering of events, all this bitter sorrow should never be. There came a low, tremulous knock as an interruption to her thoughts, and Maggie's swollen eyes and tearstained face appeared at the door with a message.

"If you please, Miss Ester, she wants you."

"Who?" asked Ester, with trembling lips and a sinking at her heart.

"Miss Abbie, ma'am; she asked for you and said would you come to her as soon as you could."

But it was hours after that before Ester brought herself to feel that she *could* go to her. Nothing had

ever seemed so hard to her to do. How to look, how
to act, what to say, and above all, what *not* to say to this
poor, widowed bride. These questions were by no
means answered when she suddenly, in desperate
haste, decided that if it must be done, the sooner it was
over the better, and she made all speed to prepare
herself for the visit; and yet there was enough of
Ester's personal self left, even on that morning, to send
a little quiver of complacency through her veins as she
bathed her tearstained face and smoothed her disordered hair. Abbie had sent for *her*. Abbie wanted her;
she had sent twice. Evidently she had turned to her
for help. Miserably unable as she felt herself to give it,
still it was a comfort to feel that she was the one
selected from the household for companionship. Ester
knew that Mrs. Ried had been with her daughter for
a few moments and that Ralph had rushed in and out
again, too overcome to stay, but Ester had asked no
questions and received no information concerning
her. She pictured her lying on the bed, with disordered hair and swollen eyes, given over to the aban-
donment of grief, or else the image of stony despair;
and it was with a very trembling hand that at last she
softly turned the knob and let herself into the morning room, which she and Abbie had enjoyed together;
and just as she pushed open the door, a neighboring
clock counted out twelve strokes, and it was at twelve
o'clock that Abbie was to have become a wife! Midway into the room Ester paused, and as her eyes rested
on Abbie, a look of bewildering astonishment gathered on her face. In the little easy chair by the open
window, one hand keeping the place in the partly
closed book, sat the young creature whose life had so
suddenly darkened around her. The morning robe of
soft pure white was perfect in its neatness and simplic-

ity, the brown curls clustered around her brow with their wonted grace and beauty, and while under her eyes indeed there were heavy rings of black, yet the eyes themselves were large and full and tender. As she held out the disengaged hand, there came the soft and gentle likeness of a smile over her face; and Ester, bewildered, amazed, frightened, stood almost as transfixed as if she had been one of those who saw the angel sitting at the door of the empty tomb. She stood a moment, then a sudden revulsion of feeling overcoming her, hurried forward, and dropping on her knees, bowed her head over the white hand and the half-open Bible and burst into a passion of tears.

"Dear Ester!" This said Abbie in the softest, most soothing of tones. The mourner turned comforter!

"Oh, Abbie, Abbie, how can you bear it—how *can* you live?" burst forth from the heart of this friend who had come to comfort this afflicted one!

There was a little bit of silence now and a touching tremble to the voice when it was heard again.

"'The Lord knoweth them that are his.' I try to remember that. Christ knows it all, and he loves me, and he is all-powerful; and yet he leads me through this dark road; therefore it *must* be right."

"But," said Ester, raising her eyes and staying her tears for very amazement, "I do not understand—I do not see. How *can* you be so calm, so submissive, at least just now—so soon—and you were to have been married today?"

The blood rolled in great purple waves over neck and cheek and brow, and then receded, leaving a strange, almost deathlike, pallor behind it. The small hands were tightly clasped, with a strange mixture of pain and devotion in the movement, and the white lips moved for a moment, forming words that met no mortal ear—then the sweet, low, tender voice sounded again.

"Dear Ester, I pray. There is no other way. I pray all the time. I keep right by my Savior. There is just a little, a very little, veil of flesh between him and between my—my husband and myself. Jesus loves me, Ester. I know it now just as well as I did yesterday. I do not and cannot doubt him."

A mixture of awe and pain and astonishment kept Ester moveless and silent, and Abbie spoke no more for some moments. Then it was a changed, almost bright voice.

"Ester, do you remember we stood together alone for a moment yesterday? I will tell you what he said, the last words that were intended for just me only, that I shall hear to a little while; they are *my* words, you know, but I shall tell them to you so you may see how tender Christ is, even in his most solemn chastenings. 'See here,' he said, 'I will give you a word to keep until we meet in the morning: "The Lord watch between thee and me while we are absent one from another."' I have been thinking, while I sat here this morning, watching the coming of this new day, which you know is his first day in heaven, that perhaps it will be on some such morning of beauty as this that my long, long day will dawn, and that I will say to him as soon as ever I see his face again: 'The word was a good one; the Lord has watched between us, and the night is gone.' Think of it, Ester, I shall *surely* say that some-day—some summer morning."

The essence of sweetness and the sublimity of faith which this young Christian threw into these jubilant words cannot be repeated on paper; but, thank God, they can in the heart—they are but the echo of those sure and everlasting words: "My grace is sufficient for thee." As for Ester, who had spent her years groveling in the dust of earth, it was the recital of such an experience as she had not deemed it possible for humanity to reach. And still she knelt immovable and silent, and Abbie broke the silence yet again.

"Dear Ester, do you know I have not seen him yet, and I want to. Mother does not understand, and she would not give her consent, but she thinks me safe while you are with me. Would you mind going down with me just to look at his face again?"

Oh, Ester would mind it *dreadfully*. She was actually afraid of death. She was afraid of the effect of such a scene upon this strange Abbie. She raised her head, shivering with pain and apprehension, and looked a volume of petition and remonstrance; but ere she spoke Abbie's hand rested lovingly on her arm, and her low sweet voice continued the pleading:

"You do not quite understand my mood, Ester. I am not unlike others; I have wept bitter tears this past night; I have groaned in agony of spirit; I have moaned in the very dust. I shall doubtless have such struggles again. This is earth, and the flesh is weak; but now is my hour of exaltation—and while it is given me now to feel a faint overshadowing of the very glory which surrounds him, I want to go and look my last upon the dear clay which is to stay here on earth with me."

And Ester rose up and wound her arm about the tiny frame which held this brave true heart, and without another spoken word the two went swiftly down the stairs and entered the silent, solemn parlor. Yet, even while she went, a fierce throb of pain shook Ester's heart as she remembered how they had arranged to descend the staircase on this very day—in what a different manner, and for what a different purpose. Apparently no such thought as this touched

Abbie. She went softly and yet swiftly forward to the still form, while Ester waited in almost breathless agony to see what would result from this trial of faith and nerve; but what a face it was upon which death had left its seal! No sculptured marble was ever so grand in its solemn beauty as was this clay-molded face, upon which the glorious smile born not of earth rested in full sweetness. Abbie, with clasped hands and slightly parted lips, stood and almost literally drank in the smile; then, sweet and low and musical, there broke the sound of her voice in that great solemn room.

"So he giveth his beloved sleep."

Not another word or sound disturbed the silence. And still Abbie stood and gazed on the dear, dead face. And still Ester stood near the door and watched with alternations of anxiety and awe the changeful expressions on the scarcely less white face of the living, until at last, without sound or word, she dropped upon her knees, a cloud of white drapery floating around her, and clasped her hands over the lifeless breast. Then on Ester's face the anxiety gave place to awe, and with softly moving fingers she opened the door, and with noiseless tread went out into the hall and left the living and the dead alone together.

There was one more scene for Ester to endure that day. Late in the afternoon, as she went to the closed room, there was bending over the manly form a gray-haired old woman. By whose friendly hands she had been permitted to enter, Ester did not stop to wonder. She had seen her but once before, but she knew at a glance the worn, wrinkled face; and as if a picture of the scene hung before her, she saw that old, queer form, leaning trustfully on the strong arm, lying nerveless now, being carefully helped through the pushing throng—being reverently cared for as if she had been his mother; and *she,* looking after the two, had wondered if she should ever see them again. Now she stood in the presence of them both, yet what an unmeasurable ocean rolled between them! The faded, tearful eyes were raised to her face after a moment, and a quivering voice spoke her thoughts aloud, rather than addressed anybody. "He gave his life for poor old useless me, and it was such a beautiful life, and was needed, oh so much; but what am I saying, God let it be him instead of me, who wanted so to go—and after trusting him all along, am I, at my time of life, going to murmur at him now? He came to see me only yesterday"—this in a more natural tone of voice, addressed to Ester—"he told me good-bye. He said he was going on a long journey with his wife; and now, may the dear Savior help the poor darling, for he has gone on his long journey without her."

Ester waited to hear not another word. The heavy sense of pain because of Abbie, which she had carried about with her through all that weary day, had reached its height with that last sentence: "He has gone on his long journey without her."

She fled from the room, up the stairs, to the quiet little chamber which had been given to her for her hours of retirement, locked and bolted the door, and commenced pacing up and down the room in agony of soul.

It was not all because of Abbie that this pain knocked so steadily at her heart, at least not all out of sympathy with her bitter sorrow. There was a fearful tumult raging in her own soul; her last stronghold had been shattered. Of late she had come to think that Abbie's Christian life was but a sweet reflection of Mr. Foster's strong, true soul; that she leaned not on Christ, but on the arm of flesh. She had told herself very confidently that if *she* had such a friend as he had been to Abbie, she should be like her. In her hours of rebellion she had almost angrily reminded herself that it was not strange that Abbie's life could be so free from blame; *she* had someone to turn to in her needs. It was a very easy matter for Abbie to slip lightly over the petty trials of her life, so long as she was surrounded and shielded by that strong, true love. But now, ah now, the arm of flesh had faltered, the strong staff had broken, and broken, too, only a moment, as it were, before it was to have been hers in name as well as in spirit. Naturally, Ester had expected that the young creature, so suddenly shorn of her best and dearest, would falter and faint and utterly fail. And when, looking on, she saw the triumph of the Christian's faith, rising even over death, sustained by no human arm, and yet wonderfully, triumphantly sustained, even while she bent for the last time over that which was to have been her earthly all—looking and wondering, there suddenly fell away from her the stupor of years, and Ester saw with wide-open eyes and thoroughly awakened soul that there was something in this Christian religion that Abbie had and she had not.

And thus it was that she paced her room in that strange agony that was worse than grief and more sharp than despair. No use now to try to lull her conscience back to quiet sleep again—that time was past; it was thoroughly and sharply awake; the same all-wise hand, which had tenderly freed one soul from its bonds of clay and called it home, had as tenderly and as wisely, with the same stroke, cut the cords that bound this other soul to earth, loosed the scales from her long-closed eyes, broke the sleep that had well nigh lulled her to ruin; and now heart and brain and conscience were thoroughly and forever awake.

When at last, from sheer exhaustion, she ceased her excited pacing up and down the room and sank into a chair, her heart was not more stilled. It seemed to her, long after, in thinking of this hour, that it was given to her to see deeper into the recesses of her own depravity than ever mortal had seen before. She began years back, at that time when she thought she had given her heart to Christ, and reviewed step by step all the weary way, up to this present time; and she found nothing but backslidings, and inconsistencies, and confusion—denials of her Savior, a closed Bible, a neglected closet, a forgotten cross. Oh, the bitterness, the unutterable agony of that hour! Surely Abbie, on her knees struggling with her bleeding heart, and yet feeling all around and underneath her the everlasting arms, knew nothing of desolation such as this.

Fiercer and fiercer waged the warfare, until at last every root of pride, or self-complacence, or self-excuse was utterly cast out. Yet did not Satan despair. Oh, he meant to have this poor, sick, weak lamb, if he could get her; no effort should be left unmade. And when he found that she could be no more coaxed and lulled and petted into peace, he tried that darker, heavier temptation—tried to stupefy her into absolute despair. *No,* she said within her heart, *I am not a Christian; I never have been one; I never can be one. I've been a miserable, self-deceived hypocrite all my life. I have had a name to live and am dead. I would not let myself be awakened; I have struggled against it; I have been only too glad to stop myself from thinking about it. I have been just a miserable stumbling block, with no excuse to offer; and now I feel myself deserted, justly so. There can be no rest for such*

*as I. I have no Savior; I have insulted and denied him; I
have crucified him again, and now he has left me to myself.*

Thus did that father of lies continue to pour into
this weary soul the same old story which he has
repeated for so many hundred years, with the same old
foundation: "I—I—I." And strange to say, this poor
girl repeated the experience which has so many times
been lived, during these past hundreds of years, in the
very face of that other glorious pronoun, in very
defiance, it would seem, to that old, old, explanation:
"Surely *he* hath borne our griefs and carried our
sorrows." *"He* was wounded for our transgressions; *he*
was bruised for our iniquities. The chastisement of our
peace was upon *him;* and with *his stripes* we are
healed."

Yes, Ester knew those two verses. She knew yet
another, which said: "All we, like sheep, have gone
astray. We have turned everyone to his own way: *and
the Lord hath laid on him the iniquity of us all."*

And yet she dared to sit with hopeless, folded hands,
with heavy despairing eyes, and repeat that sentence: "I
have no Savior now." And many a wandering sheep has
dared, even in its repenting hour, to insult the great
Shepherd thus. Ester's Bible lay on the window seat—
the large, somewhat worn Bible which Abbie had lent
her, to "mark just as much as she pleased"; it lay open
as if it had opened of itself to a familiar spot. There were
heavy markings around several of the verses, markings
that had not been made by Ester's pencil. Some power
far removed from that which had been guiding her
despairing thoughts prompted her to reach forth her
hand for the book and fix her attention on those
marked verses, and the words were these: "For thus saith
the high and lofty One that inhabiteth eternity, whose
name is Holy; I dwell in the high and holy place, with

him also that is of a contrite and humble spirit, to revive the spirit of the humble, and to revive the heart of the contrite ones. For I will not contend forever, neither will I be always wroth: for the spirit should fail before me, and the souls which I have made. For the iniquity of his covetousness was I wroth, and smote him: I hid me, and was wroth, and he went on frowardly in the way of his heart. I have seen his ways, and will heal him: I will lead him also, and restore comforts unto him and to his mourners. I create the fruit of the lips; Peace, peace to him that is far off, and to him that is near, saith the Lord; and *I will heal him.*"

Had an angel spoken to Ester, or was it the dear voice of the Lord himself? She did not know. She only knew that there rang through her very soul two sentences as the climax of all these wonderful words: "Peace, peace to him that is far off"—and—"I will heal him."

A moment more, and with the very promise of the Crucified spread out before her, Ester was on her knees; and at first, with bursts of passionate, tearful pleading, and later with low, humble, contrite tones, and finally with the sound in her voice of that peace which comes only to those to whom Christ is repeating: "I have blotted out as a cloud thy transgressions, and as a thick cloud thy sins," did Ester pray.

"Do you know, dear Ester, there must have been two new joys in heaven today? First they had a newcomer among those who walk with him in white, for they are worthy; and then they had that shout of triumph over another soul for whom Satan has struggled fiercely and whom he has forever lost." This said Abbie as they nestled close together that evening in the "purple twilight."

And Ester answered simply and softly: "Amen."

19

SUNDRIES

MEANWHILE the days moved on; the time fixed for Ester's return home had long passed, and yet she tarried in New York.

Abbie clung to her, wanted her for various reasons; and the unselfish, pitying mother, far away, full of tender sympathy for the stricken bride, smothered a sigh of weariness, buried in her heart the thought of her own need of her eldest daughter's presence and help, and wrote a long, loving letter, jointly to the daughter and niece, wherein she gave her full consent to Ester's remaining away, so long as she could be a comfort to her cousin.

Two items worthy of record occurred during these days. The first time the family gathered at the dinner table after the one who had been so nearly a son of the house had been carried to his rest in that wonderful and treasured city of Greenwood, Ralph, being helped by John, as usual, to his glass of wine, refused it with a short, sharp, almost angry, *"No.* Take it away and never offer me the accursed stuff again. We should have had him with us today but for that. I'll never touch another drop of it as long as I live."

Which startling words Mr. and Mrs. Ried listened to without comment, other than a half-frightened look bestowed on Abbie to see how she would bear this mention of her dead; and she bore it this way. Turning her eyes, glistening with tears, full on her brother's face, she said, with a little quiver of tender gladness in her voice:

"Oh, Ralph, I knew it had a silver lining, but I did not think God would let me see it so soon."

Then Mr. and Mrs. Ried concluded that both their children were queer and that they did not understand them. The other item was productive of a dissertation on propriety from Mrs. Ried.

Ralph and his father were in the back parlor, the former standing with one arm resting on the mantel while he talked with his father, who was half buried in a great easy chair—that easy chair in his own elegant parlor and his handsome son standing before him in that graceful attitude were Mr. Ried's synonyms for perfect satisfaction; and his face took on a little frown of disappointment as the door opened somewhat noisily, and Mrs. Ried came in wearing a look expressive of thoroughly defined vexation. Ralph paused in the midst of his sentence and wheeled forward a second easy chair for his mother, then returned to his former position and waited patiently for the gathered frown to break into words, which event instantly occurred.

"I really do not think, Mr. Ried, that this nonsense ought to be allowed; besides being a very strange, unfeeling thing to do, it is in my opinion positively indecent—and I *do* think, Mr. Ried, that you ought to exercise your authority for once."

"If you kindly inform me what you are supposed to be talking about and where my authority is specially needed at this time, I might be induced to consider the matter."

This, from the depths of the easy chair, in its owner's most provokingly indifferent tone, which fortunately Mrs. Ried was too much preoccupied to take special note of, and she continued her storm of words.

"Here, it is not actually quite a week since he was buried, and Abbie must needs make herself and her family appear perfectly ridiculous by making her advent in public."

Mr. Ried came to an upright posture, and even Ralph asked a startled question:

"Where is she going?"

"Why, where do you suppose, but to that absurd little prayer meeting, where she always would insist upon going every Thursday evening. I used to think it was for the pleasure of a walk home with Mr. Foster; but why she should go tonight is incomprehensible to me."

"Nonsense!" said Mr. Ried, settling back into the cushions. "A large public that will be. I thought at the very least she was going to the opera. If the child finds any comfort in such an atmosphere, where's the harm? Let her go."

"Where's the harm! Now, Mr. Ried, that is just as much as you care for appearances *sometimes,* and at other times you can be quite as particular as *I* am; though I certainly believe there is nothing that Abbie might take a fancy to do that you would not uphold her in."

Mr. Ried's reply was uttered in a tone that impressed one with the belief that he was uttering a deliberate conviction.

"You are quite right as regards that, I suspect. At least I find myself quite unable to conceive of anything connected with her that could by any twisting be made other than just the thing."

Mrs. Ried's exasperated answer was cut short by the entrance of Abbie, attired as for a walk or ride, the extreme pallor of her face and the largeness of her soft eyes enhanced by the deep mourning robes which fell around her like the night.

"Now, Abbie," said Mrs. Ried, turning promptly to her, "I did hope you had given up this strangest of all your strange whims. What *will* people think?"

"People are quite accustomed to seeing me there, dear Mother, at least all the people who will see me tonight; and if *ever* I needed help, I do just now."

"I should think it would be much more appropriate to stay at home and find help in the society of your own family. That is the way other people do who are in affliction."

Mrs. Ried had the benefit of a full, steady look from Abbie's great solemn eyes now as she said:

"Mother, I want God's help. No other will do me any good."

"Well," answered Mrs. Ried, after just a moment of rather awestruck silence, "can't you find that help anywhere but in that plain, common little meeting-house? I thought people with your peculiar views believed that God was everywhere."

An expression not unlike that of a hunted deer shone for a moment in Abbie's eyes. Then she spoke, in tones almost despairing:

"O Mother, *Mother,* you *cannot* understand."

Tone or words, or both, vexed Mrs. Ried afresh, and she spoke with added sharpness.

"At least I can understand this much, that my daughter is very anxious to do a thing utterly unheard of in its propriety, and I am thoroughly ashamed of you. If I were Ester I should not like to uphold you in such a singularly conspicuous parade. Remember, you have no one *now* but John to depend upon as an escort."

Ralph had remained a silent, immovable listener to this strange, sad conversation up to this moment. Now he came suddenly forward with a quick, firm tread and encircled Abbie's trembling form with his arm, while with eyes and voice he addressed his mother.

"In that last proposition you are quite mistaken, my dear mother. Abbie chances to have a brother who considers himself honored by being permitted to accompany her anywhere she may choose to go."

Mrs. Ried looked up at her tall, haughty son in unfeigned astonishment and for an instant was silent.

"Oh," she said at last, "if you have chosen to rank yourself on this ridiculous fanatical side, I have nothing more to say."

As for Mr. Ried, he had long before this shaded his eyes with his hand and was looking through half-closed fingers with mournful eyes at the sable robes and pallid face of his golden-haired darling, apparently utterly unconscious of or indifferent to the talk that was going on.

But will Ralph ever forget the little sweet smile which illumined for a moment the pure young face as she turned confiding eyes on him?

Thenceforth there dawned a new era in Abbie's life. Ralph, for reasons best known to himself, chose to be released from his vacation engagements in a neighboring city and remained closely at home. And Abbie went as usual to her mission class, to her Bible class, to the teacher's prayer meeting, to the regular church prayer meeting, everywhere she had been wont to go, and she was always and everywhere accompanied and sustained by her brother.

As for Ester, these were days of great opportunity and spiritual growth to her.

So we bridge the weeks between and reach the afternoon of a September day, bright and beautiful, as the month draws toward its closing; and Ester is sitting alone in her room in the low easy chair by the open window, and in her lap lies an open letter, while she, with thoughtful, earnest eyes seems to be reading, not it, but the future, or else her own heart. The letter is from Sadie, and she has written thus:

MY DEAR CITY SISTER—

Mother said tonight, as we were promenading the dining room for the sake of exercise, and also to clear off the table (Maggie had the toothache and was off duty): "Sadie, my dear child, haven't you written to Ester yet? Do you think it is quite right to neglect her so, when she must be very anxious to hear from home?" Now, you know, when Mother says, "Sadie, my dear child," and looks at me from out those reproachful eyes of hers, there is nothing short of mixing a mess of bread that I would not do for her. So here I am—place, third-story front; time, 11:30 P.M.; position, foot of the bed (Julia being soundly sleeping at the head), one gaiter off and one gaiter on, somewhat after the manner of my son John so renowned in history. Speaking of bread, how abominably that article can act. I had a solemn conflict with a batch of it this morning. Firstly, you must know, I forgot it. Mother assured me it was ready to be mixed before I awakened, so it must have been before that event took place that the forgetfulness occurred; however, be that as it may, after I was thoroughly awake, and up, and *down,* I still forgot it. The fried potatoes were frying themselves fast to that abominable black dish in which they are put to sizzle and which, by the way, is the most nefarious article in the entire kitchen list to get clean (save and excepting the dishcloth). Well, as I was saying, they burned themselves, and I ran to the rescue. Then Minie wanted me to go to the yard with her to see a dear cunning little brown and gray thing with some greenish spots that walked and spoke to her. The interesting stranger proved to be a fair-sized frog! While examining into and explaining minutely the nature and character and occupations of the entire frog family, the mixture in the tin pail, behind the kitchen stove, took that opportunity to *sour.* My! what a bubble it was in, and what an interesting odor it emitted, when at last I returned from frogdom to the ordinary walks of life and gave it my attention. Maggie was above her elbows in the wash-tub, so I seized the pail, and in dire haste and dismay ran up two flights of stairs in search of Mother. I suppose you know what followed. I assure you, I think mothers and soda are splendid! What a remarkable institution that ingredient is. While I made sour into sweet with the aid of its soothing proclivities, I moralized; the result of which was that after I had squeezed and mushed and rolled over, and thumped and patted my dough the requisite number of times, I tucked it away under blankets in a corner and went out to the piazza to ask Dr. Douglass if he knew of an article in the entire round of Materia Medica which could be given to human beings when they were sour and disagreeable, and which, after the manner of soda in dough, would immediately work a reform. On his acknowledging his utter ignorance of any such principle, I advanced the idea that cooking was a much more developed science than medicine; thence followed an animated discussion.

But in the meantime what do you suppose that bread was doing? Just spreading itself in the most remarkable manner over the nice blanket under which I had cuddled it! Then I had an amazing time. Mother said the patting process must all be done over again; and there was abundant opportunity for more moralizing. That bread developed the most remarkable stick-to-it-ive-ness that I ever beheld. I assure you, if total depravity is a mark of humanity, then I believe my dough is human.

Well, we are still alive, though poor Mr. Holland is, I fear, very little more than that. He was thrown from his carriage one evening last week and brought home insensible. He is now in a raging fever and very ill indeed. For once in their lives both doctors agree. He is delirious most of the time; and his delirium takes the very trying form which leads him to imagine that only Mother can do anything for him. The doctors think he fancies she is his own mother and that he is a boy again. All this makes matters rather hard on Mother. She is frequently with him half the night; and often Maggie and I are left to reign supreme in the kitchen for the entire day. Those are the days that try men's souls, especially women's.

I am sometimes tempted to think that all the book knowledge the world contains is not to be compared to knowing just what, and how, and when to do in the kitchen. I quite think so for a few hours when Mother, after a night of watching in a sickroom, comes down to undo some of my blundering. She is the patientest, dearest, lovingest, kindest mother that ever a mortal had, and just because she is so patient shall I rejoice over the day when she can give a little sigh of relief and leave the kitchen, calm in the assurance that it will be right side up when she returns. Ester, how *did* you make things go right? I'm sure I try harder than I ever knew you to, and yet salt will get into cakes and puddings, and sugar into potatoes. Just here I'm conscience smitten. I beg you will not construe one of the above sentences as having the remotest allusion to your being sadly missed at home. Mother said I was not even to *hint* such a thing, and I'm sure I haven't. I'm a *remarkable* housekeeper. The fall term at the academy opened week before last. I have hidden my schoolbooks behind that old barrel in the north-east corner of the attic. I thought they would be safer there than below-stairs. At least I was sure the bread would do better in the oven because of their ascent.

To return to the scene of our present trials: Mr. Holland is, I suppose, very dangerously sick; and poor Mrs. Holland is the very embodiment of despair. When I look at her in prospective misery, I am reminded of poor, dear cousin Abbie (to whom I would write if it didn't seem a sacrilege), and I conclude there is really more misery in this world of ours that I had any idea of. I've discovered why the world was made round. It must be to typify our lives—sort of a treadmill existence, you know; coming constantly around to the things which you thought you had done yesterday and put away; living over again today the sorrows which you thought were vanquished last week. I'm sleepy, and it is nearly time to bake cakes for breakfast. The top of the morning to you, as Patrick O'Brien greets Maggie.

Yours nonsensically,
SADIE

Over this letter Ester had laughed and cried, and finally settled, as we found her, into quiet thought. When Abbie came in after a little and nestled on an ottoman in front of her with an inquiring look, Ester placed the letter in her hands without note or comment, and Abbie read and laughed considerably, then grew more sober, and at last folded the letter with a very thoughtful face.

"Well," said Ester at last, smiling a little.

And Abbie answered: "Oh, Ester."

"Yes," said Ester, "you see, they need me."

Then followed a somewhat eager, somewhat sorrowful talk, and then a moment of silence fell between them, which Abbie broke by a sudden question:

"Ester, isn't this Dr. Douglass gaining some influence over Sadie? Have I imagined it, or does she speak of him frequently in her letters in a way that gives me an idea that his influence is not for good?"

"I'm afraid it is very true; his influence over her seems to be great, and it certainly is not for good. The man is an infidel, I think. At least he is very far indeed from being a Christian. Do you know I read a verse in my Bible this morning which, when I think of my past influence over Sadie, reminds me bitterly of myself. It was like this: 'While men slept his enemy came and sowed tares.' If I had not been asleep I might have won Sadie for the Savior before this enemy came."

"Well," Abbie answered gently, not in the least contradicting this sad statement, but yet speaking hopefully, "you will try to undo all this now."

"Oh, Abbie, I don't know. I am so weak—like a child just beginning to take little steps alone, instead of being the strong disciple that I might have been. I distrust myself. I am afraid."

"I'm not afraid for you," Abbie said, speaking very earnestly. "Because in the first place you are unlike the little child, in that you must never even try to take one step *alone*. And besides, there are more verses in the Bible than that one. See here, let me show you mine."

And Abbie produced her little pocket Bible and pointed with her finger while Ester read: "When I am weak, then am I strong." Then turning the leaves rapidly as one familiar with the strongholds of that tower of safety, she pointed again, and Ester read: "What time I am afraid, I will trust in thee."

20

AT HOME

IT was almost five o'clock of a sultry October day, one
of those days which come to us sometimes during that
golden month, like a regretful turning back of the
departing summer; a day which, coming to people
who have much hard, pressing work, and who are
wearied and almost stifled with the summer's heat,
makes them thoroughly uncomfortable, not to say
cross. Almost five o'clock, and in the great dining
room of the Rieds, Sadie was rushing nervously back
and forth, very much in the same manner that Ester
was doing on that first evening of our acquaintance,
only there was not so much method in her rushing.
The curtains were raised as high as the tapes would
take them, and the slant rays of the yellow sun were
streaming boldly in, doing their bravest to melt into
oil the balls of butter on the table, for poor, tired,
bewildered Sadie had forgotten to let down the
shades, and had forgotten the ice for the butter, and
had laid the tablecloth crookedly, and had no time to
straighten it. This had been one of her trying days. The
last fierce look of summer had parched anew the

fevered limbs of the sufferer upstairs and roused to sharper conflict the bewildered brain. Mrs. Ried's care had been earnest and unremitting, and Sadie, in her unaccustomed position of mistress belowstairs, had reached the very verge of bewildered weariness. She gave nervous glances at the inexorable clock as she flew back and forth. There were those among Mrs. Ried's boarders whose business made it almost a necessity that they should be promptly served at five o'clock. Maggie had been hurriedly summoned to do an imperative errand connected with the sickroom; and this inexperienced butterfly, with her wings sadly drooping, was trying to gather her scattered wits together sufficiently to get that dreadful tea table ready for the thirteen boarders who were already waiting for the summons.

"What *did* I come after?" she asked herself impatiently as she pressed her hand to her frowning forehead and stared about the pantry in a vain attempt to decide what had brought her there in such hot haste. "Oh, a spoon—no, a fork, I guess it was. Why, I don't remember the forks at all. As sure as I'm here, I believe they are, too, instead of being on the table; and—oh, my patience, I believe those biscuits are burning. I wonder if they are done. Oh, dear me!" And the young lady, who was Mr. Hammond's star scholar, bent with puzzled, burning face and received hot whiffs of breath from the indignant oven while she tried to discover whether the biscuits were ready to be devoured. It was an engrossing employment. She did not hear the sound of carriage wheels near the door, nor the banging of trunks on the side piazza. She was halfway across the dining room, with her tin of puffy biscuits in her hands, the puzzled, doubtful look still on her face, before she felt the touch of two soft, living arms around her neck, and turning quickly, she screamed, rather than said: "Oh, Ester!" And suddenly seating her tin of biscuits on one chair and herself on another, Sadie covered her face with both hands and actually cried.

"Why, Sadie, you poor dear child, what *can* be the matter?"

And Ester's voice was full of anxiety, for it was almost the first time that she had ever seen tears on that bright young face.

Sadie's first remark caused a sudden revulsion of feeling. Springing suddenly to her feet, she bent anxious eyes on the chair full of biscuits.

"Oh, Ester," she said, *"are* those biscuits done, or will they be sticky and hateful in the middle?"

How Ester laughed! Then she came to the rescue. *"Done*—of course they are, and beautifully, too. Did you make them? Here, I'll take them out. Sadie, where is Mother?"

"In Mr. Holland's room. She has been there nearly all day. Mr. Holland is no better, and Maggie has gone on an errand for them. Why have you come? Did the fairies send you?"

"And where are the children?"

"They have gone to walk. Minie wanted Mother every other minute, so Alfred and Julia have carried her off with them. Say, you, *dear* Ester, how *did* you happen to come? How shall I be glad enough to see you?"

Ester laughed. "Then I can't see any of them," she said by way of answer. "Never mind then, we'll have some tea. You poor child, how very tired you look. Just seat yourself in that chair, and see if I have forgotten how to work."

And Sadie, who was thoroughly tired and more

nervous than she had any idea she could be, leaned luxuriously back in her mother's chair with a delicious sense of unresponsibility about her and watched a magic spell come over the room. Down came the shades in a twinkling, and the low red sun looked in on them no more; the tablecloth straightened itself; pickles and cheese and cake got out of their confused proximity and marched each to their appropriate niche on the well-ordered table; a flying visit into well-remembered regions returned hard, sparkling, ice-crowned butter. And when at last the fragrant tea stood ready to be served, and Ester, bright and smiling, stationed herself behind her mother's chair, Sadie gave a little relieved sigh, and then she laughed.

"You're straight from fairyland, Ester; I know it now. That tablecloth has been crooked in spite of me for a week. Maggie lays it, and I *cannot* straighten it. I don't get to it. I travel five hundred miles every night to get this supper ready, and it's never ready. I have to bob up for a fork or a spoon, or I put on four plates of butter and none of bread. Oh, there is witch work about it, and none but thoroughbred witches can get everything, every little insignificant, indispensable thing on a table. I can't keep house."

"You poor kitten," said Ester, filled with very tender sympathy for this pretty young sister and feeling very glad indeed that she had come home. "Who would think of expecting a butterfly to spin? You shall bring those dear books down from the attic tomorrow. In the meantime, where is the tea bell?"

"Oh, we don't ring," said Sadie, rising as she spoke. "The noise disturbs Mr. Holland. Here comes my first lieutenant, who takes charge of that matter. My sister, Miss Ried, Dr. Douglass."

And Ester, as she returned the low, deferential bow

bestowed upon her, felt anew the thrill of anxiety which had come to her of late when she thought of this dangerous stranger in connection with her beautiful, giddy, unchristian sister.

On the whole, Ester's homecoming was pleasant. To be sure it was a wonderful change from her late life; and there was perhaps just the faintest bit of a sigh as she drew off her dainty cuffs and prepared to wipe the dishes which Sadie washed, while Maggie finished her interrupted ironing. What would John, the stylish waiter at Uncle Ralph's, think if he could see her now, and how funny Abbie would look engaged in such employment; but Sadie looked so bright and relieved and rested, and chatted so gayly that presently Ester gave another little sigh and said:

"Poor Abbie! how very, *very* lonely she must be tonight. I wish she were here for you to cheer her, Sadie."

Later, while she dipped into the flour preparatory to relieving Sadie of her fearful task of sponge setting, the kitchen clock struck seven. This time she laughed at the contrast. They were just going down to dinner now at Uncle Ralph's. Only the night before last she was there herself. She had been out that day with Aunt Helen, and so was attired in the lovely blue silk and the real laces, which were Aunt Helen's gift, fastened at the throat by a tiny pearl, Abbie's last offering. Now they were sitting down to dinner without her, and she was in the great pantry five hundred miles away, wide calico apron quite covering up her traveling dress, sleeves rolled above her elbows, and engaged in scooping flour out of the barrel into her great wooden bowl! But then how her mother's weary, careworn face had brightened and glowed into pleased surprise as she caught the first glimpse of her; how lovingly she had folded her in those dear *motherly* arms and said, actually with lips all a tremble: "My *dear* daughter! what an unexpected blessing and what a kind providence that you have come just now." Then Alfred and Julia had been as eager and jubilant in their greeting as though Ester had been always to them the very perfection of a sister; and hadn't little Minie crumpled her dainty collar into an unsightly rag and given her "Scotch kisses," and "Dutch kisses," and "Yankee kisses," and genuine, sweet baby kisses in her uncontrollable glee over dear "Auntie Essie."

And besides, oh besides! this Ester Ried who had come home was not the Ester Ried who had gone out from them only two months ago. A whole lifetime of experience and discipline seemed to her to have been crowded into those two months. Nothing of the past awakened more keen regret in this young girl's heart than the thought of her undutiful, unsisterly life. It was all to be different now. She thanked God that he had let her come back to that very kitchen and dining room to undo her former work. The old sluggish, selfish spirit had gone from her. Before this, everything had been done for Ester Ried; now it was to be done for Christ—*everything,* even the mixing up of that flour and water; for was not the word given: "*Whatsoever* ye do, do all to the glory of God?" How broad that word was, "whatsoever." Why, that covered every movement—yes, and every word. How *could* life have seemed to her dull and uninteresting and profitless?

Sadie hushed her busy tongue that evening as she saw in the moonlight Ester kneeling to pray; and a kind of awe stole over her for a moment as she saw that the kneeler seemed unconscious of any earthly presence. Somehow it struck Sadie as a different matter from any kneeling which she had ever watched in the moonlight before.

And Ester, as she rested her tired, happy head upon her own pillow, felt this word ringing sweetly in her heart: "And ye are Christ's, and Christ is God's."

21

———— ✦ ————

TESTED

ESTER was winding the last smooth coil of hair around her head when Sadie opened her eyes the next morning.

"My!" she said. "Do you know, Ester, it is perfectly delightful to me to lie here and look at you and remember that I shall not be responsible for those cakes this morning? They shall want a pint of soda added to them for all that I shall need to know or care."

Ester laughed. "You will surely have *your* pantry well stocked with soda," she said gayly. "It seems to have made a very strong impression on your mind."

But the greeting had chimed with her previous thoughts and sounded pleasant to her. She had come home to be the helper; her mother and Sadie should feel and realize after this how very much of a helper she could be. That very day should be the commencement of her old, new life. It was baking day—her detestation heretofore, her pleasure now. No more useful day could be chosen. How she would dispatch the pies and cakes and biscuits, to say nothing of the

———————————

wonderful loaves of bread. She smiled brightly on her young sister as she realized in a measure the weight of care which she was about to lift from her shoulders; and by the time she was ready for the duties of the day, she had lived over in imagination the entire routine of duties connected with that busy, useful, happy day. She went out from her little clothespress wrapped in armor—the pantry and kitchen were to be her battlefield, and a whole host of old temptations and trials were there to be met and vanquished. So Ester planned, and yet it so happened that she did not once enter the kitchen during all that long, busy day, and Sadie's young shoulders bore more of the hundred little burdens of life that Saturday than they had ever felt before. Descending the stairs, Ester met Dr. Van Anden for the first time since her return. He greeted her with a hurried "good morning," quite as if he had seen her only the day before, and at once pressed her into service:

"Miss Ester, will you go to Mr. Holland immediately? I cannot find your mother. Send Mrs. Holland from the room; she excites him. Tell her *I* say she must come immediately to the sitting room; I wish to see her. Give Mr. Holland a half teaspoonful of the mixture in the wineglass every ten minutes, and on no account leave him until I return, which will be as soon as possible."

And seeming to be certain that his directions would be followed, the doctor vanished.

For only about a quarter of a minute did Ester stand irresolute. Dr. Van Anden's tone and manner were full of his usual authority—a habit with him which had always annoyed her. She shrank with a feeling amounting almost to terror from a dark, quiet room and the position of nurse. Her base of operations, according to her own arrangements, had been the light, airy kitchen, where she felt herself needed at this very moment. But one can think of several things in a quarter of a minute. Ester had very lately taken up the habit of securing one Bible verse as part of her armor to go with her through the day. On this particular morning the verse was: "Whatsoever thy hand findeth to do, do it with thy might." Now if her hands had found work waiting for her down this first flight of stairs instead of down two as she had planned, what was that to her? Ester turned and went swiftly to the sickroom, dispatched the almost frantic wife according to the doctor's peremptory orders, gave the mixture as directed, waited patiently for the doctor's return, only to hear herself installed as head nurse for the day; given just time enough to take a very hurried second table meal with Sadie, listen to her half-pitiful, half-comic complainings, and learn that her mother was down with a sick headache.

So it was that this first day at home drew toward its closing; and not one single thing that Ester had planned to do, and do so well, had she been able to accomplish. It had been very hard to sit patiently there and watch the low breathings of that almost motion-less man on the bed before her, to rouse him at set intervals sufficiently to pour some mixture down his unwilling lips, to fan him occasionally, and that was all. It had been hard, but Ester had not chafed under it; she had recognized the necessity—no nurse to be found, her mother sick, and the young, frightened, as well as worn-out wife not to be trusted. Clearly she was at the post of duty. So as the red sun peeped in a good-night from a little corner of the closed curtain, it found Ester not angry, but *very* sad. *Such* a weary day! And this man on the bed was dying; both doctors had *looked* that at each other at least a dozen times that day. How her life of late was being mixed up with death. She had just passed through one sharp lesson, and here at the threshold awaited another. Different from that last though—oh, *very* different—and herein lay some of the sadness. Mr. Foster had said "everything was ready for the long journey, even should there be no return." Then she went back for a minute to the look of glory on that marble face and heard again that wonderful sentence: *"So* he giveth his beloved sleep." But this man here! everything had not been made ready by him. So at least she feared. Yet she was conscious, professed Christian though she had been, living in the same house with him for so many years, that she knew very little about him. She had seen much of him, had talked much with him, but she had never mentioned to him the name of Christ, the name after which she called herself. The sun sank lower, it was almost gone; this weary day was nearly done; and very sad and heavyhearted felt this young watcher— the day begun in brightness was closing in gloom. It was not all so clear a path as she had thought; there were some things that she could not undo. Those days of opportunity, in which she might at least have invited this man to Jesus, were gone; it seemed alto- gether probable that there would never come another. There was a little rustle of the drapery about the bed, and she turned suddenly to meet the great searching eyes of the sick man bent full upon her. Then he spoke in low, but wonderfully distinct and solemn tones. And the words he slowly uttered were yet more startling:

"Am I going to die?"

Oh, what *was* Ester to say? How those great bright eyes searched her soul! Looking into them, feeling the awful solemnity of the question, she could not answer no; and it seemed almost equally impossible to tell him yes. So the silence was unbroken, while she trembled in every nerve and felt her face blanch before the continued gaze of those mournful eyes. At length the silence seemed to answer him; for he turned his head suddenly from her, and half buried it in the pillow, and neither spoke nor moved.

That awful silence! That moment of opportunity, perhaps the last of earth for him, perhaps it was given to her to speak to him the last words that he would ever hear from mortal lips. What *could* she say? If she only knew how—only had words. Yet *something* must be said.

Then there came to Ester one of those marked Bible verses which had of late grown so precious, and her voice, low and clear, filled the blank in the room.

"God is our refuge and strength, a very present help in trouble."

No sound came from the quiet figure on the bed. She could not even tell if he had heard, yet perhaps he might, and so she gathered them, a little string of wondrous pearls, and let them fall with soft and gentle cadence from her lips.

"Commit thy way unto the Lord; trust also in him, and he shall bring it to pass."

"The Lord is nigh unto all them that call upon him—the Lord is gracious, and full of compassion."

"Thus saith the Lord, your Redeemer, the Holy One of Israel, I, even I, am he that blotteth out thy transgressions for mine own sake, and will not remember thy sins."

"Look unto me and be ye saved, all ye ends of the earth; for I am God, and there is none else."

"Incline your ear, and come unto me; hear and your soul shall live."

Silence for a moment, and then Ester repeated in tones that were full of sweetness that one little verse which had become the embodiment to her of all that was tender and soothing and wonderful: "What time I am afraid I will trust in thee." Was this man, moving toward the very verge of the river, afraid? Ester did not know, was not to know, whether those gracious invitations from the Redeemer of the world had fallen once more on unheeding ears, or not; for with a little sigh, born partly of relief, and partly of sorrow that the opportunity was gone, she turned to meet Dr. Van Anden and was sent for a few moments out into the light and glory of the departing day to catch a bit of its freshness.

It was as the last midnight stroke of that long, long day was being given that they were gathered about the dying bed. Sadie was there, solemn and awe-stricken. Mrs. Ried had arisen from her couch of suffering and nerved herself to be a support to the poor young wife. Dr. Douglass, at the side of the sick man, kept anxious watch over the fluttering pulse. Ester, on the other side, looked on in helpless pity, and other friends of the Hollands were grouped about the room. So they watched and waited for the swift down-coming of the angel of death. The death damp had gathered on his brow, the pulse seemed but a faint tremble now and then, and those whose eyes were used to death thought that his lips would never frame mortal sound again, when suddenly the eyelids raised, and Mr. Holland, fixing a steady gaze upon the eyes bent on him from the foot of the bed, whither Ester had slipped to make more room for her mother and Mrs. Holland, said in a clear, distinct tone, one unmistakable word— "Pray!"

Will Ester ever forget the start of terror which

thrilled her frame as she felt that look and heard that word? She cast a quick, frightened glance around her of inquiry and appeal; but her mother and herself were the only ones present whom she, had reason to think ever prayed. Could she, *would* she, that gentle, timid, shrinking mother? But Mrs. Ried was supporting the now almost fainting form of Mrs. Holland and giving anxious attention to her. "He says pray!" Sadie murmured in low, frightened tones. "Oh, where is Dr. Van Anden?"

Ester knew he had been called in great haste to the house across the way, and ere he could return, this waiting spirit might be gone—gone without a word of prayer. Would Ester want to die so, with no voice to cry for her to that listening Savior? But then, no human being had ever heard her pray. Could she?— must she? Oh, for Dr. Van Anden—a Christian doctor! Oh, if that infidel stood anywhere but there, with his steady hand clasping the fluttering pulse, with his cool, calm eyes bent curiously on her—but Mr. Holland was dying; perhaps the everlasting arms were not underneath him—and at this fearful thought, Ester dropped upon her knees, giving utterance to the deepest need in the first uttered words, "Oh, Holy Spirit, teach me just what to say!" Her mother, listening with startled senses as the familiar voice fell on her ear, could but think that *that* petition was answered; and Ester felt it in her very soul. Dr. Douglass, her mother, Sadie, all of them were as nothing—there was only this dying man and Christ, and she pleading that the passing soul might be met even now by the Angel of the covenant. There were those in the room who never forgot that prayer of Ester's. Dr. Van Anden, entering hastily, paused midway in the room, taking in the scene in an instant of time, and then was on his knees, uniting his silent petitions with hers. So fervent and persistent was the cry for help that even the sobs of the stricken wife were hushed in awe, and only the watching doctor, with his finger on the pulse, knew when the last fluttering beat died out, and the death angel pressed his triumphant seal on pallid lip and brow.

"Dr. Van Anden," Ester said as they stood together for a moment the next morning, waiting in the chamber of death for Mrs. Ried's directions, "was— did he—" with an inclination of her head toward the silent occupant of the couch—"did he ever think he was a Christian?"

The doctor bent on her a grave, sad look and slowly shook his head.

"Oh, Doctor! you cannot think that he—" and Ester stopped, her face blanching with the fearfulness of her thought.

"Shall not the Judge of all the earth do right?" This was the doctor's solemn answer. After a moment, he added: "Perhaps that one eagerly spoken word, 'pray,' said as much to the ears of him whose thoughts are not our thoughts, as did that old-time petition— 'Remember me when thou comest into thy kingdom.'"

Ester never forgot that, and the following day, while the corpse of one whom she had known so well lay in the house; and when she followed him to the quiet grave and watched the red and yellow autumn leaves flutter down around his coffin—dead leaves, dead flowers, dead hopes, death everywhere—not just a going up higher, as Mr. Foster's death had been—this was solemn and inexorable death. More than ever she felt how impossible it was to call back the days that had slipped away while she slept and do their ne-glected duties. She had come for this, full of hope; and now one of those whom she had met many times each day for years, and never said Jesus to, was at this moment being lowered into his narrow house, and, though God had graciously given her an inch of time and strength to use it, it was as nothing compared with those wasted years, and she could never know, at least never until the call came for her, whether or not at the eleventh hour this "poor man cried, and the Lord heard him" and received him into paradise.

Dr. Van Anden moved around to where she was standing with tightly clasped hands and colorless lips. He had been watching her, and this was what he said: "Ester, shall you and I ever stand again beside a new-made grave, receiving one whom we have known ever so slightly, and have to settle with our consciences and our Savior, because we have not invited that one to come to Jesus?"

And Ester answered, with firmly drawn lips, "As that Savior hears me and will help me, *never!*"

22

"Little Plum Pies"

ESTER was in the kitchen, trimming off the puffy crusts of endless pies—the old brown calico morning dress, the same huge bib apron which had been through endless similar scrapes with her—everything about her looking exactly as it had three months ago, and yet so far as Ester and her future—yes, and the future of everyone about her was concerned, things were very different. Perhaps Sadie had a glimmering of some strange changes as she eyed her sister curiously and took note that there was a different light in her eye and a sort of smoothness on the quiet face that she had never noticed before. In fact, Sadie missed some wrinkles which she had supposed were part and parcel of Ester's self.

"How I *did* hate that part of it," she remarked, watching the fingers that moved deftly around each completed sphere. "Mother said my edges always looked as if a mouse had marched around them nibbling all the way. My! how thoroughly I hate housekeeping. I pity the one who takes me for better or worse—always provided there exists such a poor victim on the face of the earth."

"I don't think you hate it half so much as you imagine," Ester answered kindly. "Anyway, you did nicely. Mother says you were a great comfort to her."

There was a sudden mist before Sadie's eyes.

"Did Mother say that?" she queried. "The blessed woman, what a very little it takes to make a comfort for her. Ester, I declare to you, if ever angels get into kitchens and pantries and the like, Mother is one of them. The way she bore with my endless blunderings was perfectly angelic. I'm glad, though, that her day of martyrdom is over, and mine, too, for that matter."

And Sadie, who had returned to the kingdom of spotless dresses and snowy cuffs, and above all, to the dear books and the academy, caught at that moment the sound of the academy bell, and flitted away. Ester filled the oven with pies, then went to the side doorway to get a peep at the glowing world. It was the very perfection of a day—autumn meant to die in wondrous beauty that year. Ester folded her bare arms and gazed. She felt little thrills of a new kind of restlessness all about her this morning. She wanted to do something grand, something splendidly good. It was all very well to make good pies; she had done that, given them the benefit of her highest skill in that line—now they were being perfected in the oven, and she waited for something. If ever a girl longed for an opportunity to show her colors, to honor her leader, it was our Ester. Oh yes, she meant to do the duty that lay next for her, but she perfectly ached to have that next duty be something grand, something that would show all about her what a new life she had taken on.

Dr. Van Anden was tramping about in his room, over the side piazza, a very unusual proceeding with him at that hour of the day; his windows were open, and he was singing, and the fresh lake wind brought tune and words right down to Ester's ear:

> "I would not have the restless will
> that hurries to and fro,
> Seeking for some great thing to do,
> Or wondrous thing to know;
> I would be guided as a child,
> And led where'er I go.
> I ask thee for the daily strength,
> To none that ask denied,
> A mind to blend with outward life,
> While keeping at thy side;
> Content to fill a little space
> If thou be glorified."

Of course, Dr. Van Alden did not know that Ester Ried stood in the doorway below and was at that precise moment in need of just such help as this; but then what mattered that, so long as the Master did?

Just then another sense belonging to Ester did its duty and gave notice that the pies in the oven were burning; and she ran to their rescue, humming meantime:

> "Content to fill a little space
> If thou be glorified."

Eleven o'clock found her busily paring potatoes—hurrying a little, for in spite of swift, busy fingers, their work was getting a little the best of Maggie and her, and one pair of very helpful hands was missing.

Alfred and Julia appeared from somewhere in the outer regions, and Ester was too busy to see that they both carried rather woebegone faces.

"Hasn't Mother got back yet?" queried Alfred.

"Why, no," said Ester. "She will not be back until tonight—perhaps not then. Didn't you know Mrs. Carleton was worse?"

Alfred kicked his heels against the kitchen door in a most disconsolate manner.

"Somebody's always sick," he grumbled out at last. "A fellow might as well not have a mother. I never saw the beat—nobody for miles around here can have a toothache without borrowing Mother. I'm just sick and tired of it."

Ester had nearly laughed, but catching a glimpse of the forlorn face, she thought better of it, and said:

"Something is awry now, I know. You never want Mother in such a hopeless way as that unless you're in trouble; so you see, you are just like the rest of them, everybody wants Mother when they are in any difficulty."

"But she is my mother, and I have a right to her, and the rest of 'em haven't."

"Well," said Ester soothingly, "suppose I be mother this time. Tell me what's the matter, and I'll act as much like her as possible."

"You!" And thereupon Alfred gave a most uncomplimentary sniff. "Queer work you'd make of it."

"Try me," was the good-natured reply.

"I ain't going to. I know well enough you'd say, 'Fiddlesticks' or, 'Nonsense,' or some such word, and finish up with, 'Just get out of my way.'"

Now, although Ester's cheeks were pretty red over this exact imitation of her former ungracious self, she still answered briskly:

"Very well, suppose I should make such a very rude and unmotherlike reply, fiddlesticks and nonsense would not shoot you, would they?"

At which sentence Alfred stopped kicking his heels against the door and laughed.

"Tell us about it," continued Ester, following up her advantage.

"Nothing to tell, much, only all the folks are going to sail on the lake this afternoon and going to have a picnic in the grove, the very last one before snow, and I meant to ask Mother to let us go, only how was I going to know that Mrs. Carleton would get sick and come away down here after her before daylight; and I know she would have let me go, too; and they're going to take things, a basketful each one of 'em—and they wanted me to bring little bits of pies, such as Mother bakes in little round tins, you know, plum pies, and she would have made me some, I know; she always does; but now she's gone, and it's all up, and I shall have to stay at home like I always do, just for sick folks. It's mean, anyhow."

Ester smothered a laugh over this curious jumble and asked a humble question:

"Is there really nothing that would do for your basket but little bits of plum pies?"

"No," Alfred explained earnestly, "because, you see, they've got plenty of cake and such stuff; the girls bring that, and they do like my pies awfully. I most always take 'em. Mr. Hammond likes them, too; he's going along to take care of us, and I shouldn't like to go without the little pies, because they depend upon them."

"Oh," said Ester, "girls go, too, do they?" And she looked for the first time at the long, sad face of Julia in the corner.

"Yes, and Jule is in just as much trouble as I am, 'cause they are all going to wear white dresses, and she's tore hers, and she says she can't wear it till it's ironed, 'cause it looks like a rope, and Maggie says she can't and won't iron it today, *so;* and Mother was going to mend it this very morning, and— Oh, fudge! it's no use talking, we've got to stay at home, Jule, so now." And the kicking heels commenced again.

Ester pared her last potato with a half-troubled, half-amused face. She was thoroughly tired of baking for that day and felt like saying fiddlesticks to the little plum pies; and that white dress was torn criss-cross and everyway, and ironing was always hateful; besides it *did* seem strange that when she wanted to do some great, nice thing, so many plum pies and torn dresses should step right into her path. Then unconsciously she repeated:

> *"Content to fill a little space*
> *If Thou be glorified."*

Could he be glorified, though, by such very little things? Yet hadn't she wanted to gain an influence over Alfred and Julia, and wasn't this her first opportunity; besides there was that verse: "Whatsoever thy hand findeth to do . . ." At that point her thoughts took shape in words.

"Well, sir, we'll see whether Mother is the only woman in this world after all. You tramp down to the cellar and bring me up that stone jar on the second shelf, and we'll have those pies in the oven in a twinkling; and that little woman in the corner, with two tears rolling down her cheeks, may bring her white dress and my workbox and thimble, and put two irons on the stove, and my word for it, you shall both be ready by three o'clock, spry and span, pies and all."

By three o'clock on the afternoon in question Ester was thoroughly tired, but little plum pies by the dozen were cuddling among snowy napkins in the willow basket, and Alfred's face was radiant as he expressed his satisfaction after this fashion:

"You're just jolly, Ester! I didn't know you could be so good. Won't the boys chuckle over these pies, though? Ester, there's just seven more than Mother ever made me."

"Very well," answered Ester gayly; "then there will be just seven more chuckles this time than usual."

Julia expressed her thoughts in a way more like her. She surveyed her skillfully mended and beautifully smooth white dress with smiling eyes; and as Ester tied the blue sash in a dainty knot and stepped back to see that all was as it should be, she was suddenly confronted with this question:

"Ester, what does make you so nice today? You didn't ever used to be so."

How the blood rushed into Ester's cheeks as she struggled with her desire to either laugh or cry, she hardly knew which. These were very little things which she had done, and it was shameful that, in all the years of her elder sisterhood, she had never sacrificed even so little of her own pleasure before; yet it was true, and it made her feel like crying—and yet there was rather a ludicrous side to the question, to think that all her beautiful plans for the day had culminated in plum pies and ironing. She stooped and kissed Julia on the rosy cheek and answered gently, moved by some inward impulse:

"I am trying to do all my work for Jesus nowadays."

"You didn't mend my dress and iron it, and curl my hair, and fix my sash for him, did you?"

"Yes, every little thing."

"Why, I don't see how. I thought you did them for me."

"I did, Julia, to please you and make you happy; but Jesus says that that is just the same as doing it for him."

Julia's next question was very searching:

"But, Ester, I thought you had been a member of the church a good many years. Sadie said so. Didn't you ever try to do things for Jesus before?"

A burning blush of genuine shame mantled Ester's face, but she answered quickly:

"No, I don't think I ever really did."

Julia eyed her for a moment with a look of grave wonderment, then suddenly stood on tiptoe to return the kiss as she said:

"Well, I think it is nice, anyway. If Jesus likes to have you be so kind and take so much trouble for me, why then he must love me, and I mean to thank him this very night when I say my prayers."

And as Ester rested for a moment in the armchair on the piazza and watched her little brother and sister move briskly off, she hummed again those two lines that had been making unconscious music in her heart all day:

> *"Content to fill a little space*
> *If Thou be glorified."*

23

CROSSES

THE large church was *very* full; there seemed not to be another space for a human being. People who were not much given to frequenting the house of God on a weekday evening had certainly been drawn thither at this time. Sadie Ried sat beside Ester in their mother's pew, and Harry Arnett, with a sober look on his boyish face, sat bolt upright in the end of the pew, while even Dr. Douglass leaned forward with graceful nonchalance from the seat behind them, and now and then addressed a word to Sadie.

These people had been listening to such a sermon as is very seldom heard—that blessed man of God whose name is clear to hundreds and thousands of people, whose hair is whitened with the frosts of many a year spent in the Master's service, whose voice and brain and heart are yet strong, and powerful, and "mighty through God," the Reverend Mr. Parker, had been speaking to them, and his theme had been the soul, and his text had been: "What shall it profit a man if he gain the whole world and lose his own soul?"

I hope I am writing for many who have had the

honor of hearing that appeal fresh from the great brain and greater heart of Mr. Parker. Such will understand the spell under which his congregation sat even after the prayer and hymn had died into silence. Now the gray-haired veteran stood bending over the pulpit, waiting for the Christian witnesses to the truth of his solemn messages; and for that he seemed likely to wait. A few earnest men, veterans too in the cause, gave in their testimony—and then occurred one of those miserable, disheartening, disgraceful pauses which are met with nowhere on earth among a company of intelligent men and women, with liberty given them to talk, save in a prayer meeting! Still silence, and still the aged servant stood with one arm resting on the Bible and looked down almost beseechingly upon that crowd of dumb Christians.

"Ye are my witnesses, saith the Lord," he repeated in earnest, pleading tones.

Miserable witnesses they! Was not the Lord ashamed of them all, I wonder? Something like this flitted through Ester's brain as she looked around upon that faithless company and noted here and there one who certainly ought to "take up his cross." Then some slight idea of the folly of that expression stuck her. What a fearful cross it was, to be sure! What a strange idea to use the same word in describing it that was used for that bloodstained, nail-pierced cross on Calvary. Then a thought, very startling in its significance, came to her. Was that cross borne only for men? Were they the only ones who had a thank-offering because of Calvary? Surely *her* Savior hung there, and bled, and groaned, and died for HER. Why should not she say, "By his stripes *I* am healed?" What if she should? What would people think? No, not that either. What would Jesus think? That, after all, was the important question. Did she really believe that if she should say in the hearing of that assembled company, "I love Jesus," that Jesus, looking down upon her and hearing how her timid voice broke the dishonoring silence, would be displeased, would set it down among the long list of "ought not to have dones"? She tried to imagine herself speaking to him in her closet after this manner: "Dear Savior, I confess with shame that I have brought reproach upon thy name this day, for I said, in the presence of a great company of witnesses, that I loved thee!" In defiance of her education and former belief upon this subject, Ester was obliged to confess, then and there, that all this was extremely ridiculous. "Oh, well," said Satan, "it's not exactly *wrong*, of course; but then it isn't very modest or ladylike; and, besides, it is unnecessary. There are plenty of men to do the talking." "But," said common sense, "I don't see why it's a bit more unladylike than the ladies' colloquy at the lyceum was last evening. There were more people present than are here tonight; and as for the men, they are perfectly mum. There seems to be plenty of opportunity for somebody." "Well," said Satan, "it isn't customary at least, and people will think strangely of you. Doubtless it would do more harm than good."

The most potent argument, "People will think strangely of you," smothered common sense at once, as it is apt to do, and Ester raised her head from the bowed position which it had occupied during this whirl of thought and considered the question settled. Someone began to sing, and of all the words that *could* have been chosen, came the most unfortunate ones for this decision:

> "On my head he poured his blessing,
> Long time ago;

Now he calls me to confess him
Before I go.
My past life, all vile and hateful,
He saved from sin;
I should be the most ungrateful
Not to own him.
Death and hell he bade defiance,
Bore cross and pain;
Shame my tongue this guilty silence,
And speak his name."

This at once renewed the struggle, but in a different form. She no longer said, "Ought I?" but "Can I?" Still the spell of silence seemed unbroken save by here and there a voice, and still Ester parleyed with her conscience, getting as far now as to say: "When Mr. Jones sits down, if there is another silence, I will try to say something"—not quite meaning, though, to do any such thing, and proving her word false by sitting very still after Mr. Jones sat down, though there was plenty of silence. Then when Mr. Smith said a few words, Ester whispered the same assurance to herself, with exactly the same result. The something *decided* for which she had been longing, the opportunity to show the world just where she stood, had come at last, and this was the way in which she was meeting it. At last she knew by the heavy thuds which her heart began to give that the question was decided, that the very moment Deacon Graves sat down, she would rise; whether she would say anything or not would depend upon whether God gave her anything to say—but at least she could stand up for Jesus. But Mr. Parker's voice followed Deacon Graves'; and this was what he said:

"Am I to understand by your silence that there is not a Christian man or woman in all this company who has an unconverted friend whom he or she would like to have us pray for?"

Then the watching Angel of the Covenant came to the help of this trembling, struggling Ester, and there entered into her heart such a sudden and overwhelming sense of longing for Sadie's conversion that all thought of what she would say, and how she would say it, and what people would think, passed utterly out of her mind; and rising suddenly, she spoke, in clear and wonderfully earnest tones:

"Will you pray for a dear, dear friend?"

God sometimes uses very humble means with which to break the spell of silence which Satan so often weaves around Christians; it was as if they had all suddenly awakened to a sense of their privileges.

Dr. Van Anden said, in a voice which quivered with feeling: "I have a brother in the profession for whom I ask your prayers that he may become acquainted with the great Physician."

Request followed request for husbands and wives, mothers and fathers, and children. Even timid, meek-faced, low-voiced Mrs. Ried murmured a request for her children who were out of Christ. And when at last Harry Arnett suddenly lifted his handsome boyish head from its bowed position and said in tones which conveyed the sense of a decision, "Pray for *me*," the last film of worldliness vanished; and there are those living today who have reason never to forget that meeting.

"Is it your private opinion that our good doctor got up a streak of disinterested enthusiasm over my unworthy self this evening?" This question Dr. Douglass asked of Sadie as they lingered on the piazza in the moonlight. Sadie laughed gleefully. "I am sure I don't know. I'm prepared for anything strange that can possibly happen. Mother and Ester between them have turned the world upside down for me tonight. In case you are the happy man, I hope you are grateful?"

"Extremely! Should be more so perhaps if people would be just to me in private and not so alarmingly generous in public."

"How bitter you are against Dr. Van Anden," Sadie said, watching the lowering brow and sarcastic curve of the lip with curious eyes. "How much I should like to know precisely what is the trouble between you!"

Dr. Douglass instantly recovered his suavity. "Do I appear bitter? I beg your pardon for exhibiting so ungentlemanly a phase of human nature; yet hypocrisy does move me to—" And then occurred one of those sudden periods with which Dr. Douglass always seemed to stop himself when anything not quite courteous was being said. "Just forget that last sentence," he added. "It was unwise and unkind; the trouble between us is not worthy of a thought of yours. I wish I could forget it. I believe I could if he would allow me."

At this particular moment the subject of the above conversation appeared in the door. Sadie gave a slight start; the thought that Dr. Van Anden had heard the talk was not pleasant. She need not have feared; he had just come from his room, and from his knees.

He spoke abruptly and with a touch of nervousness: "Dr. Douglass, may I have a few words with you in private?"

Dr. Douglass's "Certainly, if Miss Sadie will excuse us," was both prompt and apparently courteous, though the tone said almost as plainly as words could have done, "To what can I be indebted for this honor?"

Dr. Van Anden led the way into the brightly lighted vacant parlor; and there Dr. Douglass stationed himself directly under the gaslight, where he could command a full view of the pale, somewhat anxious face of his companion, and waited with that indescribable air made up of nonchalance and insolence. Dr. Van Anden dashed into his subject:

"Dr. Douglass, ten years ago you did what you could to injure me. I thought then purposely; I think now that perhaps you were sincere. Be that as it may, I used language to you then, which I, as a Christian man, ought never to have used. I have repented it long ago, but in my blindness I have never seen that I ought to apologize to you for it until this evening. God has shown me my duty. Dr. Douglass; I ask your pardon for the angry words I spoke to you that day."

The gentleman addressed kept his full bright eyes fixed on Dr. Van Anden and answered him in the quietest and at the same time iciest of tones:

"You are certainly very kind, now that your anger has had time to cool during these ten years, to accord me the merit of being *possibly* sincere. Now I was more *Christian* in my conclusions; I set you down as an honest blunderer. That I have had occasion since to change my opinion is nothing to the purpose; but it would be pleasanter for both of us if apologies could restore our friend, Mrs. Lyons, to life."

During this response Dr. Van Anden's face was a study. It had passed in quick succession through so many shades of feeling—anxiety, anger, disgust, and finally surprise—and apparently a dawning sense of a new development, for he made the seemingly irrelevant reply:

"Do you think *I* administered that chloroform?"

Dr. Douglass's coolness forsook him for a moment. "Who did?" he queried, with flashing eyes.

"Dr. Gilbert."

"Dr. Gilbert?"

"Yes, sir."

"How does it happen that I never knew it?"

"I am sure I do not know." Dr. Van Anden passed his hand across his eyes and spoke in sadness and weariness. "I had no conception that you were not aware of it until this moment. It explains in part what was strangely mysterious to me; but even in that case, it would have been, as you said, a blunder, not a criminal act. However, we cannot undo *that* past. I desire, above all other things, to set myself right in your eyes as a Christian man. I think I may have been a stumbling-block to you. God only knows how bitter is the thought. I have done wrong; I should have acknowledged it years ago. I can only do it now. Again I ask you, Dr. Douglass, will you pardon those bitterly spoken words of mine?"

Dr. Douglass bowed stiffly, with an increase of hauteur visible in every line of his face.

"Give yourself no uneasiness on that score, Dr. Van Anden, nor on any other, I beg you, so far as I am concerned. My opinion of Christianity is peculiar perhaps, but has not altered of late; nor is it likely to do so. Of course, every gentleman is bound to accept the apology of another, however tardily it may be offered. Shall I bid you good-evening, sir?"

And with a very low, very dignified bow, Dr. Douglass went back to the piazza and Sadie. And groaning in spirit over the tardiness of his effort, Dr. Van Anden returned to his room and prayed that he might renew his zeal and his longing for the conversion of that man's soul.

"Have you been receiving a little fraternal advice?" queried Sadie, her mischievous eyes dancing with fun over the supposed discomfiture of one of the two gentlemen, she cared very little which.

"Not at all. On the contrary, I have been giving a little of that mixture in a rather unpalatable form, I fear. I haven't a very high opinion of the world, Miss Sadie."

"Including yourself, do you mean?" was Sadie's demure reply.

Dr. Douglass looked the least bit annoyed; then he laughed and answered with quiet grace:

"Yes, including even such an important individual as myself. However, I have one merit which I consider very rare—sincerity."

Sadie's face assumed a half-puzzled, half-amused expression as she tried by the moonlight to give a searching look at the handsome form leaning against the pillar opposite her.

"I wonder if you *are* as sincere as you pretend to be," was her next complimentary sentence. "And also I wonder if the rest of the world is as unlimited a set of humbugs as you suppose. How do you fancy you happened to escape getting mixed up with the general humbugism of the world? This Mr. Parker, now, talks as though he felt it and meant it."

"He is a first-class fanatic of the most outrageous sort. There ought to be a law forbidding such ranters to hold forth, on pain of imprisonment for life."

"Dr. Douglass," said Sadie, speaking with grave dignity, "I would rather not hear you speak of that old gentleman in such a manner. He may be a fanatic and a ranter, but I believe he means it, and I can't help respecting him more than any cold-blooded moralist that I ever met. Besides, I cannot forget that my honored father was among the despised class of whom you speak so scornfully."

"My dear friend," and Dr. Douglass's tone was as gentle as her mother's could have been, "forgive me if I have pained you; it was not intentional. I do not know what I have been saying—some unkind things perhaps, and that is always ungentlemanly; but I have been greatly disturbed this evening, and that must be my apology. Pardon me for detaining you so long in the evening air. May I advise you, professionally, to go in immediately?"

"May I advise you unselfishly to get into a better humor with the world in general, and Dr. Van Anden in particular, before you undertake to talk with a lady again?" Sadie answered in her usual tones of raillery; all her dignity had departed. "Meantime, if you would like to have unmolested possession of this piazza to assist you in tramping off your evil spirit, you shall be indulged. I'm going to the west side. The evening air and I are excellent friends." And with a mocking laugh and bow Sadie departed.

"I wonder," she soliloquized, returning to gravity the moment she was alone, "I wonder what the man has been saying to him now? How unhappy those two gentlemen make themselves. It would be a consolation to know right from wrong. I just wish I believed in everybody as I used to. The idea of this gray-headed minister being a hypocrite! That's absurd. But then the idea of Dr. Van Anden being what he is! Well, it's a queer world. I believe I'll go to bed."

24

GOD'S WAY

BE it understood that Dr. Douglass was very much
astonished and not a little disgusted with himself. As
he marched defiantly up and down the long piazza he
tried to analyze his state of mind. He had always
supposed himself to be a man possessed of keen
powers of discernment, and yet withal exercising con-
siderable charity toward his erring fellowmen, willing
to overlook faults and mistakes, priding himself not a
little on the kind and gentlemanly way in which he
could meet ruffled human nature of any sort. In fact,
he dwelt on a sort of pedestal from the height of
which he looked calmly and excusingly down on
weaker mortals. This, until tonight: now he realized, in
a confused, blundering sort of way, that his pedestal
had crumbled, or that he had tumbled from its height,
or at least that something new and strange had happened. For instance, what had become of his powers
of discernment? Here was this miserable doctor, who
had been one of the thorns of his life, whom he had
looked down upon as a canting hypocrite. Was he,
after all, mistaken? The explanation of tonight looked

like it; he had been deceived in that matter which had years ago come between them; he could see it very plainly now. In spite of himself, the doctor's earnest, manly apology would come back and repeat itself to his brain and demand admiration.

Now Dr. Douglass was honestly amazed at himself, because he was not pleased with this state of things. Why was he not glad to discover that Dr. Van Anden was more of a man than he had ever supposed? This would certainly be in keeping with the character of the courteous, unprejudiced gentleman that he had hitherto considered himself to be; but there was no avoiding the fact that the very thought of Dr. Van Anden was exasperating, more so this evening than ever before. And the more his judgment became convinced that he had blundered, the more vexed did he become.

"Confound everybody!" he exclaimed at length, in utter disgust. "What on earth do I care for the contemptible puppy that I should waste thought on him? What possessed the fellow to come whining around me tonight and set me in a whirl of disagreeable thought? I ought to have knocked him down for his insufferable impudence in dragging me out publicly in that meeting." This he said aloud; but something made answer down in his heart: *Oh, it's very silly of you to talk in this way. You know perfectly well that Dr. Van Anden is not a contemptible puppy at all. He is a thoroughly educated, talented physician, a formidable rival, and you know it; and he didn't whine in the least this evening; he made a very manly apology for what was not so very bad after all, and you more than half suspect yourself of admiring him.*

"Fiddlesticks!" said Dr. Douglass aloud to all this

information and went off to his room in high dudgeon.

The next two days seemed to be very busy ones to one member of the Ried family. Dr. Douglass sometimes appeared at mealtime and sometimes not, but the parlor and the piazza were quite deserted, and even his own room saw little of him. Sadie, when she chanced by accident to meet him on the stairs, stopped to inquire if the village was given over to smallpox, or any other dire disease which required his constant attention; and he answered her in tones short and sharp enough to have been Dr. Van Anden himself:

"It is given over to madness," and moved rapidly on.

This encounter served to send him on a long tramp into the woods that very afternoon. In truth, Dr. Douglass was overwhelmed with astonishment at himself. Two such days and nights as the last had been he hoped never to see again. It was as if all his pet theories had deserted him at a moment's warning, and the very spirit of darkness had taken up his abode in their place. Go whither he would, do what he would, he was haunted by these new, strange thoughts. Sometimes he actually feared that he, at least, was losing his mind, whether the rest of the world was or not. Being an utter unbeliever in the power of prayer, knowing indeed nothing at all about it, he would have scoffed at the idea that Dr. Van Anden's impassioned, oftrepeated petitions had aught to do with him at this time. Had he known that at the very time in which he was marching through the dreary woods, kicking the red and yellow leaves from his path in sullen gloom, Ester, in her little clothespress, on her knees, was pleading with God for his soul, and that through him Sadie might be reached, I presume he would have laughed. The result of this long communion with himself was as follows: that he had overworked and underslept, that his nervous system was disordered, that in the meantime he had been fool enough to attend that abominable sensation meeting, and the man actually had wonderful power over the common mind and used his eloquence in a way that was quite calculated to confuse a not perfectly balanced brain. It was no wonder, then, in his state of bodily disorder, that the sympathetic mind should take the alarm. So much for the disease; now for the remedy. He would study less; at least he would stop reading half the night away; he would begin to practice some of his preaching and learn to be more systematic, more careful of this wonderful body, which could cause so much suffering; he would ride fast and long; above all, he would keep away from that church and that man, with his fanciful pictures and skillfully woven words.

Having determined his plan of action, he felt better. There was no sense, he told himself, in yielding to the sickly sentimentalism which had bewitched him for the past few days; he was ashamed of it and would have no more of it. He was master of his own mind, he guessed; always had been and always *would* be. And he started on his homeward walk with a good deal of alacrity and much of his usual composure settling on his face.

Oh, would the gracious Spirit which had been struggling with him leave him indeed to himself? "O God," pleaded Ester, "give me this one soul in answer to my prayer. For the sake of Sadie, bring this strong pillar obstructing her way to thyself. For the sake of Jesus, who died for them both, bring them both to yield to him."

Dr. Douglass paused at the place where two roads

forked and mused, and the subject of his musing was
no more important than this: Should he go home by
the river path or through the village? The river path
was the longer, and it was growing late, nearly teatime; but if he took the main road he would pass his
office, where he was supposed to be, as well as several
houses where he ought to have been, besides meeting probably several people whom he would rather
not see just at present. On the whole, he decided to
take the river road and walked briskly along, quite in
harmony with himself once more, enjoying the autumn beauty spread around him. A little white speck
attracted his attention; he almost stopped to examine
it, then smiled at his curiosity and moved on. "A bit
of waste paper probably," he said to himself. "Yet
what a curious shape it was, as if it had been carefully
folded and hidden under that stone. Suppose I see
what it is? Who knows but I shall find a fortune
hidden in it?" He turned back a step or two and
stooped for the little white speck. One corner of it
was nestled under a stone. It was a ragged, rumpled,
muddy fragment of a letter or an essay, which rain
and wind and water had done their best to annihi-
late, and finally, seeming to become weary of their
plaything, had tossed it contemptuously on the
shore, and a pitying stone had rolled down and
covered and preserved a tiny corner. Dr. Douglass
eyed it curiously, trying to decipher the mud-stained
lines, and being in a dreamy mood, wondered meanwhile what young, fair hand had penned the words
and what of joy or sadness filled them. Scarcely a
word was readable, at least nothing that would gratify his curiosity, until he turned the bit of leaf, and
the first line, which the stone had hidden, shone out
distinctly: "Sometimes I cannot help asking myself

why I was made—" Here the corner was torn off, and whether that was the end of the original sentence or not, it was the end to him. God sometimes uses very simple means with which to confound the wisdom of this world. Such a sudden and extraordinary revulsion of feeling as swept over Dr. Douglass he had never dreamed of before. He did not stop to question the strangeness of his state of mind, nor why that bit of soiled, torn paper should possess so fearful a power over him. He did not even realize at the moment that it was connected with this bewilderment; he only knew that the foundation upon which he had been building for years seemed suddenly to have been torn from under him by invisible hands, and left his feet sinking slowly down on nothing; and his inmost soul took suddenly up that solemn question with which he had never before troubled his logical brain: "I cannot help asking myself why I was made." There was only one other readable word on that paper, turn it whichever way he would, and that word was "God"; and he started and shivered when his eye met this, as if some awful voice had spoken it to his ear.

"What unaccountable witchcraft has taken possession of me?" he muttered at length. And turning suddenly, he sat himself down on an old decaying log by the riverside and gave himself up to real, honest, solemn thought.

"Where is Dr. Douglass?" queried Julia, appearing at the dining room door just at teatime. "There is a boy at the door says they want him at Judge Beldon's this very instant."

"He's *nowhere*," answered Sadie solemnly, pausing in the work of arranging cups and saucers. "It's my private opinion that he has been and gone and hung himself. He passed the window about one o'clock, looking precisely as I should suppose a man would who was about to commit that interesting act, since which time I've answered the bell seventeen times to give the same melancholy story of his whereabouts."

"My!" exclaimed the literal Julia, hurrying back to the boy at the door. She comprehended her sister sufficiently to have no faith in the hanging statement, but honestly believed in the seventeen sick people who were waiting for the doctor.

The church was very full again that evening. Sadie had at first declared herself utterly unequal to another meeting that week, but had finally allowed herself to be persuaded into going and had nearly been the cause of poor Julia's disgrace because of the astonished look which she assumed as Dr. Douglass came down the aisle, with his usual quiet composure of manner, and took the seat directly in front of them. The sermon was concluded. The text: "See, I have set before thee this day life and good, and death and evil," had been dwelt upon in such a manner that it seemed to some as if the aged servant of God had verily been shown a glimpse of the two unseen worlds waiting for every soul and was painting from actual memory the picture for them to look upon. That most solemn of all solemn hymns had just been sung:

> "There is a time, we know not when,
> A point, we know not where,
> that marks the destiny of men
> 'Twixt glory and despair.
> There is a line, by us unseen,
> that crosses every path,
> The hidden boundary between
> God's mercy and his wrath."

Silence had but fairly settled on the waiting congregation when a strong, firm voice broke in upon it, and the speaker said:

"I believe in my soul that I have met that point and crossed that line this day. I surely met God's mercy and his wrath, face-to-face, and struggled in their power. Your hymn says, To cross that boundary is to die; but I thank God that there are two sides to it. I feel that I have been standing on the very line that my feet had well-nigh slipped. Tonight I step over onto mercy's side. Reckon me henceforth among those who have chosen life."

"Amen," said the veteran minister with radiant face.

"Thank God," said the earnest pastor with quivering lip.

Two heads were suddenly bowed in the silent ecstasy of prayer—they were Ester's and Dr. Van Anden's. As for Sadie, she sat straight and still as if petrified with amazement, as she well-nigh felt herself to be, for the strong, firm voice belonged to Dr. Douglass!

An hour later Dr. Van Anden was pacing up and down the long parlor with quick, excited steps, waiting for he hardly knew what, when a shadow fell between him and the gaslight. He glanced up suddenly, and his eyes met Dr. Douglass, who had placed himself in precisely the same position in which he had stood when they had met there before. Dr. Van Anden started forward, and the two gentlemen clasped hands as they had never in their lives done before. Dr. Douglass broke the beautiful silence first with earnestly spoken words:

"Doctor, will you forgive all the past?"

And Dr. Van Anden answered: "Oh, my brother in Christ!"

As for Ester, she prayed in her clothespress, thankfully for Dr. Douglass, more hopefully for Sadie, and knew not that a corner of the poor little letter which had slipped from Julia's hand and floated down the stream one summer morning, thereby causing her such a miserable, *miserable* day, was lying at that moment in Dr. Douglass's notebook, counted as the most precious of all his precious bits of paper. Verily, "his ways are not as our ways."

25

SADIE SURROUNDED

"OH," said Sadie, with a merry toss of her brown curls, *"don't* waste any more precious breath over me, I beg. I'm an unfortunate case, not worth struggling for. Just let me have a few hours of peace once more. If you'll promise not to say 'meeting' again to me, I'll promise not to laugh at you once after this long drawn out spasm of goodness has quieted and you have each descended to your usual level once more."

"Sadie," said Ester in a low, shocked tone, *"do* you think we are all hypocrites and mean not a bit of this?"

"By *no* means, my dear sister of charity, at least not all of you. I'm a firm believer in diseases of all sorts. This is one of the violent kind of highly contagious diseases; they must run their course, you know. I have not lived in the house with two learned physicians all this time without learning that fact, but I consider this very nearly at its height and live in hourly expectation of the turn. But, my dear, I don't think you need worry about me in the least. I don't believe I'm a fit subject for such trouble. You know I never took whooping cough nor measles, though I have been exposed a great many times."

To this Ester only replied by a low, tremulous, "Don't, Sadie, please."

Sadie turned a pair of mirthful eyes upon her for a moment and, noting with wonder the pale, anxious face and quivering lip of her sister, seemed suddenly sobered.

"Ester," she said quietly, "I don't think you are playing good; I *don't* positively. I believe you are thoroughly in earnest, but I think you have been through some very severe scenes of late, sickness and watching and death, and your nerves are completely unstrung. I don't wonder at your state of feeling, but you will get over it in a little while and be yourself again."

"Oh," said Ester tremulously, "I pray God I may *never* be myself again; not the old self that you mean."

"You will," Sadie answered with roguish positiveness. "Things will go crosswise: the fire won't burn, and the kettle won't boil, and the milk pitcher will tip over, and all sorts of mischievous things will go on happening after a little bit, just as usual, and you will feel like having a general smashup of everything in spite of all these meetings."

Ester sighed heavily. The old difficulty again—things would not be undone. The weeds which she had been carelessly sowing during all these past years had taken deep root and would not give place. After a moment's silence she spoke again.

"Sadie, answer me just one question. What do you think of Dr. Douglass?"

Sadie's face darkened ominously. "Never mind what I think of *him*," she answered in short, sharp tones, and abruptly left the room.

What she *did* think of him was this: that he had become that which he had affected to consider the most despicable thing on earth—a hypocrite. Remember, she had no personal knowledge of the power of the Spirit of God over a human soul. She had no conception of how so mighty a change could be wrought in the space of a few hours, so her only solution of the mystery was that to serve some end which he had in view, Dr. Douglass had chosen to assume a new character.

Later, on that same day, Sadie encountered Dr. Douglass; rather, she went to the side piazza equipped for a walk, and he came eagerly from the west end to speak with her.

"Miss Sadie, I have been watching for you. I have a few words that are burning to be said."

"Proceed," said Sadie, standing with demurely folded hands and a mock gravity in her roguish eyes.

"I want to do justice at this late day to Dr. Van Anden. I misjudged him, wronged him, perhaps prejudiced you against him. I want to undo my work."

"Some things can be done more easily than they can be undone," was Sadie's grave and dignified reply. "You certainly have done your best to prejudice me against Dr. Van Anden not only, but against all other persons who hold his peculiar views, and you have succeeded splendidly. I congratulate you."

That look of absolute pain which she had seen once or twice on this man's face swept over it now as he answered her.

"I know—I have been blind and stupid, *wicked*, anything you will. Most bitterly do I regret it now; most eager am I to make reparation."

Sadie's only answer was: "What a capital actor you

would make, Dr. Douglass. Are you sure you have not mistaken your vocation?"

"I know what you think of me." This with an almost quivering lip and a voice strangely humble and as unlike as possible to any which she had ever heard from Dr. Douglass before. "You think I am playing a part. Though what my motive could be I cannot imagine, can you? But I do solemnly assure you that if ever I was sincere in anything in all my life, I am now concerning this matter."

"There is a most unfortunate if in the way, Doctor. You see, the trouble is, I have very serious doubts as to whether you ever were sincere in anything in your life. As to motives, a first-class anybody likes to try his power. You will observe that I have a very poor opinion of the world."

The doctor did not notice the quotation of his favorite expression, but answered with a touch of his accustomed dignity:

"I may have deserved this treatment at your hands, Miss Sadie. Doubtless I have, although I am not conscious of ever having said to you anything which I did not *think* I *meant*. I have been a *fool*. I am willing—yes, and anxious to own it. But there are surely some among your acquaintances whom you can trust if you cannot me. I—"

Sadie interrupted him. "For instance, that first-class fanatic of the most objectionable stamp, the man who Dr. Douglass thought, not three days ago, ought to be bound by law to keep the peace. I suppose you would have me unhesitatingly receive every word he says?"

Dr. Douglass's face brightened instantly, and he spoke eagerly:

"I remember those words, Miss Sadie, and just how honestly I spoke them, and just how bitterly I felt when I spoke them, and I have no more sure proof that this thing is of God than I have in noting the wonderful change which has come over my feelings in regard to that blessed man. I pray God that he may be permitted to speak to your soul with the tremendous power that he has to mine. Oh, Sadie, I have led you astray; may I not help you back?"

"I am not a weather vane, Dr. Douglass, to be whirled about by every wind of expediency; besides, I am familiar with one verse in the Bible, of which you seem never to have heard: 'Whatsoever a man soweth, that shall he also reap.' You have sowed well and faithfully; be content with your harvest."

I do not know what the pale, grave lips would have answered to this mocking spirit, for at that moment Dr. Van Anden and the black ponies whizzed around the corner and halted before the gate.

"Sadie," said the doctor, "are you in the mood for a ride? I have five miles to drive."

"Dr. Van Anden," answered Sadie promptly, "the last time you and I took a ride together we quarreled."

"Precisely," said the doctor, bowing low. "Let us take another now and make up."

"Very well," was the gleeful answer which he received, and in another minute they were off.

For the first mile or two he kept a tight rein and let the ponies skim over the ground in the liveliest fashion, during which time very little talking was done. After that he slackened his speed and, leaning back in the carriage, addressed himself to Sadie:

"Now we are ready to make up."

"How shall we commence?" asked Sadie gravely.

"Who quarreled?" answered the doctor sententiously.

"Well," said Sadie, "I understand what you are

waiting for. You think I was very rude and unladylike in my replies to you during that last interesting ride we took. You think I jumped at unwarrantable conclusions and used some unnecessarily sharp words. I think so myself, and if it will be of any service to you to know it, I don't mind telling you in the least."

"That is a very excellent beginning," answered the doctor heartily. "I think we shall have no difficulty in getting the matter all settled. Now, for my part, it won't sound as well as yours, because however blunderingly I may have said what I did, I said it honestly, in good faith, and with a good and pure motive. But I am glad to be able to say in equal honesty that I believe I was overcautious, that Dr. Douglass was never so little worthy of regard as I supposed him to be, and that nothing could have more rejoiced my heart than the noble stand which he has so recently taken. Indeed his conduct has been so noble that I feel honored by his acquaintance."

He was interrupted by a mischievous laugh.

"A mutual admiration society," said Sadie in her most mocking tone. "Did you and Dr. Douglass have a private rehearsal? You interrupted him in a similar rhapsody over your perfections."

Instead of seeming annoyed, Dr. Van Anden's face glowed with pleasure.

"Did he explain to you our misunderstanding!" he asked eagerly. "That was very noble in him."

"Of *course*. He is the soul of nobility—a villain yesterday and a saint today. I don't understand such marvelously rapid changes, Doctor."

"I know you don't," the doctor answered quietly. "Although you have exaggerated both terms, yet there is a great and marvelous change, which must be experienced to be understood. Will you never seek it for yourself, Sadie?"

"I presume I never shall, as I very much doubt the existence of any such phenomenon."

The doctor appeared neither shocked nor surprised, but favored her with a cool and quiet reply:

"Oh no, you don't doubt it in the least. Don't try to make yourself out that foolish and unreasonable creature—an unbeliever in what is as clear to a thinking mind as is the sun at noonday. You and I have no need to enter into an argument concerning this matter. You have seen some unwise and inconsistent acts in many who are called by the name of Christian. You imagine that they have staggered your belief in the verity of the thing itself. Yet it is not so. You had a dear father who lived and died in the faith, and you no more doubt the fact that he is in heaven today, brought there by the power of the Savior in whom he trusted, than you doubt your own existence at this moment."

Sadie sat silenced and grave; she was very rarely either. Perhaps Dr. Van Anden was the one person who could have thus subdued her, but in her inmost heart she felt his words to be true; that dear, *dear* father, whose weary suffering life had been one long evidence to the truth of the religion which he professed—yes, it was so; she no more doubted that he was at this moment in that blessed heaven toward which his hopes had so constantly tended than she doubted the shining of that day's sun—so he, being dead, yet spoke to her. Besides, her keen judgment had, of late, settled back upon the belief that Dr. Van Anden lived a life that would bear watching—a true, earnest, manly life; also that he was a man not likely to be deceived. So, sitting back there in the carriage, and appearing to look at nothing, and be interested in nothing, she allowed herself to take in again the firm conviction that whatever most lives were, there was always that father—safe, *safe* in the Christian's heaven—and there were besides some few, a very few, she thought; but there were *some* still living whom she knew, yes, actually *knew,* were fitting for that same faraway, safe place. No, Sadie had stood upon the brink, was standing there still, indeed; but reason and the long-buried father still kept her from toppling over into the chasm of settled unbelief. "Blessed are the dead which die in the Lord from henceforth: Yea, saith the Spirit, that they may rest from their labors; and their words do follow them."

But something must be said. Sadie was not going to sit there and allow Dr. Van Anden to imagine that she was utterly quieted and conquered; she would rather quarrel with him than have that. He had espoused Dr. Douglass's cause so emphatically, let him argue for him now; there was nothing like a good sharp argument to destroy the effect of unpleasant personal questions—so she blazed into sudden indignation:

"I think Dr. Douglass is a hypocrite!"

Nothing could have been more composed than the tone in which she was answered:

"Very well. What then?"

This question was difficult to answer, and Sadie remaining silent, her companion continued:

"Mr. Smith is a drunkard; therefore I will be a thief. Is that Miss Sadie Ried's logic?"

"I don't see the point."

"Don't you? Wasn't that exclamation concerning Dr. Douglass a bit of hiding behind the supposed sin of another—a sort of a reason why you were not a Christian, because somebody else pretended to be? Is that sound logic, Sadie? When your next neighbor in class peeps in her book, and thereby disgraces herself, and becomes a hypocrite, do you straightway declare that you will study no more? You see it is fashionable, in talking of this matter of religion, to drag out the shortcomings and inconsistencies of others and try to make of them a garment to cover our own sins; but it is very senseless, after all, and you will observe, is never done in the discussion of any other question."

Clearly, Sadie must talk in a commonsense way with this straightforward man, if she talked at all. Her resolution was suddenly taken, to say for once just what she meant; and a very grave and thoughtful pair of eyes were raised to meet the doctor's when next she spoke.

"I think of these things sometimes, Doctor, and though a great deal of it seems to be humbug, it is as you say—I know *some* are sincere, and I know there is a right way. I have been more than half tempted many times during the last few weeks to discover for myself the secret of power, but I am deterred by certain considerations which you would doubtless think very absurd, but which, joined with the inspiration which I receive from the ridiculous inconsistencies of others, have been sufficient to deter me hitherto."

"Would you mind telling me some of the considerations?"

And the moment Sadie began to talk honestly, the doctor's tones lost their half-indifferent coolness and expressed a kind and thoughtful interest.

"No," she said hesitatingly. "I don't know that I need, but you will not understand them; for instance, if I were a Christian I should have to give up one of my favorite amusements—almost a passion, you know, dancing is with me, and I am not ready to yield it."

"Why should you feel obliged to do so if you were a Christian?"

Sadie gave him the benefit of a very searching look. "Don't *you* think I would be?" she queried after a moment's silence.

"I haven't said what I thought on that subject, but I feel sure that it is not the question for you to decide at present; first settle the all-important one of your personal acceptance of Christ, and then it will be time to decide the other matter, for or against, as your conscience may dictate."

"Oh, but," said Sadie positively, "I know very well what my conscience would dictate, and I am not ready for it."

"Isn't dancing an innocent amusement?"

"For *me,* yes, but not for a Christian."

"Does the Bible lay down one code of laws for you and another for Christians?"

"I think so—it says, 'Be not conformed to this world.'"

"Granted, but does it anywhere say to those who are of the world, '*You* have a right to do just what you like; that direction does not apply to you at all, it is all intended for those poor Christians'?"

"Dr. Van Anden," said Sadie with dignity, "don't you think there should be a difference between Christians and those who are not?"

"Undoubtedly I do. Do *you* think that every person ought or ought *not* to be a Christian?"

Sadie was silent and a little indignant. After a moment she spoke again, this time with a touch of hauteur:

"I think you understand what I mean, Doctor, though you would not admit it for the world. I don't suppose I feel very deeply on the subject, else I would not advance so trivial an excuse; but this is honestly my state of mind. Whenever I think about the matter at all, this thing comes up for consideration. I think it would be very foolish for me to argue against dancing, for I don't know much about the arguments, and care less. I know only this much: that there is a very distinctly defined inconsistency between a profession of religion and dancing, visible very generally to the eyes of those who make no profession; the other class doesn't seem so able to see it; but there exists very generally among us worldlings a disposition to laugh a little over dancing Christians. Whether this is a well-founded inconsistency, or only a foolish prejudice on our part, I have never taken the trouble to try to determine, and it would make little material difference which it was—it is enough for me that such is the case; and it makes it very plain to me that if I were an honest professor of that religion which leads one of its teachers to say he will eat no meat while the world stands if it makes his brother to offend, I should be obliged to give up my dancing. But since I am not one of that class, and thus have no such influence, I can see no possible harm in my favorite amusement and am not ready to give it up; and that is what I mean by its being innocent for me and not innocent for professing Christians."

Dr. Van Anden made no sort of reply, if Sadie could judge from his face; he seemed to have grown weary of the whole subject; he leaned back in his carriage and let the reins fall loosely and carelessly. His next proceeding was most astounding; coolly possessing himself of one of the small gloved hands that lay idly in Sadie's lap, he said in a quiet, matter-of-fact tone: "Sadie, would you allow me to put my arm around you?"

In an instant the indignant blood surged in waves over Sadie's face; the hand was angrily withdrawn, and the graceful form drawn to an erect height, and it is impossible to describe the freezing tone of astonished indignation in which she ejaculated, "Dr. Van Anden!"

"Just what I expected," returned that gentleman in a composed manner, bestowing a look of entire satisfaction upon his irate companion. "And yet, Sadie, I hope you will pardon my obtuseness, but I positively cannot see why, if it is proper and courteous, and all that sort of thing, I, who am a friend of ten years' standing, should not enjoy the same privilege which you accord to Fred Kenmore, to whom you were introduced last week and with whom I heard you say you danced five times."

Sadie looked confused and annoyed, but finally she laughed; for she had the good sense to see the folly of doing anything else under existing circumstances.

"That is the point which puzzles me at present," continued the doctor in a kind, grave tone. "I do not understand how young ladies of refinement can permit, under certain circumstances and often from comparative strangers, attentions which, under other circumstances, they repel with becoming indignation. Won't you consider the apparent inconsistency a little? It is the only suggestion which I wish to offer on the question at present. When you have settled that other important matter, this thing will present itself to your clear-seeing eyes in other and more startling aspects. Meantime, this is the house at which I must call. Will you hold my horses, Miss Sadie, while I dispatch matters within?"

26

❖

CONFUSION—CROSS-BEARING—
CONSEQUENCE

BUT the autumn days were not *all* bright, and glowing, and glorious. One morning it rained—not a soft,
silent, and warm rain, but a gusty, windy, turbulent
one; a rain that drove into windows ever so slightly
raised and hurled itself angrily into your face whenever you ventured to open a door. It was a day in
which fires didn't like to burn, but smoldered, and
sizzled, and smoked; and people went around shivering, their shoulders shrugged up under little dingy,
unbecoming shawls, and the clouds were low, and gray,
and heavy—and everything and everybody seemed
generally out of sorts.

Ester was no exception; the toothache had kept her
awake during the night, and one cheek was puffy and
stiff in the morning, and one tooth still snarled threat-
eningly whenever the slightest whisper of a draft came
to it. The high-toned, exalted views of life and duty
which had held possession of her during the past few

weeks seemed suddenly to have deserted her. In short, her body had gained that mortifying ascendency over the soul which it will sometimes accomplish, and all her hopes and aims and enthusiasms seemed blotted out. Things in the kitchen were uncomfortable. Maggie had seized on this occasion for having the mumps, and acting upon the advice of her sympathizing mistress, had pinned a hot flannel around her face and gone to bed. The same unselfish counsel had been given to Ester, but she had just grace enough left to refuse to desert the camp when dinner must be in readiness for twenty-four people in spite of nerves and teeth. Just here, however, the supply failed her, and she worked in ominous gloom.

Julia had been pressed into service and was stoning raisins, or eating them; a close observer would have found it difficult to discover which. She was certainly rasping the nerves of her sister in a variety of those endless ways by which a thoughtless, restless, questioning child can almost distract a troubled brain. Ester endured with what patience she could the ceaseless drafts upon her and worked at the interminable cookies with commendable zeal. Alfred came with a bang and a whistle, and held open the side door while he talked. In rushed the spiteful wind, and all the teeth in sympathy with the aching one set up an immediate growl.

"Mother, I don't see any. Why, where is Mother?" questioned Alfred; and was answered with an emphatic:

"Shut that door!"

"Well, but," said Alfred, "I want Mother. I say, Ester, will you give me a cookie?"

"No!" answered Ester with energy. "Did you hear me tell you to shut that door this instant?"

"Well now, don't bite a fellow." And Alfred looked curiously at his sister. Meantime the door closed with a heavy bang. "Mother, say, Mother," he continued as his mother emerged from the pantry, "I don't see anything of that hammer. I've looked everywhere. Mother, can't I have one of Ester's cookies? I'm awful hungry."

"Why, I guess so, if you are really suffering. Try again for the hammer, my boy; don't let a poor little hammer get the better of you."

"Well," said Alfred, "I won't," meaning that it should answer the latter part of the sentence; and seizing a cookie, he bestowed a triumphant look upon Ester and a loving one upon his mother, and vanished amid a renewal of the whistle and bang.

This little scene did not serve to help Ester; she rolled away vigorously at the dough, but felt some way disturbed and outraged, and finally gave vent to her feelings in a peremptory order.

"Julia, don't eat another raisin; you've made away with about half of them now."

Julia looked aggrieved. "Mother lets me eat raisins when I pick them over for her," was her defense; to which she received no other reply than:

"Keep your elbows off the table."

Then there was silence and industry for some minutes. Presently Julia recovered her composure and commenced with:

"Say, Ester, what makes you prick little holes all over your biscuits?"

"To make them rise better."

"Does everything rise better after it is pricked?"

Sadie was paring apples at the end table and interposed at this point:

"If you find that to be the case, Julia, you must be

very careful after this, or we shall have Ester pricking you when you don't rise in time for breakfast in the morning."

Julia suspected that she was being made a dupe of and appealed to her older sister:

"*Honestly,* Ester, *do* you prick them so they will rise better?*"

"Of course. I told you so, didn't I?"

"Well, but why does that help them any? Can't they get up unless you make holes in them, and what is all the reason for it?"

Now, these were not easy questions to answer, especially for a girl with the toothache, and Ester's answer was not much to the point.

"Julia, I declare, you are enough to distract one. If you ask any more questions I shall certainly send you upstairs out of the way."

Her scientific investigations thus nipped in the bud, Julia returned again to silence and raisins, until the vigorous beating of some eggs roused anew the spirit of inquiry. She leaned eagerly forward with a:

"Say, Ester, please tell me why the whites all foam and get thick when you stir them, just like beautiful white soapsuds." And she rested her elbow, covered with its blue sleeve, plump into the platter containing the beaten yolks. You must remember Ester's face-ache, but even then I regret to say that this disaster culminated in a decided box on the ear for poor Julia and in her being sent weeping upstairs. Sadie looked up with a wicked laugh in her bright eyes and said demurely:

"You didn't keep your promise, Ester, and let me live in peace, so I needn't keep mine, and I consider you pretty well out of the spasm which has lasted for so many days."

"Sadie, I am really ashamed of you." This was Mrs. Ried's grave, reproving voice; and she added kindly: "Ester, poor child, I wish you would wrap your face up in something warm and lie down awhile. I am afraid you are suffering a great deal."

Poor Ester! It had been a hard day. Late in the afternoon, as she stood at the table and cut the bread, and cake, and cheese, and cold meat for tea; when the sun had made a rift in the clouds and was peeping in for good night; when the throbbing nerves had grown quiet once more, she looked back upon this weary day in shame and pain. How very little her noble resolves, and efforts, and advances had been worth after all. How far back she seemed to have gone in that one day—not strength enough to bear even the little crosses that befell an ordinary quiet life! How she had lost the so-lately-gained influence over Alfred and Julia by a few cross words! How much reason she had given Sadie to think that her attempts at following the Master were, after all, only spasmodic and visionary! But Ester had been to that little clothespress upstairs in search of help and forgiveness, and now she clearly saw there was something to do besides mourn over her failures. It was hard to do it, too. Ester's spirit was proud, and it was very humbling to confess herself in the wrong. She hesitated and shrank from the work until she finally grew ashamed of herself for that; and at last, without turning her head from her work or giving her resolve time to falter, she called to the twins, who were occupying seats in one of the dining room windows and talking low and soberly to each other:

"Children, come here a moment, will you?"

The two had been very shy of Ester since the morning's trials and were at that moment sympathizing with each other in a manner uncomplimentary to her. However, they slid down from their perch and slowly answered her call.

Ester glanced up as they entered the storeroom and then went on cutting her cheese, but speaking in low, gentle tones:

"I want to tell you two how sorry I am that I spoke so crossly and unkindly to you this morning. It was very wrong in me. I thought I never should displease Jesus so again, but I did, you see; and now I am very sorry indeed, and I want you to forgive me."

Alfred looked aghast. This was an Ester that he had never seen before, and he didn't know what to say. He wriggled the toes of his boots together and looked down at them in puzzled wonder. At last he faltered out:

"I didn't know your cheek ached till Mother told me, or else I'd have shut the door right straight. I'd ought to, *anyhow,* cheek or no cheek."

This last in a lower tone and more looking down at his boots. It was new work for Alfred, this voluntarily owning himself in the wrong.

Julia burst forth eagerly. "And I was very careless and naughty to keep putting my elbows on the table after you had told me not to, and I am ever so sorry that I made you such a lot of trouble."

"Well, then," said Ester, "we'll all forgive each other, shall we, and begin over again? And, children, I want you to understand that I *am* trying to please Jesus; and when I fail it is because of my own wicked heart, not because there is any need of it if I tried harder; and I want you to know how anxious I am that you should love this same Jesus now while you are young and get him to help you."

Their mother called the children at this moment,

and Ester dismissed them each with a kiss. There was a little rustle in the flour room, and Sadie, whom nobody knew was downstairs, emerged therefrom with suspiciously red eyes but a laughing face and approached her sister.

"Ester," said she, "I'm positively afraid that you are growing into a saint, and I know that I'm a sinner. I consider myself mistaken about the spasm—it is evidently a settled disease."

While the bell tolled for evening service, Ester stood in the front doorway and looked doubtfully up and down the damp pavements and muddy streets, and felt her stiff cheek. How much she seemed to need the rest and help of God's house tonight; and yet:

Julia's little hand stole softly into hers. "We've been talking about what you said you wanted us to do, Alfred and I have. We've talked about it a good deal lately. *We* most wish so, too."

Ere Ester could reply other than by an eager grasp of the small hand, Dr. Douglass came out. His horses and carriage were in waiting.

"Miss Ried," he said, pausing irresolutely with his foot on the carriage step and finally turning back, "I am going to drive down to church this evening, as I have a call to make afterward. Will you not ride down with me? It is unpleasant walking."

Ester's grave face brightened. "I'm so glad," she answered eagerly. "I *did* want to go to church tonight, and I was afraid it would be imprudent on account of my tooth."

Alfred and Julia sat right before them in church; and Ester watched them with a prayerful, and yet a sad heart. What right had she to expect an answer to her petitions when her life had been working against them all that day? And yet the blood of Christ was all-powerful, and there was always *his* righteousness to plead; and she bent her head in renewed supplications for these two. "And it shall come to pass, that before they call, I will answer; and while they are yet speaking, I will hear."

Into one of the breathless stillnesses that came, while beating hearts were waiting for the requests that they hoped would be made, broke Julia's low, trembling, yet singularly clear voice:

"Please pray for me."

There was a little choking in Alfred's throat and a good deal of shuffling done with his boots. It was so much more of a struggle for the sturdy boy than the gentle little girl; but he stood manfully on his feet at last, and his words, though few, were fraught with as much meaning as any which had been spoken there that evening, for they were distinct and decided:

"Me, too."

27

❧

THE TIME TO SLEEP

LIFE went swiftly and busily on. With the close of December the blessed daily meetings closed; rather they closed with the first week of the new year, which the church kept as a sort of jubilee week in honor of the glorious things that had been done for them.

The new year opened in joy for Ester; many things were different. The honest, straightforward little Julia carried all her earnestness of purpose into this new life which had possessed her soul; and the sturdy brother had naturally too decided a nature to do anything halfway, so Ester was sure of this young sister and brother. Besides, there was a new order of things between her mother and herself; each had discovered that the other was bound on the same journey, and that there were delightful resting places by the way.

For herself, she was slowly but surely gaining. Little crosses that she stooped and resolutely took up grew to be less and less until they, some of them, merged into positive pleasures. There were many things that cast rays of joy all about her path; but there was still one heavy abiding sorrow. Sadie went giddily and gleefully on her downward way. If she perchance seemed to have a serious thought at night, it vanished with the next morning's sunshine, and day by day Ester realized more fully how many tares the enemy had sown while she was sleeping. Sometimes the burden grew almost too heavy to be borne, and again she would take heart of grace and bravely renew her efforts and her prayers. It was about this time that she began to recognize a new feeling. She was not sick exactly, and yet not quite well. She discovered, considerably to her surprise, that she was falling into the habit of sitting down on a stair to rest ere she had reached the top of the first flight; also, that she was sometimes obliged to stay her sweeping and clasp her hands suddenly over a strange beating in her heart. But she laughed at her mother's anxious face and pronounced herself quite well, quite well, only perhaps a little tired.

Meantime all sorts of plans for usefulness ran riot in her brain. She could not go away on a mission because her mission had come to her. For a wonder she realized that her mother needed her. She took up bravely and eagerly, so far as she could see it, the work that lay around her; but her restless heart craved more, more. She *must* do something outside this narrow circle for the Master. One evening her enthusiasm, which had been fed for several days on a new scheme that was afloat in the town, reached its height. Ester remembered afterward every little incident connected with that evening—just how cozy the little family sitting room looked with her for its only occupant; just how brightly the coals glowed in the open grate; just what a brilliant color they flashed over the crimson cushioned rocker which she had vacated when she heard Dr. Van Anden's steps in the hall and went to speak to him. She was engaged in writing a letter to Abbie, full of eager schemes and busy, bright work. "I am astonished that I ever thought there was nothing worth living for," she wrote. "Why, life isn't half long enough for the things that I want to do. This new idea just fills me with delight. I am so eager to get to work—" Thus far when she heard that step and, springing up, went with eagerness to the door

"Doctor, are you in haste? Haven't you just five minutes for me?"

"Ten," answered the doctor promptly, stepping into the bright little room.

In her haste, not even waiting to offer him a seat, Ester plunged at once into her subject.

"Aren't you the chairman of that committee to secure teachers for the evening school?"

"I am."

"Have you all the help you want?"

"Not by any means. Volunteers for such a self-denying employment as teaching factory girls are not easy to find."

"Well, Doctor, do you think—would you be willing to propose my name as one of the teachers? I should so like to be counted among them."

Instead of the prompt thanks which she expected, to her dismay Dr. Van Anden's face looked grave and troubled. Finally he slowly shook his head with a troubled:

"I don't think I can, Ester."

Such an amazed, grieved, hurt look as swept over Ester's face.

"It is no matter," she said at last, speaking with an effort. "Of course I know little of teaching and perhaps could do no good; but I thought if help was scarce you might—well, never mind."

And here the doctor interposed. "It is not that, Ester—" with the troubled look deepening on his face—"I assure you we would be glad of your help, but," and he broke off abruptly and commenced a sudden pacing up and down the room. Then stopped before her with these mysterious words: "I don't know how to tell you, Ester."

Ester's look now was one of annoyance, and she spoke quickly.

"Why, Doctor, you need tell me nothing. I am not a child to have the truth sugarcoated. If my help is not needed, that is sufficient."

"Your help is exactly what we need, Ester, but your health is not sufficient for the work."

And now Ester laughed. "Why, Doctor, what an absurd idea. In a week I shall be as well as ever. If that is all, you may surely count me as one of your teachers."

The doctor smiled faintly and then asked: "Do you never feel any desire to know what may be the cause of this strange lassitude which is creeping over you, and the sudden flutterings of heart, accompanied by pain and faintness, which take you unawares?"

Ester's face paled a little, but she asked, quietly enough: "How do you know all this?"

"I am a physician, Ester. Do you think it is kindness to keep a friend in ignorance of what very nearly concerns him, simply to spare his feelings for a little?"

"Why, Dr. Van Anden, you do not think—you do not mean that—tell me *exactly what* you mean."

But the doctor's answer was grave, anxious, absolute *silence.*

Perhaps the silence answered her—perhaps her own heart told the secret to her, for a sudden gray pallor overspread her face. For an instant the room darkened and whirled around her, then she staggered as if she would have fallen, then she reached forward and caught hold of the little red rocker and sank into it, and leaning both elbows on the writing table before her, buried her face in her hands. Afterward Ester called to mind the strange whirl of thoughts which thrilled her brain at that time. Life in all the various phases that she had thought it would bear for her, all the endless plans that she had made, all the things that she had meant to *do* and *be,* came and stared her in the face. Nowhere in all her plannings crossed by that strange creature Death; someway she had never planned for that. Could it be possible that he was to come for her so soon, before any of these things were done? Was it possible that she must leave Sadie, bright, brilliant, unsafe Sadie, and go away where she could work for her no more? Then, like a picture spread before her, there came back that day in the cars, on her way to New York, the Christian stranger, who was not a stranger now, but her friend, and was in heaven—the earnest little old woman with her thoughtful face and that strange sentence on her lips: "Maybe my coffin will do it better than I can." Well, maybe *her* coffin could do it for Sadie. Oh, the blessed thought! Plans? Yes, but perhaps God had plans too. What mattered hers compared to *his?* If he would that she should do her earthly work by lying down very soon in the unbroken calm of the "rest that remaineth," what was that to her? Presently she spoke without raising her head.

"Are you very certain of this thing, Doctor, and is it to come to me soon?"

"That last we cannot tell, dear friend. You *may* be with us years yet, and it *may* be swift and sudden. I think it is worse than mistaken kindness, it is foolish wickedness, to treat a Christian woman like a little child. I wanted to tell you before the shock would be dangerous to you."

"I understand." When she spoke again it was in a more hesitating tone. "Does Dr. Douglass agree with you?" And the quick, pained way in which the doctor answered showed her that he understood.

"Dr. Douglass will not *let* himself believe it."

Then a long silence fell between them. The doctor kept his position, leaning against the mantel, but never for a moment allowed his eyes to turn away from that motionless figure before him. Only the loving, pitying Savior knew what was passing in that young heart.

At last she arose and came toward the doctor with a strange sweetness playing about her mouth and a strange calm in her voice.

"Dr. Van Anden, I am *so* much obliged to you. Don't be afraid to leave me now. I think I need to be quite alone."

And the doctor, feeling that all words were vain and useless, silently bowed and softly let himself out of the room.

The first thing upon which Ester's eye alighted when she turned again to the table was the letter in which she had been writing those last words: "Why life isn't half long enough for the things that I want to do." Very quietly she picked up the letter and committed it to the glowing coals upon the grate. Her mood had changed.

By degrees, very quietly and very gradually, as such bitter things *do* creep in upon a family, it grew to be an acknowledged fact that Ester was an invalid. Little by little her circle of duties narrowed; one by one her various plans were silently given up. The dear mother first, and then Sadie, and finally the children, grew into the habit of watching her footsteps and saving her from the stairs, from the lifting, from every possible burden. Once in a long while, and then, as the weeks passed, more frequently, there would come a day in which she did not get down further than the little sitting room, but was established amid pillows on the couch, "enjoying poor health" as she playfully phrased it.

So softly and silently and surely the shadow crept and crept until June brought roses and Abbie. Ester received her in her own room, propped up among the pillows in her bed. Gradually they grew accustomed to that also as God in his infinite mercy has planned that human hearts shall grow used to the inevitable. They even told each other hopefully that the warm weather was what depressed her so much, and as the summer heat cooled into autumn she would grow stronger. And she had bright days in which she really seemed to grow strong and which deceived everybody save Dr. Van Anden and herself.

During one of those bright days, Sadie came from school full of a new idea and curled herself in front of Ester's couch to entertain her with it.

"Mr. Hammond's last," she said. "Such a curious idea, as like him as possible, and like nobody else. You know that our class will graduate in just two years from this time, and there are fourteen of us, an even number, which is lucky for Mr. Hammond. Well, we are each, don't you think, to write a letter, as sensible, honest, and piquant as we can make it; historic, sentimental, poetic, or otherwise, as we please, so that it be the honest exponent of our views. Then we are to make a grand exchange of letters among the class, and the young lady who receives my letter, for instance, is to keep it sealed, and under lock and key, until graduation day, when it is to be read before scholars, faculty, and trustees, and my full name announced as the signature; and all the rest of us are to perform in like manner."

"What is supposed to be the object?" queried Abbie.

"Precisely the point which oppressed us, until Mr. Hammond complimented us by announcing that it was for the purpose of discovering how many of us, after making use of our highest skill in that line, could write a letter that after two years we should be willing to acknowledge as ours."

Ester sat up, flushed and eager. "That is a very nice idea," she said brightly. "I'm so glad you told me of it. Sadie, I'll write you a letter for that day. I'll write it tomorrow, and you are to keep it sealed until the evening of that day on which you graduate. Then when you have come up to your room and are quite alone, you are to read it. Will you promise, Sadie?"

But Sadie only laughed merrily and said: "You are growing sentimental, Ester, as sure as the world. How can I make any such promise as that? I shall probably chatter to you like a magpie instead of reading anything."

This young girl utterly ignored so far as was possible the fact of Ester's illness, never allowing it to be admitted in her presence that there were any fears as to the result. Ester had ceased trying to convince her, so now she only smiled quietly and repeated her petition.

"Will you promise, Sadie?"

"Oh yes, I'll promise to go to the mountains of the moon on foot and alone, across lots—*anything* to amuse you. You're to be pitied, you see, until you get over this absurd habit of cuddling down among the pillows."

So a few days thereafter she received with much apparent glee the dainty sealed letter addressed to herself and dropped it in her writing desk, but ere she turned the key there dropped a tear or two on the shining lid.

Well, as the long, hot summer days grew longer and fiercer, the invalid drooped and drooped, and the home faces grew sadder. Yet there still came from time to time those rallying days, wherein Sadie confidently pronounced her to be improving rapidly. And so it came to pass that so sweet was the final message that the words of the wonderful old poem proved a fitting description of it all.

> *"They thought her dying when she slept,*
> *And sleeping when she died."*

Into the brightness of the September days there intruded one, wherein all the house was still, with that strange, solemn stillness that comes only to those homes where death has left a seal. From the doors floated the long crape signals, and in the great parlors were gathering those who had come to take their parting look at the white, quiet face. "ESTER RIED, aged 19," so the coffin plate told them. Thus early had the story of her life been finished.

Only one arrangement had Ester made for this last scene in her life drama.

"I am going to preach my own funeral sermon," she had said pleasantly to Abbie one day. "I want everyone to know what seemed to me the most important thing in life. And I want them to understand that when I came just to the end of my life it stood out the most important thing still—for Christians, I mean. My sermon is to be preached for them. No, it isn't either; it applied equally to all. The last time I went to the city I found in a bookstore just the kind of sermon I wanted preached. I bought it. You will find the package in my upper bureau drawer, Abbie. I leave it to you to see that they are so arranged that everyone who comes to look at *me* will be sure to see them."

So on this day, amid the wilderness of flowers and vines and mosses that had possession of the rooms, ranged along the mantel, hanging in clusters on the walls, were beautifully illuminated texts—and these were some of the words that they spoke to those who silently gathered in the parlors:

"And that knowing the time, that now it is high time to awake out of sleep."

"But wilt thou know, O vain man, that faith without works is dead?"

"What shall we do that we might work the works of God?"

"Whatsoever thy hand findeth to do, do it with thy might; for there is no work, nor device, nor knowledge, nor wisdom in the grave whither thou goest."

"I must work the work of him that sent me, while it is day: the night cometh when no man can work."

"Awake to righteousness and sin not."

"Awake thou that sleepest, and arise from the dead, and Christ shall give thee light."

"Redeeming the time, because the days are evil."

"Let us not sleep as do others, but let us watch, and be sober."

Chiming in with the thoughts of those who knew by whose direction the illuminated texts were hung, came the voice of the minister, reading:

"And I heard a voice from heaven saying unto me,

Write, Blessed are the dead which die in the Lord from henceforth: Yea, saith the Spirit, that they may rest from their labors; and their works do follow them."

So it was that Ester Ried, lying quiet in her coffin, was reckoned among that number who "being dead, yet speaketh."

28

At Last

THE busy, exciting, triumphant day was done. Sadie
Ried was no longer a schoolgirl; she had graduated.
And although a dress of the softest, purest white had
been substituted for the blue silk, in which she had so
long ago planned to appear, its simple folds had swept
the platform of Music Hall in as triumphant a way as
ever she had planned for the other. More so, for Sadie's
wildest flights of fancy had never made her valedicto-
rian of her class, yet that she certainly was. In some
respects it had been a merry day—the long-sealed
letters had been opened and read by their respective
holders that morning, and the young ladies had discovered, amid much laughter and many blushes, that
they were ready to pronounce many of the expressions which they had carefully made only two years
before "ridiculously out of place" or "absurdly sentimental."

"Progress," said Mr. Hammond, turning for a moment to Sadie, after he had watched with an amused
smile the varying play of expression on her speaking
face, while she listened to the reading of her letter.

"You were not aware that you had improved so much in two years, now, were you?"

"I was not aware that I ever was such a simpleton!" was her half-provoked, half-amused reply.

Tonight she loitered strangely in the parlors, in the halls, on the stairs, talking aimlessly with anyone who would stop; it was growing late. Mrs. Ried and the children had long ago departed. Dr. Van Anden had not yet returned from his evening round of calls. Everybody in and about the house was quiet ere Sadie, with slow, reluctant steps, finally ascended the stairs and sought her room. Arrived there, she seemed in no haste to light the gas; moonlight was streaming into the room, and she put herself down in front of one of the low windows to enjoy it. But it gave her a view of the not far distant cemetery, and gleamed on a marble slab, the lettering of which she knew perfectly well was—"Ester, daughter of Alfred and Laura Ried, died Sept. 4, 18—, aged 19. Asleep in Jesus—Awake to everlasting life." And that reminded her, as she had no need to be reminded, of a letter with the seal unbroken, lying in her writing desk—a letter which she had promised to read this evening—promised the one who wrote it for her, and over whose grave the moonlight was now wrapping its silver robe. Sadie felt strangely averse to reading that letter; in part, she could imagine its contents, and for the very reason that she was still "halting between two opinions," "almost persuaded," and still on that often fatal "almost" side, instead of the "altogether," did she wait and linger and fritter away the evening as best she could, rather than face that solemn letter. Even when she turned resolutely from the window, and lighted the gas, and drew down the shade, she waited to put everything tidy on her writing table, and then, when she had finally turned the key in her writing desk, to read over half a dozen old letters, and bits of essays, and scraps of poetry ere she reached down for that little white envelope, with her name traced by the dear familiar hand that wrote her name no more. At last the seal was broken, and Sadie read:

MY DARLING SISTER:

I am sitting today in our little room—yours and mine. I have been taking in the picture of it; everything about it is dear to me, from our father's face smiling down on me from the wall, to the little red rocker in which he sat and wrote, in which I sit now, and in which you will doubtless sit, when I have gone to him. I want to speak to you about that time. When you read this, I shall have been gone a long, long time, and the bitterness of the parting will all be past; you will be able to read calmly what I am writing. I will tell you a little of the struggle. For the first few moments after I knew that I was soon to die, my brain fairly reeled; it seemed to me that I *could* not. I had so much to live for, there was so much that I wanted to do; and most of all other things, I wanted to see you a Christian. I wanted to live for that, to work for it, to undo if I could some of the evil that I knew my miserable life had wrought in your heart. Then suddenly there came to me the thought that perhaps what my life could not do, my coffin would accomplish— perhaps that was to be God's way of calling you to himself; perhaps he meant to answer my pleading in that way, to let my grave speak for me as my crooked, marred, sinful living might never be able to do. My darling, then I was content; it came to me so suddenly as that almost the certainty that God meant to use me thus, and I love you so, and I long so to see you come to him, that I am more than willing to give up all that this life seemed to have for me and go away, if by that you be called to Christ.

And Sadie, dear, you will know before you read this, how much I had to give up. You will know very soon all that Dr. Douglass and I looked forward to being to each other—but I give it up, give him up, more than willingly—joyfully—glad that my Father will accept the sacrifice, and make you his child. Oh, my darling, what a life I have lived before you! I do not wonder that, looking at me, you have grown into the habit of thinking that there is nothing in religion—you have looked at me, not at Jesus, and there has been no reflection of his beauty in me, as there should have been, and the result is not strange. Knowing this, I am the more thankful that God will forgive me and use me as a means to bring you home at last. I speak confidently. I am sure, you see, that it will be; the burden, the fearful burden that I have carried about with me so long, has gone away. My Redeemer and yours has taken it from me. I shall see you in heaven. Father is there, and I am going, oh *so* fast, and Mother will not be long behind, and Alfred and Julia have started on the journey, and you *will* start. Oh, I know it—we shall all be there! I told my Savior I was willing to do anything, *anything,* so my awful mockery of a Christian life that I wore so long might not be the means of your eternal death. And he has heard my prayer. I do not know when it will be; perhaps you will still be undecided when you sit in our room and read these words. Oh, I hope, I *hope* you will not waste two years more of your life, but if you do, if as you read these last lines that I shall ever write, the question is unsettled, I charge you by the memory of your sister, by the love you bear her, not to wait another *moment*—not one. Oh, my darling, let me beg this at your hands; take it as my dying petition—renewed after two years of waiting. Come to Jesus now.

That question settled, then let me give you one word of warning. Do not live as I have done—my life has been a failure—five years of stupid sleep, while the enemy waked and worked. Oh, God, forgive me! Sadie, never let that be your record. Let me give you a motto—Press toward the mark. The mark is high; don't look away from or forget it, as I did; don't be content with simply sauntering along, looking toward it now and then, but take in the full meaning of that earnest sentence and live it—Press toward the mark!

And now good-bye. When you have finished reading this letter, do this last thing for me: If you are already a Christian, get down on your knees and renew your covenant; resolve anew to live and work, and suffer and die, for Christ. If you are not a Christian—Oh, I put my whole soul into this last request—I beg you kneel and give yourself up to Jesus. My darling, good-bye until we meet in heaven.

ESTER RIED.

The letter dropped from Sadie's nerveless fingers. She arose softly, and turned down the gas, and raised the shade—the moonlight still gleamed on the marble slab. Dr. Van Anden came with quick, firm tread up the street. She gave a little start as she recognized the step, and her thoughts went out after that other lonely doctor, who was to have been her brother, and then back to the long, earnest letter and the words, "I give him up"—and she realized, as only those can who know by experience what a giving up that would be, how much her sister longed for her soul. And then, moved by a strong, firm resolve, Sadie knelt in the solemn moonlight, and the long, long struggle was ended. Father and sister were in heaven, but on earth, this night, their prayers were being answered.

"Blessed are the dead which die in the Lord from henceforth: Yea, saith the Spirit, that they may rest from their labors; and their works do follow them."

THE END

If you enjoyed the sweet, romantic stories in the Grace Livingston Hill Library . . .

. . . you'll be swept away by the Grace Livingston Hill novels

Check your local bookstore for the 100 titles available in this series.